The Year of the Storm

JOHN MANTOOTH

BERKLEY BOOKS, NEW YORK

THE BERKLEY PUBLISHING GROUP
Published by the Penguin Group
Penguin Group (USA) Inc.
375 Hudson Street, New York, New York 10014, USA

USA I Canada I UK I Ireland I Australia I New Zealand I India I South Africa I China

Penguin Books Ltd., Registered Offices: 80 Strand, London WC2R 0RL, England
For more information about the Penguin Group, visit penguin.com.

This book is an original publication of The Berkley Publishing Group.

Library of Congress Cataloging-in-Publication Data

Mantooth, John, 1971–
The year of the storm / John Mantooth. —Berkley trade paperback edition.
pages cm
ISBN 978-0-425-26574-1
1. Missing persons—Fiction.   2. Storms—Fiction.   3. Strangers—Fiction.   I. Title.
PR9199.4.M337Y43 2013
813'.6—dc23
2013003379

PUBLISHING HISTORY
Berkley trade paperback edition / June 2013

PRINTED IN THE UNITED STATES OF AMERICA

10 9 8 7 6 5 4 3 2 1

Cover photo: Shutterstock. Cover design: George Long.
Interior text design by Laura K. Corless.

The Brewing Tempest

I was fourteen the first time I came in contact with a real storm. It cut a line right down the center of my life, pulling my sister and mother away from me and cleanly dividing that year into a before and after so radically different that I've come to think of fourteen as not only the longest year of my life, but also the most important because it was the last year of childhood and the first year of the rest of my life, a life that would be forever marked as different in subtle and insidious ways from the people around me.

Fourteen was the year my mother and sister disappeared, the year I lost my mind. The year I learned secrets that will stay with me until I am no longer able to think of them.

And fourteen, most of all, was the year of the storm.

———

"Mantooth's voice is masculine and powerful, flavoring the pages with the Alabama wilderness, the turmoil of family and how all these elements work to shape and nurture teenage boys into men."

—Frank Bill

For Becky, with gratitude.

Acknowledgments

Many people helped this book make it into print. Without agent Beth Fleisher's keen insight and unwavering patience, this book would still be just a manuscript languishing on my hard drive. Amanda Ng, my editor, also deserves a huge thanks for nudging the book in the right direction and being an indispensable source of knowledge and good advice. My writing group read this book first and then again after each revision (sorry guys). Sam W. Anderson, Kim Despins, Kurt Dinan, Petra Miller, and Erik Williams are the best writing group any writer could hope to have. Thanks, guys, I'll probably never repay what you have given to me so freely. Thanks also to all my friends, supporters, and kind first readers. I won't try to list them all, but there are a few that I would be remiss not to mention: John Rector, Frank Bill, Benjamin Percy, Dan Chaon, Joey Kennedy, Holly Goddard Jones, Usman Taneer Malik, Bracken MacLeod, Kevin Wallis, Beverly Bambury, Ian Rogers, John Langan, Paul Tremblay, Laird Barron, Jamie Nelson, Mary Rees, John Hornor Jacobs, Erik Smetana, Frank J. Mueller III, and Lawrence Wharton.

Finally, deepest thanks and love for my wife, Becky. This book is as much yours as it is mine because you gave me the freedom to write it.

The most beautiful thing we can experience is the mysterious. It is the source of all true art and all science. He to whom this emotion is a stranger, who can no longer pause to wonder and stand rapt in awe, is as good as dead: His eyes are closed.

—ALBERT EINSTEIN

One person's craziness is another person's reality.

—TIM BURTON

Chapter One

DANNY

A storm is a kind of magic.

I've lived through a lot of them, but none of them were like the ones I experienced when I was fourteen.

Watch the news in the spring. You'll see footage of flooding and devastation and broken homes scattered like wood chips from an almighty Skilsaw, any previous illusion of constancy the houses held shattered in short seconds of earsplitting fury. As I grow older, I watch these scenes on the nightly news a little differently. Of course I still grieve for the people whose homes and lives have been uprooted by the weather, but I also study the pictures and video a little more closely. I look for the way things have been altered, the way one world is gone and another moves in to take its place, and if this isn't a kind of terrible magic, then I don't know what is. After the news, when the lights are off and I lie atop the covers, not even pretending that sleep might eventually transport me away from these nagging thoughts, I marvel at the way scientists can deconstruct a thing, pulling it apart fiber by fiber until the whole of it is unwound and every piece labeled and comprehended. I tell myself that if the right scientist could get hold of my life, if that scientist could put the events of my fourteenth year under a microscope, he'd be able to explain them away. But then the magic would be gone, and *that* would keep me up at night too.

Now, I'm almost thirty, and I make weekly visits to a therapist who insists I call him Dwight instead of Dr. Reynolds. He slaps me on the back at the beginning of every session and hugs me at the end, just before letting his hand linger until I stuff a check in it. Oh, he's not a bad guy, and he seems genuinely fascinated by my story. He likes to explain everything in psychological terms and ask a lot of leading questions. Sometimes I think he's even on to something when he talks about "subconscious mythmaking" and "the profundity of illusion." But other times—and these are the nights I sleep best—I dismiss his words as easily as the straight-line winds dismiss trees, snapping them like brittle sticks. When I think like this, I remember it all, and if there are pieces of the puzzle that I can't work into place, I ignore them and focus on the pieces that do fit. And these pieces are the people—Pike and Seth and Cliff and even my little sister, Anna. Most of all, I focus on the great things that the brain is capable of and how like a storm it can be, wild and ravaging, erasing landscapes and building new ones in the wink of a eye.

I was fourteen the first time I came in contact with a real storm. It cut a line right down the center of my life, pulling my sister and mother away from me and cleanly dividing that year into a before and after so radically different that I've come to think of fourteen as not only the longest year of my life, but also the most important because it was the last year of childhood and the first year of the rest of my life, a life that would be forever marked as different in subtle and insidious ways from the people around me.

Fourteen was the year my mother and sister disappeared, the year I lost my mind. The year I learned secrets that will stay with me until I am no longer able to think of them.

And fourteen, most of all, was the year of the storm.

Despite dealing with the presumed deaths of my mother and sister, at fourteen I still believed that magic and God were the same thing, or if they weren't, that they were wound so tightly together and threaded through the spaces of our lives as to become a length of double-braided rope whose ends had not yet begun to fray.

My father was forty-one when I was fourteen, and like me, he was knocked back by the storm. But unlike me, his world then was a rigid place. Neither magic nor God existed for him except in books and memories. Storms were storms, and any transformation that came from them was incidental, swept away in a flood of adult problems.

Before my mother and sister vanished, we weren't a perfect family, but we were complete, a strong knot of individual strings, each wrapped over the other. If one string pulled too tight while another string fought to breathe more, how was that different from any other family? The point was that we were a knot, and then we came unwound. At fourteen, I was foolish enough to think I could tie the knot back, and we'd go on like always.

After it happened, Dad felt every kind of emotion—rage, hate, resentment, despair. But mostly, I think he was jealous. Jealous of a world that took his happiness, that swallowed it without leaving a scrap, and then went back to the same quiet, sleeping place it had always been.

But ten months into my fourteenth year, the world shifted in its slumber.

———————

Midnight, and a man I had never seen before stood outside our front door, a cigarette nub burning between his knuckles, his long white hair wild in the wind. Beside him on our front stoop was an oxygen tank he'd lugged up the steps. I watched from my bed, leaning over to peer out my upstairs window as he flicked his cigarette to the ground and stepped on it, extinguishing it against the concrete. He faced our front door, lifted a hand to knock, but faltered. Instead, he turned back to his oxygen tank, taking up the clear tubing and placing it inside his nostrils. He was still. I looked out over the yard and saw the immense oak trees swaying in the wind, saw the highway—empty and lonesome—and beyond that the great silver fields of cotton, rippling in the moonlight. On the horizon, a massive thunderhead gathered and advanced steadily toward the house.

I should have been asleep. Sleep came in fits those days, a dream of my mother's face always a few breaths away. Across the hall, Dad was snoring, and I wondered if he still dreamed about them too.

Shrugging off the covers, I stood and made my way down the steps, the same ones my sister, Anna, used to count each time she went up or down. There were twelve. Dad and I both knew that the same way we knew Anna's closet was her sanctuary from the world, the same way we knew that when a bad storm came, bad like the one that was rolling in now, Anna had no sanctuary except within herself. She was autistic and only four years old when she disappeared. She'd be five now, and though her doctors said it wasn't possible, I still wondered if she had gotten any better. It was a foolish hope, but I was fourteen and believed things that no rational person should. Things like my mother and sister were still alive.

Downstairs, I waited on the other side of the door. Would he knock? Or did he mean to simply stand outside our home, a strange presence that touched our lives without invading them? Maybe he stood outside every night while we slept. Maybe he was one of the moonshiners Dad had told me about, who lived beyond the margins of society, setting up stills in the deepest parts of the woods and living hand to mouth on what they could catch with a fishing pole or shoot with a rifle. Or he might have come from some faraway place, riding the rails like a lost hobo arriving at our house by pure chance or by some more sinister motivation. Or maybe he was the man responsible for taking those two girls back in the sixties, whose sad spirits seemed to linger and haunt these woods like fireflies in the darkest hollows of the night. Maybe he was the man who took Mom and Anna too, and now he'd come back for the rest of us. And maybe, just maybe, I'd go with him willingly.

Dropping to my knees, I moved across the den until I was under the front windows. Carefully, I lifted my head, pushing aside the curtains so that I could see out one of the lower panes. He was still standing there, illuminated by the moon, his hair glowing vivid white. Somewhere behind him, across the highway, lightning struck the cotton fields, followed by a sharp crack of thunder. The man did not jump or start or even seem to notice. He only stood at our door, filling his lungs with oxygen.

I let the curtain fall back in place, and I lay down on the floor. I'd been hearing the stories about these woods since I was a kid. Most of them were the generic campfire variety, the same urban legends reshuffled and personalized for different times, different settings, but one story was more than that. One story had the ring of authenticity. It was unique to these woods, and unlike the tales of hook hands and insane asylum escapees, it never seemed to fade away. Two girls, Tina and Rachel, lost in the woods behind our house. I grew up knowing their names just like I knew anything else. They were a part of the landscape, a part of the place where I lived. It didn't matter if I'd never seen them or heard them speak or even gotten the whole story straight about their disappearances. I felt their presences intimately, and their loss settled on the woods like a heavy fog. When I walked through the darkest parts behind my house near dusk, sometimes I thought I saw them in the gloom, floating, transparent, made from spiders' webs and dying streaks of light mingled with shadow. Their sad visages slithering round tree trunks and drifting past blooming moonvines. I shuddered, thinking that the man responsible for these disappearances might be standing in my front yard.

I'm not sure how long I lay there before I decided to check again, but when I looked up the second time, rain was hitting the roof in torrents, and the man was gone.

The next morning, I woke, back in my bed. I'd fallen asleep beside the window, but I vaguely remembered Dad picking me up in the dark hours of the morning and carrying me upstairs. It was still raining and when I fell into my own bed, in the throes of half sleep, I felt a simple, forgetful peace. It was the kind I used to feel each time my head hit the pillow and Mom leaned over me, saying the prayers I could not yet articulate, the same prayers I later repeated to myself, trying to work them out like jigsaw puzzles.

Summer meant I could sleep all day if I wanted, but I got up anyway, determined not to give in to the stifling depression that hung around our house as heavy and dank as the Alabama heat.

My best friend then was a kid named Cliff, who had a lazy eye and the biggest collection of Marvel comics I had ever seen. Together, we spent our summers chasing phantoms through the woods, imagining ourselves as Iron Man and Captain America, and lately, fantasizing about girls, specifically Rhonda Donovan and Betty Dozier. The double Ds. That was what we called them, and sometimes, in our more nerdy moments, D and D.

Usually, getting up on a summer morning meant going to Cliff's house. There were a million things to do—a trip into town to the comic book store, a day watching movies in his home theater, a jaunt into the deep woods as imaginary superheroes, a clandestine journey out to the honky-tonk on County Road Seven where we'd heard the women got drunk and danced topless.

But that morning was different. Dad came into my room as I was pulling myself from the bed.

"I found you in the den last night," he said.

"I know."

"Wonder why."

Dad did this sort of thing, this almost talking to himself that only served to make me feel like he really didn't want to talk to me at all. Which was true. He didn't want to talk to me. He hadn't wanted to talk to me since Mom and Anna disappeared. He wasn't mean

7

about it. In fact, Dad was about as gentle with me as he'd ever been, but the hardness grew inside him, in his eyes that sometimes slipped out of focus, and in his lips that were always too stiff to smile.

"The storm got to me. That's all."

He sat down on my bed.

"The sheriff called today," he said to the floor.

"And?"

He shook his head. "It's been nine months. You know that, right?"

"Yeah," I said. How could I not know that? "What did he say?"

Dad shook his head and studied the floor.

"What did he say?" I asked again.

"Same old bullshit. The woods are a dead end. The dogs have canvassed every part of it." He shook his head again, this time with more determination. "Dead ends. That's all we have. Damn dead ends. I told the sheriff—"

He stopped suddenly and looked at me, as if remembering who he was talking to. *Yeah, Dad, it's me. Remember not to tell Danny anything relevant because he's too young to understand.* It was infuriating.

"What?" I said. "What did you tell the sheriff?"

"Nothing important. He's going to do some more interviews with people at her work, extended family, that sort of thing. We've heard it all before."

"That's good news, though. Right?"

Dad looked up, his eyes skimming past my face, but not focusing until they settled on my closet where the clothes I was quickly outgrowing hung like ghosts, pieces of the past that Mom and Anna had once touched.

"Good news?" he said, almost to himself.

"Yeah, I mean, well, at least we still have some hope."

He looked at me then, and I saw that he hadn't been taking his pills. Looking back, I can't say I blame him much. The ones Dwight prescribed for me didn't work. Sure, they made sleep easier to come by, but my real issues were too deep for any medicine to touch.

The proof Dad had given up was in his face, his eyes, the way he hadn't shaved today or yesterday. Was he even going to work today? I wondered.

He shook his head. "Hope. That's funny." He looked at me for a second, expectant, as if daring me to argue with him. When I said nothing, he stood up, swinging his arms together, letting his fist connect with his palm, a gesture he used to do all the time, a gesture that seemed strangely devoid of the happy-go-lucky spirit it was meant to suggest.

"Danny," he said, speaking my name earnestly like saying it mattered somehow. "Why don't you and me do something fun today? Just the two of us?"

"What about work?" I said.

He shook his head, dismissing it. "I'll call in. I haven't missed a day in the last five months. They won't blink. Are you with me?"

"Sure. Yeah. Sounds good." I tried to sound bright, happy, but it came out shrill, needlessly high-pitched and awkward. Dad pretended not to notice. It was the one thing we had gotten good at over the last nine months: pretending.

We went for a walk in the woods.

It doesn't make sense, I know. Nine months earlier, your mother and little sister disappear into these woods, and when your father and you need some time together, some time to get away, to decompress, to try to leave behind the sadness that has overwhelmed your lives, you choose to go for a walk in the very same woods.

What can I say other than it's complicated? Both my relationship with my father and the woods. They're tied together, the woods and my father. From the time I could walk, I followed him through the trees, wondering at the solitude and dark quietness that no other place I'd been could match. In the winter, we hunted the woods, and in the spring, summer, and early fall, we walked a well-worn path to our special place to fish. We called it Big Creek because that's exactly what it was. There was a swift current and at its widest point, I could barely throw a rock to the other side. We never caught much more than wild creek fish, which are pretty small, but they make a good meal if you serve them with slaw and hush puppies and don't mind picking through the tiny bones.

It was where we went when we were happy. And more than anything, we wanted to be happy again.

The woods were bigger than us, massive and untamed, and they seemed like a great mystery. Each time we walked into them, dragging fishing gear or hunting rifles or skipping along the path, weighed down by nothing other than ambition, there was some hope—unspoken or otherwise—that we'd return at the end of the day with something life-changing.

Before we left that afternoon, Dad asked if I wanted to fish. "Had some rain," he said. "Creek will be high. Might be a river gar that's got lost from the Black Warrior."

I smiled. This was an old joke. He used to tell it to me when I was very little when I actually believed we'd catch one. I shook my head.

"Why don't we just walk? I got a feeling that the river gar will probably stay in the river."

He nodded his assent and we started off, trudging along the same path Anna and Mom had taken the day they disappeared.

In reality, I didn't enjoy fishing as much as I used to, although I still treasured any time that Dad and I had together in the woods. I wanted to go to Big Creek for a different reason. Along the banks were drifts of sand that collapsed under the weight of small animals, sucking them in. I'd seen a baby deer struggle for hours in the sand, before finally extracting his thin body and hopping feebly away. Everybody called it quicksand. It was the first thing I thought of when Mom and Anna went missing. In my mind, I saw Anna stepping into the muck, one tentative foot. I saw her thinking better of it, changing her mind, trying to pull it out, losing her balance and falling face forward. I heard Mom screaming and saw her diving in to save her daughter. Then they were both sinking, eyes upturned, struggling to glimpse the sky through the tops of the swaying trees.

According to my best friend, Cliff, quicksand was mostly a Hollywood invention and actually sinking to your death was next to impossible. Something to do with the density of the human body— I never could follow it all—but the authorities must have agreed because they made little effort to search the area, focusing most of their attention on the little cabin a couple of miles away. Whenever I tried to ask Dad about the cabin, he always shook his head and said the same thing. "Dead end."

At Big Creek, we stood and watched the current jumping the smooth rocks, saying nothing, probably thinking the same thoughts. The day was cloudy and standing under the trees near the water made it seem much later, almost dusk. Somewhere overhead, a bird began a song and another joined in, dueling the first. Dad picked up a rock and skipped it across the creek. He was a tall man, but he seemed hunched now, weak in the shoulders, bending in the slight breeze.

"What do you know about the two girls?" I said. My voice sounded louder than I had expected, and I tried to pull it back, ashamed suddenly of breaking the silence.

Dad picked up another rock and weighed it in his hand.

I wasn't sure if he heard me, and I was all set to let it go when he began to speak.

"It happened in the early sixties, when I was just a little kid. I don't remember any of it really, but I grew up with the stories, same as you. They wandered off or were kidnapped or killed. Hell, nobody knows. Law enforcement in this town." He spat into the creek. "'Frank, we're doing the best we can,'" he said, imitating Sheriff Martin's slow drawl. "'It ain't like they left a trail of crumbs.'"

"But wasn't there something about the old cabin?"

He shrugged. "That was a separate incident. Maybe they're related, but nobody knows that either."

"What happened?"

He threw the rock. It landed heavy, breaking the surface of the water and sinking. He turned and fixed me with a hard look. "I thought we were going to do something fun today."

I didn't know what to say. I looked away, not wanting to meet his eyes.

"This kind of talk is for shit," he said.

He stepped closer to the water and knelt down. He studied the stream as if reading some message in it and I took the hint. He wanted to be alone.

The quicksand was a few hundred yards upstream and I wandered that way, noticing the change in the bank as I drew closer. Gradually, it went from solid to damp to squishy. The quicksand didn't look like anything dangerous. If anything, it just looked like any other area right near the creek. The difference could not be discerned by the eye, at least not by mine. When I felt like I was getting close, I picked up a stick and poked around at the ground until I felt it give way. I tossed the stick in and it lay on the surface, too light to sink. Looking around, I found a large stone. I tossed it up in the air and it hit the quicksand with a gurgling sound and started sinking. Within seconds it was gone, disappeared from this world, as if it had never been here at all.

Chapter Two

That night I lay on the couch long after Dad had fallen asleep in the guest room (he kept both Anna's room and the old room he shared with Mom shut at all times, as if opening them up might somehow cause him to spontaneously remember). I lay in a kind of half sleep, a comic book folded on my chest. The blinds were open, and I saw the rain as it began to pelt the house. I put down my comic book and walked over to the window, flipping off all the lights in the den so I could see outside.

This one was just going to be a good soaking, the weatherman had said. No high winds or cloud-to-ground lightning. As I surveyed the front yard and saw nothing out of the ordinary, I wondered if the storm had brought the old man. Maybe he was some traveler from a different world who'd been caught in a thunderstorm and was whisked away from there to here until he ended up in our front yard.

I went back to the couch. An hour later, the rain had stopped and I was sound asleep.

A round three thirty, a noise from the back of the house woke me. I sat upright, rubbing sleep from my eyes, trying to get my bearings. There was always a moment upon first waking when Mom and Anna were still here. It usually lasted only an instant, and when that instant was gone, I felt as if someone had torn a piece of my heart away. I wondered when it would stop, *if* it would stop.

The noise had come from the back porch. I waited, very still, on the couch for it to come again. Outside, heat lightning flashed, making the den glow pale and cold and throwing shadows against the walls.

Moving slowly and deliberately in the dark, I slipped into the kitchen, opened the silverware drawer, and grabbed a knife. Creeping around the dining room table, I had the knife raised, ready to strike, ready to go for blood if the sneaky old bastard with the oxygen tank had broken into the house. I made it to the back door that led out onto our makeshift deck, where Anna used to like to stand and sing her songs, the ones that always caused me and Dad to laugh no matter how bad our moods were. Pausing near the door, I waited until the sound came again—a shuffling of feet, a slight creaking out on the porch.

Keeping my back to the wall and the knife raised, I took a deep breath, turned on the light, and flung open the door. The porch was empty.

Almost.

Muddy tracks led down the back steps and out into the yard.

I stepped outside, shutting the door behind me gently to keep from waking Dad. With the knife in my hand I felt braver perhaps than I had any right to. Following the tracks to the edge of the porch, I paused at the steps, wishing for a flashlight. The wind chimes hanging from the eaves clinked together musically and then fell quiet. The backyard was silent, thrown out of proportion from the shadows of the looming forest.

I might have gone back in for a flashlight if I hadn't caught a sudden twist of movement near the entrance to the woods.

At first, I didn't believe my eyes.

Anna or her ghost—or maybe just a figment of Anna born out of my imagination—stood near a dense cluster of trees, her arms wrapped tightly across her chest, bobbing back and forth the way she did when she was in recovery mode. That was the term Mom had coined when Anna slowly started to bring herself back from an episode.

I stepped off the porch. One step onto the muddy grass and then two, keeping my eyes on her. Something—a fallen branch or vine—caught my foot, and I stumbled forward. I had to look away—just for an instant—and when I looked back up, she was gone.

I didn't think. I just reacted, sprinting across the yard, splashing mud as I went. I made it to the very edge of the woods, what Mom had always called "the gateway to the wild," before pulling up and peering hard into an interlocking darkness, a tightly coiled mystery that I could not penetrate without light.

She was gone. Just like before. Just like Mom.

I wandered around the woods then, the knife still clutched tightly in my hand, looking for her, some sign or hint that she was still near.

It was too dark. I was set to give up and go back inside when I heard a sound nearby. It sounded like her laugh.

I walked slowly, purposefully, toward the laughing. I heard it again, now a little farther away, a little more to my left. I corrected my path and continued to walk. All around me I saw creatures twisting, writhing, reaching from the shadows. In my rational mind, I knew these were only trees and shadows and tangled kudzu vines, but my rational mind had been relegated to some nether region of my brain out here. I could hear it calling to me, but its voice was tiny, insignificant, easy to ignore.

What I couldn't ignore were the noises. Anna laughing. Anna saying one of her nonsense words. Sometimes only the slightest crack of a twig. I followed each sound, pulling myself deeper into the woods, my woods, the ones I'd grown up playing in, the ones that now seemed dangerous and unrecognizable.

I followed the sounds for a long time.

Just when I believed I'd heard the last of them, another one always came.

At some point, I looked around and realized I was near Big Creek, just a few paces from the quicksand I had visited earlier that same day. I stopped, suddenly afraid I was being lured into some kind of trap.

Then I saw her again.

This time there was no doubt. She stood just a few yards away, almost glowing in a sudden beam of moonlight, poised on the bank of the creek near what had to be the quicksand.

"Anna?" My voice came out barely a whisper.

She turned and cocked her head to the side, her eyes locking on mine. She seemed mildly surprised to see me. She waved her shy little-girl wave, the hand barely coming above her waist, her fingers wriggling.

"Hey," I said, and stepped forward. Even as I took my first step, I felt the air around me changing, losing its charge, growing cold. Anna stepped back, a look of confusion on her face. "No, don't get upset, please, Anna." With Anna it was always the same: confusion, followed by tears, followed by withdrawal. Once the process was begun, there was no stopping it. Still, I tried. I ran for her, hoping to grab her before she got away this time. I wanted very badly to touch her, to confirm that she was real.

She backed away, taking the first step, but I was fast. I reached for her arm and for a brief second, I held it in my hand. Then the wind blew or the light changed or I woke up—I couldn't be sure which—and she was gone, leaving me teetering precariously over the quicksand. I managed to keep my balance and stepped back just as another round of thunder shook the trees and the rain began to fall.

When I finally went back to sleep that same night, I dreamed of Mom. To be fair, my fourteen-year-old perception of my mother and the one I hold now are quite different. At fourteen, I still had a kid's view of her. She was my mother, the person who held me when I fell down, the woman who tucked me in at night and kissed me on the forehead. She was the alpha parent who met all my basic needs as a boy, and I loved her with an unquestioning, desperate kind of love.

In my dream that night, I saw her as I liked to remember her best: sitting with her legs crossed in the backyard at sunset, smiling as I entertained her with stories of superheroes and their secret origins. What I did not see then but had to face later was the drink she inevitably held in her hand.

In the dream, we chatted as if she had never been gone. In the dream, I was content. Then it changed. She began to speak of things I did not understand: the cabin in the swamp, the way it was always dusk, the man who crept through the trees and frightened her more than she could explain.

"He won't let us out." Now she was gone, and I only heard her voice, but it sounded far away.

"Who? Who won't let you out?"

My only answer was a bitter and abiding silence. She was gone.

I tried to linger in the dream. I tried to draw her back to me. I thought I might have heard her voice again, but the sound grew louder until it exploded in my eardrums, jarring me awake. I sat up, thinking for an instant that the whole world must be on fire.

D ad was standing at the front door, the shotgun at his shoulder, a trail of smoke drifting toward the sky. The rain had come back, a gentle brush in the trees, on the roof.

"Dad?"

"Get upstairs, Danny."

I ignored him and went over to the window and pulled back the curtains. The front yard was illuminated by the floodlights on either side of the house. It was empty, absolutely still except for the rain and the lazy smoke from the shotgun.

"What's going on?"

"Upstairs, now."

I didn't argue. Dad's tone had sharpened. I knew better than to ignore him when he sounded like that.

Upstairs, I turned off the light, parted the blinds to my room, and looked out over the yard. Beyond the big oak, I saw the road and then the glossy wet blooms of cotton shifting in the wind. Just before I let the curtain fall back into place, I saw one more thing: the tiny orange flare of a cigarette burning hot in the dark night.

Chapter Three

The next day, Cliff and I met down at the pond behind my house just as the sun positioned itself high above us, signaling midday. The pond was nameless but popular with fishermen in the area for its brim and bass. Most of the fisherman came early in the morning or at dusk. Now the pond was still and empty, a dirty, slightly rippled sheet stretched across the field.

"What are those for?" I said, pointing at the binoculars around Cliff's neck.

"What do you think they're for?" He flashed me a particularly toothy and crooked grin, the kind that reminded me that in spite of all his parents' money, he would always find getting dates a challenge.

"No idea. Bird watching?"

"Close." He held the binoculars up to his eyes. "Chick watching."

"Okay. Sounds better than bird watching, at least."

"I talked to Sarah Moss last night. She and her sister are coming to the lake today to swim."

"You talked to Sarah Moss?"

Cliff tried to play it cool. "Yeah. She called. We talked. No big deal."

I knew better. Girls did in fact call Cliff sometimes, but it was always for help with homework. It was summer, so that couldn't have been it. "Okay, come clean," I said. "Why did she call?"

Cliff gave me a sheepish grin. "All right. She called to ask me if I'd be willing to type her up some notes on our summer reading books, okay? But I talked to her. That's what counts, right?"

"Sure. If you say so."

"I do say so. And furthermore, I say that we climb this tree and get in position because Sarah and Rebecca are going to be here in bikinis. And Rebecca's like twenty. Let that sink in for a second."

I shook my head. I'd been a part of Cliff's schemes before.

"I'm going to pretend you didn't just shake your head and roll your eyes," Cliff said. "Two words: Golden. Opportunity."

I shrugged. I felt tired and completely uninvolved even if there might be an opportunity to see female flesh.

"You ever stop and think that me and you are just losers, Cliff?"

"Of course we're losers, but we're losers with binoculars. Is there a problem?"

I shook my head. "I don't know. Maybe instead of hiding in a tree, we should actually stay out here in the open and talk to them."

Cliff laughed, but I could hear genuine hurt behind it. "Easy for you to say. Your name isn't Cliff. You don't have a face full of pimples and a brain that scares girls."

"There's nothing wrong with Cliff."

"There's nothing right with it either."

Sometimes Cliff did this. He got down on himself. Maybe I would have done the same with his particular roadblocks, but today I found it irritating. He had a mother and father, a giant-sized house. I didn't, and after last night, I found myself wallowing in my own self-pity.

Cliff must have sensed this because he smiled suddenly and patted my back. "Come on. I'll let you use the binoculars first."

I shrugged and began to climb the tree.

We climbed this tree a lot, mostly when we pretended to be cops on a stakeout. Sometimes we pretended we were astronauts hanging on to a satellite in deep space after narrowly escaping our starship before it was sucked through a black hole. Sometimes, especially in the last few months or so when I began to feel the absence of Mom and Anna like two bullet-sized holes in my heart, I climbed up by myself and looked for them. I know that sounds crazy even for a kid, but that's exactly what I did.

When I reached the high, solid limb where I liked to sit, I scanned the area for anything to see. Deserted. No fisherman, no deer tentatively slipping from the dark world of the woods to the open sunlight for a drink in the pond, certainly no Sarah or Rebecca in bikinis. I repositioned myself on the limb so I could see out to the road and the cotton fields beyond. The clouds had moved on and the sun shone hot and bright on the rows of cotton, making them appear like silver liquid in the breeze. Turning back, I looked at the massive woods that lay behind the pond and my house. They stretched for a couple of miles before giving way to sloping fields and hills, and past that, County Road Seven, where Mom and Dad had forbidden me to go. It was filled with honky-tonk bars, loose women, and hard-drinking men. Dad would only shrug when I asked him about it and mumble that it was "no place for a boy." Of course, his silence on the issue only increased my desire to see it. Yet that desire paled in comparison to the fascination I felt for the woods. I'd studied them so many times, wondering if they'd swallowed Mom and Anna whole, or perhaps they'd simply slipped away through some hidden crease in the trees. The little cabin was back there somewhere. When they first disappeared, the cabin had attracted quite a bit of attention. I can still remember the police tape and the constant flow of uniformed and plainclothes cops streaming in and out. Dad and I stood, tense with anticipation, watching for several hours before the sheriff finally sauntered over, winking at me, shaking my father's hand. "Nothing," he said. Dad—this was still very early on—had taken this as good news. *Nothing* meant they were still alive. Somewhere along the way, this definition had changed. At least for Dad. *Nothing* had become synonymous with a kind of lingering and bitter regret, the weight of unending frustration—in short, no news began to equal bad news.

Some days, I liked to climb this tree and sit very still, dragging my gaze over the treetops, searching for the slight change, the little bump in the landscape where the cabin was. Then I'd be able to pick out the little smokestack on the top. According to Dad, the cabin hadn't been occupied for years, and in fact, he wasn't sure if it ever had been. This was about all I'd been able to drag out of him on the subject. Anything else I knew—or *thought* I knew—about the place was cobbled together from whispers, rumors, and innuendo. The gist of it was that the girls—those mysterious shadowy girls who seemed to haunt not only the woods, but the whole town—had something to do with the place. Whatever that might be, nobody said.

Something bumped my leg. I looked down. Cliff was balanced precariously on the limb below me, holding the binoculars up. "Take them before I fall," he said.

I took the binoculars and put them to my eyes.

"See anything interesting?" Cliff said.

I scanned the pond. "Well, the girls obviously haven't shown yet." I moved the binoculars up so I could see the woods. Slowly, I tracked them over the trees until I came to the place where the cabin was. I saw the patched shingles, the solitary, rusty smokestack. Panning down some, I saw kudzu climbing over the walls and onto the roof, covering everything in a mess of green.

"What are you looking at?" Cliff said.

"That old cabin." I pulled the binoculars from my face and handed them back to him. "You ever seen a ghost?"

"Uh, did somebody say non sequitur?"

"Huh?" I hated when Cliff used big words.

"Non sequitur. Means moving from one idea to the next without any connection between them. The old cabin. Then the question: Have I ever seen a ghost? Which, by the way, I haven't. Have you? And before you answer, please explain what this has got to do with the cabin."

"Nothing, really. It's just that the cabin is kind of spooky. The two girls and all."

"The two girls? You mean the missing girls? That's just a legend, Danny. Folklore. If two girls really did go missing in these woods, I'm positive their bodies would have been found by now. Besides, even if the girls had gone missing and *had* died, ghosts don't exist."

I shrugged, not wanting to argue the point. Anyway, that wasn't really what had been bothering me, and to Cliff's credit, he could tell.

"There's something else, right?" he said. Cliff had many faults, but he was a great listener, and more importantly, he knew me. My moods, my brooding silences. The hesitation in my conversations. He could read me like he could read his science book, which is to say irritatingly well. Still, I hesitated, not sure if I should tell him about the white-haired man I thought Dad had shot at, or about Anna. I decided on the man. The encounter with Anna seemed too personal for some reason. Besides, telling him about that would be like admitting she was a ghost, which would be like admitting she was dead. Despite the vague, almost dreamlike nature of my trip through the woods the night before, I didn't believe I'd seen a ghost. In fact, it felt strangely reassuring, like evidence that she was still alive.

"The other night there was a man at our front door. He had long, white hair. He was old. I don't know. Maybe not *old* old, but haggard, you know. Worn the hell out. He was dragging this oxygen tank thing around with him. Like—"

"Like Mr. Yates."

"Yeah, like Mr. Yates." Mr. Yates was an old man who used to be the custodian at the school before my dad took over for him when his emphysema became too much to deal with.

"Weird," Cliff said, lifting the binoculars to his eyes. "But what makes you think he's a ghost and not just some loon?"

"I don't know. Lots of things, I guess." In reality, it was one thing: Anna. The visit from Anna had seemed connected somehow, had made my thoughts turn to the supernatural. And then there was Dad shooting at what had to be the same visitor I had seen the night before.

Dad was a crack shot and he rarely missed. Yet I'd seen the light from the man's cigarette from my upstairs window after the gunfire.

"Anyway," Cliff said. "What did he want?"

"He just stood there. Like he wanted to knock on the door but couldn't decide if he should or not. The wind was blowing and it was raining and his hair kept flying everywhere. He was smoking too. Switching out hits from the oxygen with drags on his cigarette. He just stood there. It seriously creeped me out."

"So you think this guy is a ghost?"

"I didn't say that. It's just weird. It's all too weird, like something out of a movie."

"Did this apparition have a scar on his right cheek?"

"I couldn't tell. Why?"

"Long white hair, right? Messy. Greasy. Scruffy beard?"

"Yeah." I looked down and saw Cliff looking through the binoculars.

"I think I see your ghost," Cliff said.

I zoomed the binoculars in on the man's face. If anything, he looked more frightening by daylight than he had a few nights ago. His scar was long; it ran from his right eye down his cheek until it disappeared beneath his shirt collar. He muttered to himself as he paced around outside the cabin.

"What's he doing?" Cliff said.

"Looks like he's moving in." I panned out and saw that he was indeed moving in. He was carrying a large framed painting into the cabin. His pickup was filled with boxes and furniture.

"You've got to be pretty hard up to move into that place." Cliff whistled. "No running water, lights. Jeez. I hope he brought plenty of books."

I panned back to the truck. "I see a bed frame, so yeah, it looks like he's taking up residence."

"Why do you think he came to your house the other night?"

I shook my head and lowered the binoculars. "I don't know." What I didn't say was that I felt damned determined to find out.

Chapter Four

WALTER

I remember fourteen. Best and worst year of my life. Best because I learned how to be a man. Worst because I forgot how to be a boy.

The year was 1960. The year I met Seth Sykes.

Before Seth, I had friends, but they were the roughneck kind, the type of boys more interested in knocking out windows and kicking around seventh graders than doing anything worthwhile. I knew right away that Seth was different.

We liked to hang out at the pond. Me, Jake Rogan, and Ronnie Watts. The summer before, we'd built a little hut out of two-by-fours hauled over from Ronnie's place. We kept a good supply of cigarettes, moonshine, and one *Playboy*. May 1959. Had a sketch of three bathing beauties on the front. That magazine might have been the most looked-at periodical in the history of the world. I still compare every woman I see to the women in those pages. I suspect that's a sad thing in the end, but it's true, so there's no use in hiding it.

You might say it was sort of like our hangout, a place where we felt like men. It never occurred to us then that we didn't have the first clue about what it took to be real men. Ronnie, he had a saying he liked to always recite when he was sitting in the little fort, a cigarette in one hand and a bottle of Eugene Porter's moonshine in the other. "A man in his castle is a beautiful thing. All I need is some cootch and I'd have the world by its balls."

That's where we were the day Seth stumbled across us. We'd been doing nothing out of the ordinary—smoking, drinking, talking about girls, doing the things we thought made us men. Seth had been running fast and ran plumb into our little fort we'd worked so hard to build. We didn't see him so much as feel the fort shake when he hit it.

Jake put out his cigarette and went to look.

Ronnie shrugged. "Some animal, I guess."

Jake came back inside, lit another cigarette. "Men," he said, "anybody up for kicking some queerboy ass?"

I didn't believe Seth was gay. I'm not sure Jake even believed it at first. Yeah, he was different from us, but there were a lot of kids we went to school with that were different. Being from the woods like we were, we tended to see everyone as an outsider, and if you were an outsider, you were queer. It's just how we saw the world back then.

It's hard to find the right words to describe Seth. *Fragile*—that was the word that came to mind, though time would teach me this wasn't really the truth of it. No, truth was, he was as tough as thick rope. We called guys like that hard asses in 'Nam. He didn't look it, but Seth was a hard ass, through and through. Just took us a little while to figure that out, is all.

Jake wanted to make him pay for being in our woods and said we should track him down.

I told him it wasn't worth it, but that was like trying to convince an alcoholic that he didn't need another drink. Once Jake set his mind to something, he was going to do it.

"I saw this faggot," he said. "He's as queer as a three-dollar bill and he's on our turf."

That was enough for Ronnie, and I guess it was enough for me too. We went after him, running deep into the woods. We caught up with him ten minutes later at a little creek. The three of us stood on a hill, looking down on him. Seth sat at the edge of the water, his hands buried in his face. He was crying.

I don't think most people can pinpoint one certain moment when they change from a child to an adult. For me, though, it was easy. Not too long before, I would have joined Jake and Ronnie without a second thought. But for some reason, I didn't see any joy in ridiculing somebody else anymore. Especially somebody as hard up as this kid was. Maybe it was because my own family was changing— my old man was drinking more and had been out of work going on a year. Maybe it was just that I understood how sometimes a kid needed to find a place alone where he could cry his eyes out and not worry about being called a baby. Hell, maybe it was the way he cried. There was nobody here to impress—at least as far as he knew. Those tears weren't for gaining anybody's damned sympathy; they were real.

Years later, as a POW in Vietnam, I suffered moments like this when bawling my eyes out seemed like the only answer. But that was

Vietnam. Even at fourteen, I knew Seth must have been up against some pretty heavy stuff.

There was something else too. Something in his face that I recognized. Something in his eyes, maybe. I couldn't place it, but for a second, I saw it clear enough to make me dizzy. Then it was gone, and I heard Jake's voice:

"A faggot and a baby. Does the little baby queer want his mommy?"

Seth looked up, his eyes going from hurt to defiant in a hot second.

Ronnie laughed. "Look at that hair. He's a homo all right. Hey, pussy juice? You ever heard of scissors? Or maybe you're trying to grow it out so you can put it in a ponytail?"

Jake snickered. My stomach turned because I knew that every joke they made and every threat they hurled at this kid would make my own life that much harder. Pretty soon I'd have to make a choice. I couldn't just stand here with them. Silence was the same as approval. I knew that, even at fourteen. Hell, I knew it more then than I ever would.

Still, I waited. They were just throwing out some insults. We'd done that to kids hundreds of times.

"I'll bet he's got tits and a pussy," Jake said.

Seth stood up. "You won't say it to my face."

Jake slapped me on the back and laughed. "Hell, I was hoping you'd say that."

A little later, we stood in a semicircle around Seth, me on the right, Ronnie on the left, and Jake in the middle, facing Seth directly. From this closer view, I saw that Seth had a dark complexion and even darker eyes. He'd stopped crying now, and despite his long, wild hair, he didn't look like a queer at all, not now. He looked like a kid, not too different from us save one thing. His eyes. I saw in those eyes something that frightened me a little. Later, I would see similar expressions in 'Nam. Guys who had seen too much. Guys who had stepped past some invisible line that the rest of us didn't even know was there, and once they crossed that line, they changed. A silence went with them wherever they walked, and they stopped caring about their own well-being. When Jake spoke to him, he didn't even flinch; those eyes stayed right on Jake's, not moving, full of something reckless, full of something I didn't have a word for yet.

Still don't, to tell the truth, though some days it feels like it's on the tip of my tongue.

Seth was thin and at least three full inches taller than Ronnie, who was tallest in our little gang. But Ronnie wasn't just tall, he was muscular—broad shoulders with arms like small tree trunks. He'd been doing Jake's dirty work for years. Just looking at Seth, I couldn't imagine him being able to take any of us, much less Ronnie. Then I looked at his eyes again. You ever seen a cat go all bug-eyed before it pounces? That was Seth, except his eyes weren't big or anything; no, truth was, they weren't much more than slits. Didn't matter, though; the intensity, the wild-assed focus was there. And I knew. No way one of us would take him down alone.

Jake stuck his finger in Seth's chest. Obviously, Jake couldn't read the same signs I could, or maybe he just didn't care.

"Where do you live, queer?"

Seth knocked Jake's hand away.

Ronnie stepped forward. Jake held his hand up. *Wait*, the hand said. *Just wait until I need you.* Ronnie nodded and glared hard at Seth.

"Touch me again, queer, and I'll kill you." The thing about Jake was that he probably meant it. I'd once seen him hold a puppy over a fire by the scruff of its neck because it wouldn't stop barking. When the poor thing's backside began to smoke, the puppy squealed and shook and tried to bite him, but Jake held on, at least until the fire started to burn his hand. Then he took the puppy over to the pond and shoved him under. I thought he would keep him there until he was drowned, but that wasn't good enough for Jake. Jake wanted more. Jake always wanted more. He pulled the pup out and took him over to the fire to light him up again. This went on until the poor thing passed out. After that Jake tossed it aside, bored because he couldn't watch it suffer anymore.

It's hard for me to say nowadays just why I stuck with Jake as long as I did. My father liked to talk about family and the importance of sticking with your blood, but Jake was no kin of mine. Still, we'd spent enough time together that we might as well have been brothers, or at least cousins. I suppose it was loyalty as much as anything. At least that's what I liked to tell myself back then. The real reason—I know this now—is that there was part of me in Jake. A sick, twisted part that could stand by and watch a dog being tortured. Violence was a part of our lives back then. We didn't think twice about killing a rabbit or fox or any animal, really. There was some measure of comfort in watching something else suffer and knowing you didn't have to. This was in me as much as it was Jake. And when a thing like that gets inside you, it don't come out easily. Even when you want it to real bad.

So when Jake threatened to kill Seth, I had no reason to doubt he wouldn't try.

"Put your hand on my chest again and I'll knock it off again," Seth said.

Jake pointed his finger at Seth's chest a second time, but there was a key difference. This time he didn't touch him. "What are you running from?" he said.

"Don't worry about it."

"Prove you ain't a faggot."

"Don't have to."

It was like some kind of Mexican standoff. Seth was so cool under our pressure that I think it set Jake on edge. The fact that he didn't touch Seth again said something. I'd never seen Jake back down from anybody before.

"Look around you, faggot. These woods belong to me, Ronnie, and Walter. If we catch you here again, you're going home to Mommy with your nuts in a sling. *Comprende?*"

I thought it was over then. Jake was giving him an out. He didn't really want to fight this strange boy, not now. He'd wait until the odds were stacked far enough in his favor that he could humiliate Seth. It was never about just winning with Jake. He had to destroy the other person, kill their spirit. I'd seen him do it to some of the other boys at school before. But this was the summer. There wasn't a teacher here to break things up when they got tight. These were the woods, where a wildness hung in the air, strong as the scent of pine. Jake must have felt the difference. I know I did. Seth seemed too unpredictable, too intense, and out here anything could happen.

I thought it was over.

If it had been, things might have been different. Maybe I'd never have known about the slip. Maybe I wouldn't have survived 'Nam. Probably wouldn't have. The slip and Seth kept me alive over there.

It wasn't over, though. Seth said something that set Jake off. Something that I'd later wonder how he knew.

"You talk a lot about queers, don't you? I'll bet your daddy is taking it up the ass every day and night in prison. Maybe you just want to be like him."

I'd seen Jake angry before, but usually he kept it at a slow boil, just under the skin, always hot, but never full tilt. I had no idea how fast he could move. His fist had been at his waist, just hanging loose one second, and the next it was slammed up against Seth's right cheek. He hit Seth four times before anybody could react. Seth crumpled to the ground.

"You don't know nothing 'bout my daddy," he said, kicking Seth again.

I realized Jake didn't plan on stopping, so I reacted. That's something situations like this teach you. What you're made of. What you really believe. It's one thing to stand by and watch a puppy being tortured; it's not right, but it's a different thing than watching one person trying to kill another. I was proud to find out that particular bit of darkness wasn't in me.

I grabbed Jake in a bear hug, squeezing down on his chest as hard as I could. "Go easy, Jake. You've made your point."

"That bastard. Wants to talk. About my daddy. I'll kill him!" Each phrase was punctuated with another kick to Seth's midsection. I finally succeeded in pulling him away. He cursed me and struggled to break free of my grip.

"Get him off me!" he shouted to Ronnie.

Ronnie looked stunned. He didn't move.

"Just stay put, Ronnie," I said. "Jake needs to calm down before he kills somebody."

Jake twisted violently under my arms, but I didn't let go. "Get. Him. Off. Me," he said.

Ronnie shook his head.

"Remember three summers ago, Ronnie? Remember what those queers did to your—"

"Okay," Ronnie said. "Enough. Let him go."

I knew Ronnie could hurt me, but I also knew letting Jake go would get Seth hurt probably as bad or worse. I held on. Ronnie shook his head. "Your decision, Walter."

He tried to come around behind me. I turned Jake, always keeping him in front, a barrier between Ronnie and me. Seth stirred, getting up to his knees, coughing, maybe even spitting up blood.

I couldn't keep this dance up forever, but maybe I could last long enough for Seth to get away. "Get out of here," I said.

Seth made it to his feet but didn't go anywhere. Stubborn fool.

Ronnie lunged at me. I tried to move out of the way, but Jake wouldn't move with me and I was stuck. He slid through my arms and to the ground. Ronnie spun me around and I lost my balance, falling back into Seth. Seth caught me and shoved me aside before going for Jake. I hit my head on the base of an oak tree and watched from the ground as Seth managed one good lick in on Jake—a wicked shot to his nose—before Ronnie grabbed hold of him and lifted him high into the air. At first, I thought he was going to take him to the creek, maybe toss him in, but no, he walked upstream a little to where the bank turned muddy and soft. Then I knew where he was heading. For as long as I could remember there was a certain area along the creek that was like quicksand. Hell, there wasn't any *like* to it; it *was* quicksand. As a younger boy I'd thrown in rock after rock and watched, fascinated, as each disappeared from sight.

Now I watched again as Ronnie slammed Seth into the soft sand. Just like all the rocks I'd thrown, Seth began to sink.

By now, Jake was on his feet, wiping the blood from his nose. "Your ass is next," he said to me, and walked over to the quicksand. Ronnie glanced at him because he wanted Jake to tell him what to do. Seth was sinking fast, and all his flailing didn't seem to be helping much.

Jake knelt and reached one hand back, motioning for Ronnie to hold on to him. Ronnie took his arm, and Jake leaned out over the quicksand. He shoved Seth's chest hard, pushing him all the way under. Ronnie pulled Jake back and helped him regain his feet.

I watched all this through blurred vision. I knew what I was seeing wasn't right—that you couldn't make somebody sink so easy, that quicksand didn't work like that—but the knock on my head had been a doozy. I guess later, I chalked it up to that. Either way, at that moment, only one thing was clear:

Seth was gone.

Ronnie shifted, and I could tell he was nervous. He kept looking at Jake.

Jake shook his head. "Not yet."

"Jake," I said. "He's going to die."

"Shut up, Walter. Shut up or you'll be next."

"Ronnie," I tried. "Come on." Ronnie turned and looked at me. He was torn between doing the right thing and his loyalty to Jake.

The sand gurgled and Seth's right arm flailed up, waving wildly. I tried to reach for it, but Jake held me back. It didn't matter, though. The only hope I had of helping him would be if I were willing to fall in myself. Jake must have understood this because he let me go.

I turned back to Ronnie. "If you don't let him up now, he's going to die," I said. "You don't want that. None of us do."

He just looked at me. Jesus Christ.

"Take my hand," I said. If I could get one of them to cooperate, I'd be able to lean over and grab Seth. Then together, we could pull him out.

Jake shot Ronnie a look. Ronnie dropped his head.

The sand gurgled again and his arm was gone. How long had he been down there? At least two minutes, probably more. How long could a person go without breathing?

An idea hit me. It was my only chance.

I picked up a rock. It was the perfect size. Fit my hand like a baseball. Jake saw what I was planning and lunged at me. I knocked him upside the head with the rock, hit him right in the temple. The blood came fast and covered his face like a veil. His knees wobbled, and I smelled the stench of urine as he pissed himself.

Ronnie winced and slid away from me. I dropped the rock to show him I meant no harm. "You need to hold me, Ronnie. Don't let me go in."

He looked from me back to Jake and back to me again.

"He's going to die," I said. My voice cracked. I was about to cry, something I usually would have tried to hide, but not this time. This was too real, too in my face to pretend I didn't care.

I think Ronnie must have seen this and decided it was time to act, maybe past time. He nodded. "Okay."

I laid out on the ground, my elbows sinking into the sand. "Take my feet," I said, and instantly felt Ronnie's big hands around my ankles. The pull of the sand was strong, and for a minute I thought I'd plunge in headfirst, and no matter how strong Ronnie was, he wouldn't be able to pull me out. But the moment passed, and I realized if I was still, the sinking wasn't as fast.

"I need to go farther out," I said. "Do you have any good ground left?"

Ronnie moved me closer. I dug in with all my strength. I was moving my arms through the sand. It felt like moving them through wet cement. I finally touched something, a pant leg. I grabbed it just as my own chin hit the sand. I tasted the salty muck and tried to yell. I'm not sure I made much sense with the sand in my mouth, but Ronnie got the message. He pulled me back just as I got a decent grip on Seth's leg.

A few minutes later, the three of us lay on solid ground, panting. Well, not Seth. Seth was coughing up a storm. Each breath he tried to take seemed riddled with sand and grit. His lungs rattled like they were full of broken glass, but he was alive, by God.

I stumbled to my feet and stood there looking at what was left of my life. Seth—breathing, but barely. Jake—he might be dead—there was so much blood and it kept on coming. Ronnie—shaking hard, like somebody with a fever, doubled over, plumb exhausted from pulling both of us out.

At the time, I had no idea that what I'd done had set into motion the events that would shape the rest of my life.

———————

That night after I ate my supper and kissed Mama on the cheek while she listened to her radio programs, I went to the hall bathroom and locked the door. I heard my daddy outside the window with one of his buddies, popping the tops off their jugs of moonshine and muttering curses about the heat. Nobody had to tell me how that was going to end.

Thanks to a botched land deal several years ago, we were one of the few houses in this region that had running water. The lines had already been run, and we'd been ready to move—to escape what Daddy called the "city folk"—when the deal fell through, and we were left with the best of both worlds: indoor plumbing and very few neighbors. Thanks to this, I didn't have to go out to the pond to try my little experiment. That's all it was—an experiment. That's what I told myself.

But like most of the things we tell ourselves, it was a damned lie.

I stopped the sink up and let the water run until it was almost to the top. I thought about how Seth had been in the quicksand for all that time, and when he came out, he wasn't drowned or anything. Not even passed out. He was alive, maybe coughing like crazy, but he was alive.

I closed my eyes and lowered my head. The water came up around my ears and the world took on that echoing, faraway feel. My pulse throbbed in my temples, and I kept imagining hands on my back, pushing me down. I began to count.

I made it to seventy before I knew my lungs were going to explode. My pulse hammered. Ten more seconds. Twenty. Thirty. I stopped counting and opened my eyes. The white of the porcelain sink was bright. I wanted to breathe so bad, but I kept my head under anyway. I'd read somewhere that you passed out before you died when you were holding your breath.

The world shook. It was like the water was moving in the sink and not just the water; the sink moved too. I was fading, slipping away, or maybe it was the world that was slipping. The last thing I saw before sucking in a lungful of water was the sky over tall trees at dusk. Then my lungs filled up, and I began to choke. I pulled out of the sink and fell back against the window. Outside, I heard my father. "What the—?"

Coughing didn't seem to help. I couldn't remember what I had been trying to prove. I just knew I wanted to live.

Daddy lifted me off the floor, hugging me from behind. His big hands balled themselves under my rib cage, and he squeezed hard, sending the water out of my lungs and all over the bathroom mirror. He dropped me.

"Next time," he said, "try a gun."

After he left, I stayed on the floor. There was a part of me that wanted to go get his gun—I knew right where it was—and hold it under his chin and make him squirm before I pulled the trigger. But there was another part of me that was too glad to be alive to do anything as stupid as that.

Chapter Five

It was October when I heard about it. I was sitting in English class. Mrs. Harris had forgotten to pull the shades down, and outside it was one of those special fall days Alabama has: bright blue sky and red leaves, every tree blazing like a fire. I was watching a baby rabbit hop across the grass when I heard a girl speak.

"She's been gone since Saturday night. My uncle said she was just going out to check on the puppies in their barn. That was just about dark, Saturday night."

I turned around and saw Meredith Garrigan across the aisle from me. She was talking to Tina Bray, a girl I'd liked since the sixth grade.

"How old is she?" Tina asked.

Meredith shook her head. "Ten."

Tina made a face, wrinkling her nose like she was disgusted.

"I know. It's terrible."

Seth sat in the desk right in front of me. He had his head down, his usual position. Since the stuff that happened with Jake and Ronnie back in the summer, Seth and me had become casual friends, and I got used to seeing him like this in class. School was so easy for him, he barely paid attention. Once the teachers realized how smart he was, they pretty much left him alone.

Seth seemed like he wasn't listening until Meredith said, "It's terrible." Then he sat up.

"What's terrible?" he asked.

She looked a little put off. "We were talking about my cousin."

"What about your cousin?"

Just then, Mrs. Harris looked up from the essays she'd been grading. Her gaze fell on our group. I'm sure we must have looked like we were having quite the conversation, leaned over across the aisle like we were.

"Something you'd like to share with the class, Miss Bray?" Mrs. Harris always went for Tina first. I believed it was because Tina represented a lot of things in a girl that Mrs. Harris didn't like. Things like brains. Not get-the-right-answer kind of brains, but the think-for-yourself kind. To make things worse, Tina was something of a looker. First girl I can ever remember fantasizing about that wasn't in the pages of that '59 *Playboy*.

"Yes, ma'am," Tina shot back.

Mrs. Harris smiled and got up from her desk. She walked to the front of the room and addressed the rest of the class, the ones who had at least been pretending to quietly work on the sentences they were supposed to be diagramming. "Please listen, class. Miss Bray has something that she deems more important than learning the correct functions of our language." She turned to Tina. "You have the floor, Miss Bray."

Tina stood up. "Thanks. Well, a lot of things are more important than diagramming stupid sentences, but this one is especially important. Meredith was just trying to spread the word that her ten-year-old cousin is missing. Has been missing since Saturday night, as a matter of fact. Considering today is Tuesday, this is a heck of a lot more important than your brainless sentences."

A lot of things might have happened after that. I'm sure they probably did. I heard later that Mrs. Harris almost had a come-apart. She gritted her teeth and broke her ink pen. She gave Tina a look so evil that a month later when Tina herself went missing, people actually muttered about Mrs. Harris being a suspect. Truth was, I didn't notice anything at that moment except Seth. Seth broke. Right in front of us all, though I'm sure nobody else was watching, being too preoccupied with Tina and Mrs. Harris.

He started by shaking his head, slowly, side to side. It was like he refused to believe what he'd heard. His mouth dropped open and just hung there, slack. He groaned and closed his eyes. He was gone, his eyes vacant, as he dropped his head to his desk. He didn't move until the bell rang.

After school, I followed Seth to the park downtown. I realized this was the second time I'd followed him. I hoped this one turned out better than the first.

The park was already getting dark. Phillips Park. It's still there, just nobody goes anymore and the swings are all rusty. Truth is, they were rusty back then too, and on this particular day it was pretty much empty. It was the perfect place for Seth to go.

I found him huddled under a dogwood tree, arms wrapped over his knees. Damned if he wasn't shaking.

I sat down beside him and didn't say a word. He knew I was there but didn't look at me.

I waited for him to stop crying and said, "This is the second time I've chased you down."

He didn't even look at me.

"You know, you never even said thank you."

He shook his head. "You shouldn't have bothered, but thanks."

I shrugged. "You're welcome. Jake and Ronnie don't like new kids. That's all."

Seth let out a sad kind of laugh. "Is that all? Jesus, they tried to murder me."

There was an awkward pause. I didn't know what to say.

"You should have died that day," I said finally. "How'd you stay under so long? You were sunk for a good four minutes."

He brushed his long bangs out of his face. "Is that what you followed me down here for?"

"Not really, but I do wonder. I mean, that night, after it all happened, I filled the sink up with water and, you know, tried it. I barely lasted two minutes."

"That's a good way to die."

I didn't respond, and I think he realized he'd hit pretty close to home.

"You were probably thinking on the bad stuff. The way your lungs ached. How bad it hurt. That sort of thing."

I shrugged. "Nothing else to think about. You don't have much choice."

"I've got this thing," he said. "It's something I've learned. You go somewhere else. You know, inside. Once you do that, there's nothing you can't endure." He smiled weakly, and I wasn't sure if he believed his own words.

"I'm not following."

He plucked some grass and tossed it out in front of him. "You train yourself after a while to think about positive things. Here, let me show you." He reached out and grabbed the fat of my arm between his thumb and forefinger, pinching so hard I jerked away.

"Ow! What was that for?"

"To show you. All you thought about was the pain. You let it overwhelm everything else. Now, think about something that makes you really happy."

"Huh?"

"Just do it. It doesn't matter what it is, just make sure it's something good. And picture it. I mean really see it in your mind."

I thought of Tina Bray. I imagined me and her walking together in the park, her hand in mine. I saw her leaning her head on my shoulder, whispering in my ear.

"Got it?"

"Yeah, I got it."

He pinched me again.

"Holy shit, that hurts!" I said.

"But not as bad as before, right?"

I shook my head. I didn't feel a difference.

Seth shrugged. "It takes practice. The point is, the world is a different place when you come at it from in here." He tapped his forehead. "Everything sort of opens up. You look hard enough, you can find a way to escape anything. Even pain."

I rubbed my arm. "So that day, you thought about something

besides drowning, something besides all the sand and grit in your mouth and lungs, and that helped you stay under longer?"

"I guess, if that's the way you want to look at it. I wasn't really there, so I don't remember."

I took this in. Truth be told, I thought he was full of shit, but there might be something to it. He had managed to stay under much longer than I ever could.

"So where did you go that day, when Ronnie held you under?"

"Same place I always go. The swamp. But it was only a brief visit. I call it a glimpse. It's like a catnap instead of a long night's sleep."

I had no idea what he was going on about. I decided I liked Seth fine, but he was weird. I couldn't shake the sense that he believed every word he was saying.

"The swamp? A swamp doesn't sound very nice."

He shrugged. "Well, it is. It's beautiful." Maybe he saw the doubt in my face, because he added, "You wouldn't understand."

"What's that mean?"

"Nothing. I just doubt you would understand."

I stood up. "You act like your life is so hard. How bad can it be?"

He closed his eyes. I don't know, maybe he was thinking of the swamp, maybe he was just trying to decide how to answer my question. Finally, he said, "It can be bad, Walter. Really, really bad."

I believed him. Any fool could see his life was hard. I'd seen some of it firsthand. The rest was in his eyes, the way he carried himself, but I was still put off by him because I hurt too. It wasn't like he had cornered the market on pain.

"What's so bad? What about today?" I asked. "You know something about this missing girl?"

"No." The instant he said it, I knew he was lying. It was the way he ducked his head when he answered, the way he looked away and then back at me after the lie. I'd seen my daddy lie to my mama so many times, I felt like a polygraph test.

"So what's eating you?"

He shook his head. "My mother disappeared years ago. It just reminded me of her. That's all."

I could tell there was more, but I didn't want to push him. Hell, he was pretty much the only friend I had now. Jake wanted to kill me for what I'd done to him, and Ronnie would always be with Jake as long as he never learned to have a will of his own. He was the kind of person Jake lived for. I had other friends at school, but those kids were more like acquaintances because even back then, these woods were isolated. School was the only time I saw anybody besides Seth, Ronnie, and Jake. So I didn't push Seth. I figured time would eventually tell all. We sat there, talking about other stuff—movies and books, mostly—until the sun was gone and the park was completely dark.

The last thing I remember before starting home that evening was getting that feeling again. I knew Seth from somewhere. He carried it in his face, his hair, the slope of his shoulders, the same traits of someone I knew but had somehow lost.

Chapter Six

DANNY

I never really believed that my mother and sister were dead. Sometimes, I thought everyone else did except me. But then I'd remember my grandmother. She was my mother's mom, and she was a resourceful woman who had managed a farm in north Alabama and worked full-time as a real estate agent for fifteen years since her husband's death. She'd also lived through the Great Depression, two world wars, and the deaths of three of my mother's siblings. Fatalism wasn't an outlook for Gran; it was ingrained in her like a personality trait. All of this made Gran incapable of saying anything but what she thought was the truth, feelings be damned.

The last time we visited her was a few months after they disappeared.

Dad and I had driven up for a change of scenery, hoping that putting some distance between ourselves and those silent woods behind our house would help in some small way. It might have if not for Gran's stubborn fatalism. Still, I loved her for what she was—an amazing woman. Nothing could shake her, and I think it was her indomitable faith that she would survive in the face of whatever life threw her way that made me want to spend time with her even when Dad found her negativity hard to swallow and spent most of the weekend out in the garden pulling up potatoes and radishes.

We were sitting in her den watching professional wrestling, something Gran had enjoyed as far back as I could remember. I had tried, without success, to explain to her that it was fake, but she wasn't having it so I eventually gave up and enjoyed it too.

The subject of Mom and Anna hadn't come up yet, and I was fine with that. By then, I had talked to reporters, friends, neighbors, and everybody else about their disappearances. It always came back to the same thing: They were gone and nobody knew where or why. A commercial came on and Gran put down the peas she was shelling. "You got to be strong now, Danny."

I looked up from the commercial. "What?"

She stood and came over to where I was sitting on the couch, sat down, and took my hand. Squeezing it, she said, "I know it's a hard road to walk right now, being the one she left behind, but please don't think of it like that. Your mama has got problems, and always has had them. In her mind she did what she had to do." Gran squeezed my hand more tightly. "Hard truths are just that, Danny. Hard. But we've got to face them head-on. I'm going to tell you what your daddy won't tell. Your mama left you. She took Anna—God bless that child—and left. And don't you for a minute think she's coming back. That either one of them is coming back. They're not coming back, Danny." When I tried to pull away, she gripped my hand more tightly. "Your daddy isn't ready for that yet. But he will be soon enough. I know this is hard on you, but life won't never be easy. Life is relentless. It just keeps coming at you. The sooner you accept the truth, the happier you'll be."

"She didn't leave us," I said, an edge in my voice.

She let my hand go and stood, sighing.

"I'm telling you this because I think you need to know. Your mother is a selfish woman. It's no reflection on you."

I glared at her. "How do you know? What makes you so sure?" I was scolding her, something no one did to Gran.

She cocked her head at me and raised her eyebrows. "I know because I know my daughter, and I know about the choices she made. She wasn't always like this, but she changed, and now I don't think any of us will be able to reach her."

I stood up, and I could feel the blood rushing to my face. "Don't say that. Never say that." I was trembling, barely able to control my rage. I don't know what I would have said or done from there if Dad hadn't walked in.

He looked at us, about to speak. His mouth opened, and some sound came out. Then he stopped, his eyes going from Gran to me—standing over her, fists clenched—back to Gran. "What's going on?" he said.

Gran regarded me with something like pity. "Just a talk, Frank. Setting some things straight."

Dad was in no mood to get involved with anything stressful, so he only nodded and continued to the room—Mom's old room—where he was staying in the back.

Gran stood and put her hand on my shoulder. "One day you'll see I'm right, Danny." Then she picked up her shelled peas and headed back to the kitchen, leaving me alone with my anger. But as

I stood there, I felt the anger changing to fear. Gran understood the world in ways I could barely imagine. What if she was right? What if my mother had left us?

Doubt, according to the preacher whose church we stopped going to about a month after Mom and Anna vanished, was a natural part of faith. They were two vines that grew together, intertwined. That was what I remembered when I had doubts about my mother and sister.

It was hard to explain why I felt we'd be reunited. Mostly, there was a sense that I would somehow feel it when my mother passed. Her presence had been so large in my life for the first fourteen years that I felt it like a warm breeze forever at my back. The breeze was still there, and until I couldn't feel it anymore, she was alive. And if she was alive, I refused to believe she'd left us on purpose, which meant they were somewhere out there and they wanted to come home. And foolishly, I believed I could bring them back.

Cliff and I went to his house for lunch, a place I never grew tired of. His house was so large—three stories on seven acres of land—that you could literally get lost inside it. Really. It happened to me once when I was eight. His mother found me wandering on the second floor, trying to find my way back to Cliff's room on the third floor. His father had invented some kind of chip for computers in the early seventies, and now, more than twenty years later, he did nothing except count his money and tend his azaleas and roses in the walled garden behind their house. Cliff's mother was a lawyer, but not the type that argued cases in court. According to Cliff, she spent all her time poring over dusty law books and typing up long documents on their computer.

We ate shrimp sandwiches out by the pool. Yeah, shrimp. It was fresh shrimp too. Cliff's dad was fanatical about fresh seafood, so much that he had bribed the truck that delivered to the Birmingham restaurants to make a special stop out here in the country. The sandwich was good, but then again everything was good at Cliff's house. It was an odd place for me during the months after Mom and Anna's disappearance. I simultaneously craved the normalcy of being in a place with two parents, while nursing a deep-seated jealousy of what Cliff had. His parents were far from perfect, but they were there. Most of all, when I saw them together, they displayed a genuine easiness with each other, a kind of quiet confidence that my parents lacked, even when times had been good. I knew parents could fake stuff when they thought you were watching, but Cliff's parents never felt like poseurs. Rich assholes, maybe, but never poseurs.

"So, do you think he did it?" Cliff asked, his mouth stuffed full of shrimp.

"Who did what?" I knew exactly what he meant—did I think the man from the cabin killed my mother and sister—but something about the question pissed me off, so I decided to play dumb.

"You know . . . that man. Do you think he . . . was responsible?"

"Responsible for what?" Okay, I was just being a jerk now. I should have let him back out gracefully.

"You know."

"For their deaths?"

"I didn't say that."

I dropped my sandwich and stood up, suddenly not hungry anymore. I went over to the edge of the pool, kicked off my shoes and socks, sat down, and put my feet in. The water was warm. Mid-July tended to do that to swimming pools in Alabama.

"It just seems like it might be a relief, that's all."

I cocked my head but didn't turn around to look at Cliff.

"I'll drop it," he said.

I waited, splashing water with my feet in high arching sprays. If he wanted to drop it, fine. Something told me he wouldn't, though.

"All I mean to say is that it might be a relief to find out who was responsible for what happened. I mean, that way you wouldn't have to worry about . . . You know . . . Your mom being, I don't know . . ."

I sat perfectly still, daring him to say it, feeling the old anger flexing itself inside me, my muscles tensing, my pulse starting a dull thud in my head, my fists clenching and unclenching. It was an anger I'd been nursing since the day they disappeared; I'd been caring for it, tending its needs, letting it grow inside me. Always managing to keep it down, but even when I did, it was still wreaking havoc on the inside.

"What?" I said, turning. "Just finish your sentence, Cliff."

He must have seen the anger etched hard on my face because he looked down and shook his head. "Never mind."

I stalked over to him, infuriated. I grabbed his shirt collar in my fist and pulled it so hard the fabric ripped.

"You get one damned thing straight," I said. "My mother did not kidnap my sister. Do you hear me?"

Cliff looked afraid, his glasses falling down his nose, his eyes wide with something like awe.

"Do you hear me?" I said again, louder, spitting the words in his face.

"Yeah, Danny. I hear you."

I let go, disgusted with myself. I turned and felt a sudden need to cry, to sob, to call out for my mother, but I held it in. I swallowed it back down inside like bile. Then, in a flurry of motion, I ripped off my shirt and sprinted for the pool, diving in headfirst and sinking slowly to the bottom, where I would stay for as long as I was able, until my lungs burned and I had to come back up for air.

When I finally did come back to the surface, I noticed that the sky far to the west was beginning to gather clouds into a thick, black coil of impending fury.

Chapter Seven

Something clicked inside me while I was underwater. Cliff was right. It would feel better to know that someone else was responsible besides my mother. There had been rumors, innuendos, lies in the months after her disappearance. Her drinking problem, her frustration with raising two children, one of them autistic. Some people said she left on her own and took Anna with her because she knew my father could never make it with us both alone. Others—and these were the ones that bothered me most—whispered that they were both dead.

This was unthinkable to me, a notion I refused to consider, even in the lowest depths of my grief.

Despite all of the things I *didn't believe* had happened to Mom and Anna, I had very little—if anything—that I *did believe* might have happened. I was out of ideas, lost at sea, and the feeling burned inside me, spurring me to do something. Anything.

I left Cliff's house at two in the afternoon, knowing I would have at least three hours, probably more, before Dad came home. My plan—well, to be honest I didn't have a plan. I was heading for the cabin in the woods to confront the man who had stood in the rain on my front doorstep for two nights, possibly more. I was still acting on the same anger that had caused me to almost hit Cliff, the same anger that made me identify with the gathering storm above me.

I crossed the highway, noting the storm was closer than I had thought. The clouds formed a great stack of darkness, infused with what appeared to be an unnatural light, causing the edges of the cloud mass to glow a dull green. It was heading west, and from the looks of it, I'd have no more than a half hour before it hit. I broke into a run, not only to avoid the storm, but also because I feared my nerve might fail me.

Ten minutes later, I was slogging through the woods, waiting for the sky to break open. Thunder came in deep bellows and lightning had already struck one of the pines, almost bringing it down on my head. I'd made a mistake, coming here. The storm had come much faster than I'd expected, and the sky was almost completely dark now. The air felt like it was alive, so warm and wet and it hadn't even started raining yet. Another blast of lightning struck a nearby tree, and I shrieked and sprinted ahead into the darkness, now losing my way, unsure of my bearings, wishing I'd just gone home and sulked in my bed.

Then the rain came, soaking everything in giant gusts blown slantwise by the wind. I slipped and landed in the mud. Struggling to stand up, I reached for a low-hanging tree limb and heard a sharp whip crack of thunder. I felt a jolt run through my entire body, and

I smacked the ground hard. My head came down on something solid, something too hard to be the ground or even a root. I rolled over into the mud, gasping. My body tingled and I smelled smoke, something burning nearby. I looked up just in time to see a flaming tree looming over me, an inferno so spectacular that even in my panic, I admired the beauty of it, falling. I rolled, my shoulder throbbing, as the tree crashed to the ground. A burning branch brushed my face and scorched my cheek. I screamed out in pain, but the heat was soon extinguished by the downpour.

That's when I saw her again. Anna. She stood as if on the air, hovering well above the ground and debris, untouched by the storm. She said nothing. She didn't move, but I felt like she wanted me to get up to go somewhere, so I did, scrambling to my feet only to trip again over a concrete slab. I knelt and rummaged through the wet undergrowth, tearing away kudzu and weeds until I could make out a lip of concrete raised just off the muddy ground. I dug away more kudzu and mud until it was clear what I had stumbled upon: an underground shelter. I heaved open the lid, and just before going inside, I looked for Anna again.

She was gone.

Inside, the darkness was complete. I lay still, resisting the urge to vomit as I felt the shelter begin to spin around me. I couldn't see it, but I felt it, and then I did see things—flashes of water, trees, and shadows. I was turning, falling, and just before I hit the ground, I saw something else. It was only a flash, but it stayed with me. A cabin. Not the cabin I was looking for, though. This one was even more ancient, but perhaps a little bigger. It was nestled between giant oaks strung with Spanish moss, and a single light burned within. This one was bigger, older than the one Cliff and I had looked at in the binoculars, and it had a porch. Just a tumbledown, narrow walk in front of the cabin, but I was positive the other place, the one I was looking for, had no such addition.

When I woke some time later, the shelter was still. I climbed the ladder out and slogged back through the flooded lowlands trying to get my bearings and head for home.

———

It wasn't until later—much later when I was home and dry and thinking about the day—that I realized two things: I'd been struck by lightning and survived. That was one. The other was more disconcerting. I'd seen Anna again, and this time it was clear why. She had directed me to the storm shelter. Without her, I might have died out there. I wouldn't have been the only one, as two other locals were killed in the high winds on the same day.

———

That night I slept the sleep of the dead. I spent the next day completing a to-do list Dad had left for me, which had me working inside and out. I didn't get a chance to call Cliff until nearly three o'clock. But by then, I had already formulated a plan.

"Invite me to spend the night," I said.

Cliff, never one to be caught off guard, said, "Wanna spend the night?"

When Dad got home, I asked him if I could. This was just a formality in the summer. In fact, sometimes Dad seemed more than willing for me to go, and this time was no exception. He quickly agreed, even offering to drive me over.

Though the July heat was miserable, there were no signs of afternoon thunderheads, so I told him I would be fine walking.

I left him sitting on the couch watching the five o'clock news, something he and Mom always liked to do together while Anna and I were outside playing. I felt a twinge of sadness as I realized the chances of these things happening again were growing smaller every day.

We waited until eleven thirty, when Cliff was confident that both his parents were asleep. Slipping silently through the dark house, we paused just long enough at the back door to disable the alarm. Outside, it was clear and almost cool, the heat from the day lifting and sliding into memory. Above us the heavens seemed alive: a half-moon and stars beyond counting.

"Are you going to tell me where we're going?" Cliff said.

"My house."

"Why?"

"I've got a feeling. Keep your eyes peeled for smoke."

I'd already decided that if he wasn't outside my house tonight, we'd go on through the woods to his cabin, but I didn't think it would come to that. Somehow, I knew he'd be back.

We made the highway in good time and veered wide so we wouldn't approach the front of my house. Sticking to the trees, we slinked along the outskirts of the property. As the house came into view, I was surprised to see that a light was on in my parents' old room, the one Dad forbade me to go in, the one he kept under lock and key. I allowed myself a brief image of Dad inside, sitting on the bed, a photo album open and wet with his tears. This was the image I wanted. Instead, I got the increasingly cold Dad, the one who had lost his faith. The image of Dad with the photo album was fleeting because just then the light in the room went out, and Cliff and I were left in almost complete darkness save for the glow of the moon.

Cliff tapped me. I turned and saw that he was pointing to the great live oak that dominated our front yard. A thin tendril of smoke snaked around the trunk. He was there, just on the other side of the tree. I took a deep breath, feeling a surge of panic hitting me. I forced it back down and nodded at Cliff. The plan was for Cliff to stay close while I approached the man. If something bad happened—God forbid—then Cliff would run for the house to get Dad.

I stepped out of the trees and made my way across our gravel drive.

The smell of tobacco smoke was strong as I neared the tree. Though I couldn't see him yet because the oak was so thick, I heard him sucking oxygen into his nose followed by an almost inaudible cough.

When he came into view, he was lighting another cigarette. He saw me and dropped it on the ground.

"What are you doing at my house?" I said, trying to sound tougher than I was.

He held up a hand as if to ward me off.

"I asked you a question."

"I don't mean any harm."

"So why are you here? Why do you keep coming back?"

He dropped his head as if ashamed. This emboldened me, and I stepped closer to him.

"Tell me why you're here. Now."

He looked up at me then and I was close enough to see his eyes, or rather his eye. The right one shone with a clear intensity that made me weigh my next step. His left eye was dead, unresponsive, just a marble in a socket. He leaned over and picked up the cigarette he'd been lighting when I approached. Taking his time, he produced a book of matches and tore one out. He lit the match and then the cigarette, taking two long pulls before looking back at me. "You want to know why I'm here?" He nodded thoughtfully. "I'll tell you," he said.

Some part of me suddenly wanted to say *never mind*, wanted to turn tail and run. But another part, a bigger, better-developed part, wanted—no, *needed*—to know.

The next words that came out of his mouth still resound in my subconscious some sixteen years later. Some mornings, I wake up with them on my lips and ask my sleep-addled self if they could possibly be true. Some mornings the answer to that question is no. What he said that night changed everything. The words changed me and Dad and the people around us, and ultimately, I think his words saved my life.

"I know," he said, "where your mother and sister are."

I have no idea how long I stood there, openmouthed, trying to process his words. What I do know is that I never got a chance to respond because Cliff screamed bloody hell and came charging out of the woods in our direction. If the man was surprised by this development, he didn't show it.

Too stunned to speak, I simply waited for Cliff to join us. Part of me must have known his scream would alert my father, but I didn't react. Instead it was the man, dropping his cigarette to the grass and extinguishing it under one heavy-toed boot. "Snake, most likely. Bastards are everywhere these days. Better steer clear too. They're poisonous as hell. Time to get moving."

As if in confirmation of his statement, Dad's silhouette appeared in the window.

I watched as the man reached for his oxygen tank and dragged it swiftly toward the gravel drive and the woods on the other side. I followed him.

He went around Dad's truck and was almost to the trees when he stopped and turned back. "You know where I live." It wasn't a question. Then he was gone.

Cliff reached me at that same moment. He was heaving breaths in and out, laboring to get the words through. "Snake," he said. "Big freaking snake. Crawled . . ." Gasp. "Across . . . my foot."

I heard the front door open, and I grabbed Cliff's arm and pulled him down behind Dad's truck. I clamped my hand over Cliff's mouth to silence his panting. We waited. Dad muttered something and went back inside. When a few minutes passed, I let go of Cliff and slumped against the truck.

"Are we going to follow him?" Cliff said.

"No. Not tonight."

"Good."

We crept back toward the tree line. As we disappeared into the woods, Cliff said, "Watch out for snakes."

Chapter Eight

We didn't sleep.

There was too much to get our minds around. We spent the rest of the evening sitting up in chairs in front of Cliff's big-screen television. Only we didn't watch the TV. Instead, we stared at our own dark reflections in the mute screen and tried to make sense of it.

By the time the sun came up over the cotton fields, I'd come to two possible conclusions. One, the man was a crazy fool. He'd come to town and heard about Mom and Anna and decided to cause trouble. Two, he might have actually had something to do with their disappearances, a conclusion that—considering the timing of his appearance—seemed harder and harder to ignore. He was in the cabin, which seemed enough to suggest a connection. This second option made me feel sick to my stomach to think about, so I didn't. By the time I got around to articulating my thoughts to Cliff, I was thoroughly pissed because as bad as the second option was, the first wasn't much better.

"That's it," I said. "Neither one is worth a damn."

"No," Cliff said, "there's another one. Maybe, somehow, he knows where they are. I mean, he just knows. Like he didn't put them there, so he's not responsible, right? He just knows and he wants to tell you so you can help them."

I nodded. It seemed very unlikely, but I tried to ignore that and focus on the idea anyway. I think I had dismissed it simply because it held too much hope, and I'd learned that hope could sometimes be a dangerous thing.

The sunlight streamed in through the windows behind the TV now, causing me to shield my eyes and yawn. "I'm going to sleep for a couple of hours. When I wake up, I'm going to the cabin." I left the statement hanging there. I wanted him to volunteer to go with me, but I wasn't going to ask. He'd already done a lot for me, and I would understand if he didn't want to do any more.

"You know I'll go with you," Cliff said.

"Don't worry about it. That guy could be a nut."

Cliff walked over to his bed and fell on top of it heavily. "Could be? He *is* a nut. That's why you're not going alone."

That made me smile a little. Then I stretched out in the recliner and fell asleep.

One of the great heartaches I have known in my life is losing touch with Cliff Banks. I last saw him when I was twenty-seven in New York City. We'd both gone to colleges up north. Mine was the University of Massachusetts. His was Harvard. We'd had plans of meeting once a week in downtown Boston for a beer. I even remember calling him once, it must have been the first weekend I was on campus, to set up a time to get together.

"I'm already swamped," he said. "Physics is going to kill me."

"No problem. We'll do it another weekend."

"Sounds good, Dan. I'll call you."

I was about to hang up when he said, "Wait."

"Yeah?"

"What happened when we were fourteen. That summer. Do you remember?"

"Of course I remember. It was—"

"It scares me."

"Sometimes it scares me too."

"The things you said . . ."

"It really happened." I paused. "I think."

"Yeah, well, you always seemed like a reasonable kid, which is why it surprised me when you let that old man—"

"Don't," I said. "Just don't."

"Sure, Danny. I understand."

"No, you don't." It was a mean thing to say. And worse, I wondered if it was a hypocritical statement because the truth was, I didn't understand either. Not really. Not enough.

"Here's the thing, Danny. With physics . . ." He paused. "I've learned a lot about the world, the nature of things. You know, I took that class last summer. It doesn't compute. What happened, or what you say happened—"

"You heard the story too. Tell me he was lying."

"He may not have been lying. Insane people tell the truth, Dan."

I said nothing. It was a place I didn't want to go.

"Besides, it's all so vague now. Even if I believed every word he said, I didn't experience it like you did. I didn't . . ." I could hear his desire to say the word and not say it at the same time. I could hear it in the silence over the phone line.

So I said it for him. "Slip. You didn't slip. Whether you believe it or not, I did."

"Listen," he said. "This is tough for me. It was always tough for me. There's a term, maybe you've heard of it: willful amnesia. I'm starting to think it might not be a bad idea."

Willful amnesia. How many times had I repeated that phrase inside my head over the years?

"I'll call you," he said, and it was clear that he couldn't bear to talk about this any longer. "We'll get together this weekend. I'll call."

He never did.

———

When I ran into him in New York, it was as a stranger. He was sitting three seats down from me at a bar. By then, the clash between what happened to me when I was fourteen and the rational adult world I had known since was beginning to exercise a hold on my life. Some nights, I couldn't sleep for worrying about how much of it really happened. See, you start growing up, moving faster, doing more things, occupying your mind with one thing or another of little or great consequence, and you begin to lose sight of the things you once held dear: the ideals and the truths that you had clung to in your interior life because the interior life is whittled away by scratches on a calendar, obligations, and all the damned little things that make you old.

I saw him and at first, I didn't recognize him. No, that's wrong. I recognized him immediately, but I didn't place him. Seeing his face spiked something in my subconscious and put me in mind of the past. I knew I knew him. I felt dizzy with it. Then I heard him speak, saw him gesture with his hand, and I had it. Cliff. I leaned forward intending to call out his name, but at that instant, someone tapped him on the shoulder. Greetings were exchanged, beers bought amid uproarious laughter. I was left with a sense of loss so profound I immediately got up and exited the bar. Even now, I struggle to explain it. Maybe I just didn't want to make him revisit those events that obviously had caused him so much pain. More likely, I believed it would be easier to simply walk away than to confront a person from my past with whom I had shared the greatest enigma of my life.

I think one of the reasons I decided to write all of this down is because of that encounter with Cliff. It's too easy to forget. And it's even easier to pretend that you are just an ordinary person instead of that young boy who not only witnessed magic, but embraced it, reshaping the very world around him so that it lined up right and true.

Chapter Nine

Cliff woke me at ten thirty. For a brief second, I felt disoriented. I thought I was at Gran's and I'd fallen asleep in her big chair. In my reverie, Mom and Anna were still with us, and I almost called out Anna's name, somehow mistaking Cliff for her, before realizing where and *when* I was.

"I figured it was time," Cliff said.

My neck was stiff and I had a dull headache, the kind I got sometimes when I'd been overstimulated. I nodded at him. "Good call. We need to get moving."

We grabbed a box of snack cakes to eat as we walked, and I wolfed down three of them before the highway.

The day was already hot, something you got used to in Alabama, but there were no clouds that morning and the sun seemed particularly bright on my skin. I angled for a stand of pear trees in order to get out of its harsh glare.

As we slid into the dim light of the woods, I saw the remnants from the tornado. Whole segments of the forest had been decimated, making it tough going because of all the deadfall. I remembered seeing Anna, the way she had seemed to beckon to me, as if she understood something about my fate that I couldn't even begin to fathom. I was about to tell Cliff, when I thought better of it and decided to keep it to myself.

I did want to find the shelter again, to show Cliff, but for some reason I couldn't locate it. The woods looked so different now, devastated by the storm. I would be doing good just to find the old cabin again, much less the storm shelter where I'd seen Anna. Besides, I still wasn't sure what to make of that whole day anyway. Like the night I'd seen Anna near the quicksand, the time in the storm shelter seemed more like a dream than reality.

A few minutes later, we stood on top of a steep embankment, looking down at the little shack. It looked almost the same as the last time I was here, when I'd watched the police coming in and out behind yellow tape. A rutted, dirt road served as a driveway to connect the place with another similar road that wound out to the highway. You could drive back here—the man obviously had—but most people wouldn't want to put their cars through it. I noticed his mud-splattered truck, an old F-250 parked in the shade just off the makeshift drive. The yard was littered with junk, although it was evident he'd been trying to clean it up some because it had been much worse the last time I was here. A busted generator, spare tires, and the scraps of at least three push mowers sulked among the overgrown weeds and kudzu. The shack itself seemed to have sprouted vines. The kudzu fell off the roof like shaggy hair, tangling over on itself, thickening, closing off the cabin from sight. Except for the very front, where the old man had obviously cleared enough vines away to go inside. Now, the door stood open, thumping very gently in the breeze.

I looked at Cliff. "You up for this?"

"Not really."

"Me either."

We stood there a moment. I don't know about Cliff, but I was scared. You grow up in a place, taking certain things for granted. One of those things was that this cabin was a dark, brooding entity, an almost living and breathing thing that kept its secrets deep within. Watching that door thump in the breeze, almost like an invitation, didn't help either.

Yet . . .

I was here. The man said he knew where my mother and sister were. I had to go in. I just had to.

I started down the embankment, ignoring the way my insides were twisted in knots. I reached the bottom and turned back around. Cliff was still standing there. "Well?"

He shrugged, slid down the embankment, and followed me inside.

We found him on the floor beside his bed and facedown in a pool of his own vomit. The smell hit me the moment we walked in, a kind of pungent aroma that suggested raw meat. We pushed through a darkened hallway to a single room in the back. A bottle of Wild Turkey bourbon lay on the floor beside him, its amber contents seeping out and mingling with what appeared to be yellow puke.

I never assumed he was dead. Somehow that seemed out of the question. Maybe it was just my nature to always think people would survive. I certainly believed that Mom and Anna had. Still, it was alarming to see him like that, a man who had literally drunk himself into a stupor.

I picked up the man's arm gently. It was like a lead weight.

"Is he alive?" Cliff asked, his voice cracking into a whisper.

"I think so. He's just passed out." I looked around. "I wonder if this place has running water."

"Not likely," Cliff said.

I wanted to get a damp cloth and place it on his forehead. Not sure why, but it seemed like the right thing to do. Before I had a chance to move, he stirred, lifted the same arm I'd picked up, and used it to shoo me away. I stepped back and waited as he pushed himself up from his vomit. The side of his face was covered in it, the yellow semisolid stuff peppering his beard like ornaments in a bush. He reached for the blanket on his bed and used it to wipe his face before righting the bottle of Wild Turkey, preserving the very last bit. He contemplated the bottle, as if trying to decide if he should drink it, but ended up shaking his head, placing the bottle upright on a nightstand, and falling back onto his mattress.

"What's your name?" he said, his dirty T-shirt riding up past his belly and exposing a long scar that bisected his lower abdomen and curved downward beneath his blue jeans. I looked at his glass eye—it had to be glass, didn't it?—and the scar that ran down his face. The two wounds were similar, as if done by the same blade. All of these thoughts were running through my head, so much so that I didn't even give him an answer.

His good eye cut in my direction. "You got a name, don't you?"

His voice was guttural, more like the moaning of a bear than the words of a person.

"Yeah," I said, and my voice sounded foreign to me, a strange instrument that had grown dull and almost useless. "Danny."

He lifted his hand from the mattress and pointed across the room. "Danny, go get me that tank."

I turned and saw the oxygen tank on wheels leaning against an antique-looking dresser. I started for it when he said, "And a pack of smokes from the top drawer, would you?"

His name was Pike. Walter Pike.

He spoke in a deep, ancient, whiskey-stained voice. His dead eye never looked at me, and I always found myself wanting to look over my shoulder to see what it was watching. Sometimes he muttered to himself, and when he did, his eyes went distant, and he didn't seem to be in the same place as we were. It scared me, and only when he'd refocus and light another cigarette did the fear dissipate.

"I didn't think you'd come."

"You know about my mother and Anna?"

He closed one eye. The dead one stayed open and I realized whatever injury he'd suffered there must have not only taken his eye but also severed whatever nerves were needed to control the eyelid.

"Know about them? I believe I might, but it's probably not as clear-cut as you think."

"What's that supposed to mean?"

Pike ran a liver-spotted hand through his hair. "I don't hardly know myself."

I could feel Cliff's eyes watching me. I didn't look at him because once I did, I knew I'd see the skepticism there and I'd be less able to push my own away.

I shook my head, trying to make sense of it. "How can you hardly know?"

Cliff interrupted me. "Mister, if you're just blowing smoke up our asses, please stop. This is real serious stuff to Danny. We're talking about his family."

Surprisingly Pike nodded at this and dislodged a cigarette from his half-empty soft pack. "Let's go outside," he said. "It stinks in here."

Pike had us bring out wrought-iron chairs from what served as his den and set them in a half circle out in the yard. We sat in the half-light of the woods, Cliff and I shifting uneasily, while Pike alternately smoked Marlboros and took hits from his oxygen tank. Occasionally, he did that thing where he stopped and looked off in the distance. Once he even nodded as if he were hearing a voice that we couldn't.

"It's a long story. I think I'll have to tell it from the beginning for you to believe it. And even then, I'm afraid there'll be no guarantee."

I wanted to tell him to just get on with it. Spit it out and let me decide for myself.

"The hard part is deciding where the beginning begins. I think with Seth. Seth's dead now. But I'm not sure that even matters. Maybe it does. There's so much I don't know."

It was maddening. The way he'd start to say something

meaningful before detouring to begin some other thought. He was hungover, probably still groggy. I chalked it up to that.

"The reason," he continued, "I've been hanging around your house at night is that I was trying to get up the courage to talk to you, to somebody, but I think it is better you than your father. Adults, they don't believe. I've been selfish for waiting this long, but I'm afraid . . ." He trailed off, looking around anxiously, maybe for a bottle of something hard. He even shifted in his chair like he wanted to rise, to go back inside, surely for the remains of the Wild Turkey by his bedside. "I'm afraid I'm losing my mind." He beat the palm of his hand against his forehead. "Oh, if only Seth could tell you." He looked out into the woods. "You always understood it better than me," he said, and I actually turned to look for who he might be talking to. There was nothing but trees swaying in the afternoon breeze.

I looked at Cliff. Cliff gave me a look back. The guy was nuts. Still, I felt a fascination, a deep need to get at what was going on, why he was nuts, why he felt the need to inflict his madness on my family.

I spoke slowly, calmly. "Can you please just tell us what you know about my mother and sister?"

He nodded at me, his good eye fixing me with a look I couldn't read. "Yes, you deserve to hear it. Your mother and sister have vanished from this world, but they're not dead, at least I don't think they are. They've simply . . ." He paused here, as if trying to come up with just the right words. "They've simply disappeared from this world."

I was about to respond, maybe even laugh, when I heard a vehicle coming down the rutted road that led to Pike's shack.

For an instant, I thought the truck was Dad's, but then the red Silverado rounded the bend and I realized it belonged to Cliff's father.

Mr. Banks never came out here. I shot a look at Cliff. He didn't meet my eyes.

"Did you tell your dad we were coming out here?"

"Not exactly."

"Not exactly? What does that mean?"

The truck slid to a stop on the dry gravel. "It means I just mentioned we were going to be exploring over by the old cabin today."

I gave him a nasty look.

"It was the safe thing to do." He glanced at Pike, who was taking all of this in passively. "He might be a crazy man for all we know."

Pike chuckled. "You got that right."

Mr. Banks unfolded his long frame from the driver's seat and quickly headed toward us. I glanced at Pike. He was watching the man with his head tilted to the side, a look of perplexed agitation on his face.

"Get in the car, boys," he said.

"Help you?" Pike said gruffly.

Mr. Banks barely looked at him. Instead, he focused all his intensity on me, which was disconcerting to say the least, considering all the time I had spent at Cliff's over the years when he'd barely acknowledged my existence.

This obviously rubbed Pike the wrong way. He stood up and positioned himself between Cliff's father and me. He cleared his throat. "Is there something I can help you with?"

Cliff's dad shot him a withering look. "You've got some nerve coming back here."

"I grew up in these woods. Nerve ain't what I'd call it."

"What would you call it?"

Pike thought for a minute. "The right thing to do."

"What would you know about that?"

Pike seemed to consider this. "Plenty more than you know about good manners, it seems."

Cliff's dad laughed. "Manners? This is my son. He and the other boy are coming with me, and unless you want the police out here faster than you can count to five, old man, you'll stay the hell away from him."

Pike just stared at him but made no further argument.

Mr. Banks met his glare, mumbled something under his breath, and pushed his way past until he stood over me.

"Daniel," he said. "They've arrested your father."

Talking to one's father in jail for the first time is not something that's easy to forget. It was the first time I can remember feeling like our situation was spinning out of control. It seemed beyond bad luck, beyond the curves that life throws you. I felt at that moment like our family was laboring under a vicious curse and once I heard what my father had to say, the feeling grew stronger.

I took his call at Cliff's house, where I would be staying indefinitely. Dad's court-appointed attorney had already been in touch with Mr. Banks.

"Danny?" His voice was clear and loud in my ear. Somewhere in the background I heard a cell door clanging shut with an eerie finality that made me shudder.

"Hey," I said. My lips felt dry, my tongue stuck to the roof of my mouth. "What's happening?"

There was a pause. I imagined Dad's eyes roaming over the

empty cell, the cot, the plain gray walls, the floors stained with piss and blood. "Danny, I—" He faltered. "I'm sorry."

"For what?"

"For what I did."

I felt cold fingers on my spine. What had he done? I had to resist the urge to hang up the phone.

"What was it?" I said at last.

"Mr. Banks didn't tell you?"

I could hardly speak now. "No, sir."

"Jesus. I should have never gone down there."

"Where? What happened?"

"You know the place out on County Road Seven? Ghost Bells?"

It was a bar, a honky-tonk, a place I'd been expressly forbidden to go.

"Yeah. What about it?"

Dad hesitated. I could almost hear him changing his mind. He'd already told me too much. He would cut me off, tell me I was too young.

But I was wrong.

"I beat a man. At the bar. I hurt him pretty bad, Danny."

"What?" There was nothing he could say that would have surprised me more.

"It was a mistake. I let . . . I let my emotions get the best of me."

"Why?"

Dad sighed. "Danny, there are some things I haven't told you about your mother. Some things I probably shouldn't have kept from you."

I waited, again resisting—this time by force of will—the urge to hang up on him.

"Your mother—well, you know, she had some trouble with alcohol—but that's not all, Danny. Your mother, at one time, well, she was a drug addict, and she's cheated on me before, Danny."

I sucked in a deep breath. He was lying. It was easier for him to think about this sort of thing instead of her being dead. No different than Gran.

"I know this is hard to hear, Danny, but in the weeks and months before she left, she slipped back into her old—"

"Stop lying. Just stop it."

"Danny, you have to face the truth. I know she's your mother, and I know you love her, but there comes a point—"

I hung the phone up. It's not something I'm proud of. My father was in jail, and I was all he had left, yet I hung up on him. These days, when I think about regrets, I don't have many, but that's one that still gets me. I suppose in the grand scheme of things, it was a small gesture, but I can't shake the thought of him alone in that cell, believing that he'd been abandoned first by his wife, and then by his son.

B ut that's not the only thing that nags at me about that conversation these days. He'd said she "slipped." It was a word I hadn't heard yet from Pike, but I would. It's a word now that's always on my lips, as if mouthing the syllables enough times would help me break the code of my own life and see the truth of memory. *She slipped*. Yes, one way or another, I suppose she did.

Chapter Ten

WALTER

Her name was Rachel Scroggins, and they never found her. She was the first to disappear. Rach was what her friends and family called her. She was only ten and actually lived across the highway from me, about a mile to the west. Her family had a small piece of land with a barn. They raised chickens and owned three cows. She loved German shepherds, and her dog, Molly, had given birth to twelve puppies just a week before she disappeared.

Back then her disappearance obsessed the town. It wasn't on the national news or the talk shows because in the early sixties local mysteries stayed local. In the sixties, the only thing that could bring national news to Alabama was civil rights. Anything else that happened in the state was mostly just ignored. It was no different on the local level. Look back at the papers from the early sixties. You'll find very little about Rachel, but that doesn't mean we didn't care. Nothing could be further from the truth. Her name was on the lips of every person within a thirty-mile radius. We all felt the loss, the hard truth that somebody had taken a ten-year-old girl. Sure, she might have gotten lost. Those things do happen. My daddy used to tell a story of how back in 1936, a girl wandered off into the woods and didn't come back for nearly two weeks. She just got lost and confused. She panicked. She would have died in the woods if a hunter hadn't literally stumbled over her unconscious body.

This was different. People might have hoped she was lost in the woods, but in our hearts, we didn't believe that. The police had combed every bit of land within thirty miles. They had dogs. They had volunteers. But in the end, they had nothing. Not a damned thing.

My mother came into my room one night after turning off her radio programs. She sat on the edge of my bed. I was pretending to sleep, even though I couldn't because my thoughts kept jumping between Seth and Ronnie and Jake.

"She's dead," my mother said. Her voice was a whisper. I didn't move.

Mama touched my forehead with her hand. She leaned over me, and I could feel her tears soaking into my sheet. "Dead, dead, dead. Dead."

She sat there for a long time. I don't know what made her come into my room that night. I don't know if she had a vision or saw it in a dream or had inside knowledge of what was happening. To this day, I don't know. What I do know—and I knew it then too—is that she was right. The girl was dead.

A few weeks later, when Tina disappeared, Seth stayed out of school. Tina and Rachel. Their names were on everybody's lips. Tina's story was simple. Heartbreakingly simple. She'd been walking her dog, Little Rascal, one evening and never came home. The leash was found in the park, the same park where Seth and I had sat and talked after school until dark. Other than the leash, there was nothing, not a fingerprint, not a note, nothing. Even the dog was gone.

Winter was in the air. The town grew restless. My father came home less, choosing to stay over at a friend's or at the "club," which was a place that sold moonshine out on County Road Seven behind the woods. When he did come home, he was drunk. Bleary-eyed and stinking, he'd stumble through the door, looking for something to eat, or some time with my mother in the back. She always provided for him, food or sex, it didn't matter, but she did it without enthusiasm. She had a kind of fuck-you attitude that I always admired. Still, I knew she was going down fast. My father couldn't catch her, and neither could I.

It seemed like Dad's favorite pastime was ignoring me, but that was probably giving him too much credit. The truth of it was that I was a piece of furniture to him. One more thing in the room. He was more likely to sit on me or use me for a place to put his jug than talk to me. I pretended this didn't bother me, that I didn't care one way or the other if he didn't notice me. I patted myself on the back for not being a baby like Seth. All the while I knew that, deep down, Seth wasn't a baby, and I was just a pretender.

A week after Tina went missing, I walked over to Seth's house on a Saturday afternoon. Some of the kids at school had been restricted to their houses when they weren't at school because their parents worried for their safety. This wasn't an issue for me. I came and went as I pleased. Mama was in her own world, seated most of the time in her leather chair, the radio tuned to some station or another. Sometimes, I wondered if she was really listening. In 'Nam, when it got bad, I thought about Mama a lot. Still breaks my heart to think about her. There's more than one way to disappear, you know?

Seth's house is gone now. You can walk out to the spot, but all you'll see are ruins, if even that. It burned down years ago, and what was left disappeared under a maze of kudzu and vines. The kudzu has always run wild here, and even though most of it was dead because it was late fall, the dry vines still held the house as tight as a straitjacket.

The front door opened and a man who had to be Seth's father came out. He was scowling and carrying a sack under his arm. His red hair and freckled face reminded me of some distant relative I'd seen in some of Mama's old photo albums. Where the skin of the boy in the photo was pale white and dotted with freckles, this man's was a deep brown. He wore overalls and big work boots. Later, I found out he worked across the road in the cotton fields. My own father did the same when he couldn't find jobs in town doing yards and such. The fields paid better, but my father never tolerated hard labor for any length of time.

Seth's father had his head down and didn't see me until he had almost walked by. "Oh," he said, his face shifting smoothly to a grin. "You must be here for Seth."

"Yes, sir. I'm Walter Pike."

He eyed me carefully as if measuring me for a new suit. "Pike?"

"Yes, sir."

"What's your daddy's name?"

"Preston."

He nodded, and appeared to consider saying more.

"Do you know him?" I asked.

"Name sounds familiar. That's all. I've got to get to work. Go on in. Good to see he has a visitor."

He started off, but then stopped and walked back to me. He placed a hand on my shoulder, leaning in close. His breath smelled bad, like fish. "Between you and me," he said, "I worry about Seth. His mama run off and left us some time back and he ain't been the same since." He patted my shoulder. "Your mama? She a good woman?"

I thought about this for a second. "Yes, sir. I'd say she is," I said, trying to sound sure of myself even though I wasn't.

"Good. Good. A fine woman is a rare thing in this day and age. These days, the family don't mean what it used to." He smiled, showing teeth that were uneven but clean, not stained brown like my father's. "Strange times we're living in. Young girls gone astray."

I nodded. There had been some silly rumors lately suggesting the girls had been promiscuous and that had led to their downfall.

"Well, I got to get to work. I'm glad Seth's found a friend."

"Yeah, me too."

I watched him walk away, toward the road and the cotton fields beyond.

I knocked. Nobody answered, so I decided to go on in. I found Seth in his room, reading a book. I must have been quiet. Either that, or he was so caught up in the book that he didn't hear me because he just lay there on his bed, reading. The bed was the only piece of furniture in the room. Beside it, he had stacked dozens of paperbacks, creating two shaky towers of books. One window on the back wall revealed the deep woods behind his house. There were no curtains or blinds and the sun shone in. Below the window were three or four stacks of neatly folded clothes. The only other thing in the room was an old painting of what appeared to be a swamp hanging on the wall across from Seth's bed. The painting was large, but even that didn't explain how it seemed to dominate the room. I couldn't stop looking at it.

"Hey," I said.

Seth dropped his book and jumped to his feet. He acted like I'd just tossed a bomb inside his room instead of simply saying hello. "Why are you here?"

"Why wouldn't I be? We're friends, right?"

He glared at me. "I didn't invite you."

"Hell, you didn't ask me to pull your ass out of that quicksand either, but that didn't stop me."

"I would have been fine."

"'Cause you 'went somewhere,' right?"

He stepped forward, his fists clenched. "You shouldn't have come here."

I shook my head in disbelief. I'd gone out on a limb to take up for him—losing the only two friends I had in the process—and now he was going to act like this. Bullshit.

"What's wrong with you?" I said.

"You wouldn't understand."

"Of course not, because you're the only kid in the world with problems. Well, I met your dad and he didn't seem so bad. At least he was sober."

"You don't know anything about my father. He's evil."

This made me laugh. It was hard to imagine the man I'd just met as anything resembling evil. Hell, as wretched as my own father was, *evil* would not be a word I would use to describe even him.

"Evil, huh? Just because he couldn't get along with your mother doesn't make him evil. So she ran out on you. It happens to a lot of kids. They don't sit in their rooms and sulk for the rest of their lives. Maybe Jake and Ronnie were right about you."

"Say that again."

I shook my head. "You don't want a friend, do you?"

"Say that part again about Jake and Ronnie being right about me."

I was feeling pretty pissed. "I don't know, Seth. You're a weird bird. Maybe you *are* queer. Maybe you *do* like boys." As soon as the words came out of my mouth, I wanted to put them right back. Still, I let them linger because part of me couldn't help but think he had it coming.

There was a short lull when nothing happened. His face was blank and then he fixed me with a look that could have burned paper. I didn't even see his fist coming until it hit me under my chin. I fell back, my face already blooming with pain. He lunged at me and stuck his elbow into my neck, driving me against the wall. My head was forced back against the picture frame. The frame came loose from the wall and fell to the floor. I heard something crack but didn't bother to look. My chin was bleeding. Getting my fists up, I tried to locate Seth. I couldn't find him anywhere. Delirious, I stumbled over to his bed and sat down. Then I saw him. He was on the floor, hugging the picture frame to his chest.

The canvas was undamaged. Only the outer frame was cracked. I watched Seth carefully pull the frame away, brushing splinters off the canvas.

He touched the painting, running his fingers from the tall trees on the right side over to the cabin on the left and then up to the moon whose light spilled out over the painting in uneven streaks.

He picked it up and put it on the bed beside me.

"It's just a damn picture," I said.

He shook his head. "Not to me."

I scoffed at that. "It's not even very good."

Seth glared at me.

"What? Somebody you know paint it?"

"Yeah," Seth said. "I did."

If he thought this would upset me, he had another thing coming. "Whoop-dee-doo," I said.

Seth wasn't worth the anger. He was a nut, and that's probably why his mother left anyway. I felt an overwhelming urge to destroy the painting.

"No," he said. "Leave it alone." It was like he knew what I was planning, like he could look right into my eyes and see down into the deep, dark, ugly part of me that actually wanted to see him hurt, the part of me that was no damned different than Jake.

I shoved my way past him and picked it up. I tore the canvas away from the backing frame and held it in the air in front of him, my hands tensing like I was about to rip it in two.

"Tell me how you knew about Jake's dad," I said. This was

something that had been bothering me. How would a new kid have known about Jake's dad being in prison?

"Don't, Walter. Please."

I started to tear the top part. He lunged at me, but I kept it away from him, stepping up on his bed. "Answer the question."

I wanted to curse myself for what I was doing. I'd come because I wanted a friend, but I was making an enemy, and now I was too proud to stop. "Answer me or I rip it to shreds."

"My dad and I lived here years ago. He knows Jake's family and yours. I'm not sure about Ronnie's."

"What he say about my old man?"

Seth shook his head.

I began to rip.

"Stop! He didn't say nothing. He said he drank a lot. That was all."

Suddenly, I felt like laughing. "Well, he got that right."

Seth shot me a withering look. "Put it down."

"Why's it so important? What's so great about a dumb painting? Even if you did paint it."

"You wouldn't understand."

"Of course I wouldn't. My daddy's a drunk, and I don't know how it feels to be you. Jesus, man. I came over here because I wanted to be a friend, but I'm starting to get the feeling you don't want one." I dropped the painting on the bed, feeling suddenly deflated, like my life was useless and I should probably just go back to Jake, plead for mercy, and live out my days in these woods, being a damn drunk just like my father.

I stepped off the bed, taking my time to be sure that I knocked over his stacks of books, scattering them across the floor. "Standing up for you that day was a mistake."

I was all the way back out to the den before I heard his voice. "Walter. Wait."

I stopped. I was still angry, but I learned a valuable lesson that day. Anger can't hold a candle to loneliness.

He said he wanted to show me something, and when I saw it, I would understand about the painting.

I couldn't imagine what it would be, but I felt bad for threatening to rip the painting, so I agreed.

He led me outside and back into the deepest part of the woods, where Jake and Ronnie and me brought some girls last summer, telling them scary stories about the woods so that they'd squeal and hug us tight. It was spooky back here, something about the trees. Their shadows seemed to linger and spread out across the ground until you couldn't really tell what was shadow and what wasn't.

We walked slowly as a storm began to build in the sky above us. We said nothing, plowing through the densest parts of the woods. As we walked, it became clear that there was a buried past here, a community worn to rubble by time and fire and weather. A rotting fence tapered away into nothing. A stone wall that might have once been the front of a house. A pile of old junk, rusted and broken beneath smoke-charred branches. There was probably more too, but the kudzu and creepers overran everything, burying the old places as sure as if they'd been sunk into the ground.

Seth moved with an assurance that made me jealous. How was it possible that I had lived in these woods my entire life and felt confused and disoriented, while he knew exactly where he was going?

I glanced up at the darkening sky. "You sure this is a good idea? It's looking pretty ugly."

"It's right here," he said. "And the storm is a good thing. Makes it easier."

"Easier? What are you talking about?"

He ignored me. "If you ever try to find it without me and you see the little cabin, you know you've gone too far."

Cabin? I saw nothing but trees and shadows. At the time, I had no idea the "little cabin" he mentioned would be the place where my life would change forever.

"What exactly are we looking for?" I asked.

He bent down, clearing away some of the foliage. I saw a solid square block of concrete. There was an opening, a round hatch, no more than three feet in diameter, built into the top. He lifted it, revealing the arms of a ladder leading down into the darkness.

"Storm shelter. My grandmother used to live back here. I know because I found her journal in an old trunk and she wrote about this place a lot. About how the storm shelter saved her life once. About how she climbed out of it after a big storm and saw that the world had changed."

He pointed at the crumbled remains of something half hidden by the trees. An old plow lay next to it. "There's pieces of buildings everywhere. I call them ruins. They're all that's left now. It was a whole town. Called Broken Branch. Another storm, a few months after the one my grandmother survived in the shelter, destroyed everything. Including her. This time, she couldn't make it to the shelter and she died in the cellar at her own house. My dad was with her. He talks about it sometimes when he goes off into one of his moods. The cabin I mentioned? The one that you'll see over there if you go too far? That was where she died. My father rebuilt it years ago. The rest of Broken Branch is gone. His sister and him were two of the six that survived. The others moved away to start over somewhere else, I guess."

I waited for more, but Seth got quiet and just looked out at the trees. "And?"

"That's it. It's all history now, except one thing."

"What?"

"This storm shelter."

"And this is what you wanted to show me?"

"This is the doorway to what I wanted to show you. The real thing is the swamp."

"In the painting?"

"Yeah. The same one. That's where we're going."

I tried to imagine what I'd seen in the painting being out here in the woods. The cabin, maybe, but the swamp? No way. Not here. I shook my head. "This doesn't make sense."

"Forget sense, Walter. Just follow me."

He went down the ladder into darkness. I hesitated to follow, purely out of pride. I still hadn't forgotten our fight, what he'd said about my father. His foolish attachment to the painting. All of that vexed me to no end, but damned if I didn't feel a new, more powerful emotion as I took hold of the ladder: curiosity.

———

Later, I'd hear my dad talking about how the storm had been "a big 'un" and how the roof came right off Bill Morgan's house, but inside the storm shelter, I could barely hear anything at all. It was out there, sure, but it didn't seem real. Nothing seemed real inside that shelter.

We sat down on the dirt floor. Seth was across from me. It didn't matter where. He was close.

Neither of us spoke. I felt sleepy. We sat there, just soaking in the silence for a long time. Eventually, we heard the thunder as it rocked the world above us, but it was a small, faraway thing that didn't matter at all.

"The painting in my room," he said at last. "I painted it when we moved away. I couldn't go there anymore, so I painted that picture and hung it up in my room. When things got really bad, I would stare at it and dream of coming back. Then after my mom disappeared, my father decided it was time to move back."

"You're kidding, right?"

"What do you mean?"

"That painting was of a swamp. There's no swamp in these woods. I've walked them from top to bottom hundreds of times."

"You're wrong about that."

I could do nothing but grin. He was insane.

"I want to take you there."

I shook my head. "I don't understand. We're inside a storm shelter."

"You have to trust me, Walter. Can you do that?"

"Sure," I said. But it was a lie. I felt uncomfortable suddenly, and I couldn't say why.

"I've never shown anybody before."

"What are you talking about?"

"The swamp. It's where I go. I can show you." I felt his hand on me. First my shoulder, then down to my hand. I pulled away.

"What are you doing?"

"Do you want to see it or not?"

I'm sure part of me was thinking this whole thing sounded like the biggest load of bullshit I'd ever heard, but there must have been another part of me that wanted to believe in disappearing to your own place, somewhere safe and secret. More than anything, though, I was curious. I wanted to see for myself.

I let him hold on to my hand.

"Close your eyes," he said.

I did, though the darkness inside the shelter was so total it was hard to tell.

We sat like that for a long time. His hand was over mine, the silence of the shelter broken only by the thunder booming above us.

My hand felt sweaty in Seth's, and worse, I felt weird holding hands with another boy, especially one who was so widely suspected to be queer. *Just forget it, Walter*, I told myself. *He's not like that.* Still, the longer we sat there, my hand in his, the more I wanted to pull it away. I was just about to when it happened.

What *it* was is still a little unclear to me. First, the whole shelter seemed to tilt. It was like we were sitting inside a giant barrel that somebody had suddenly decided to roll over. Seth's grip tightened on my hand, and I opened my eyes. Darkness. Then I was falling; my stomach flew up into my lungs and my neck. I saw images, moving past me quickly: shadowed trees etched against a purple sky; a low moon; a brownish muck of water flying up toward me. I fell fast. I spun like someone had pushed the barrel down a hill, but there was no hill. Only free fall. I closed my eyes, bracing for impact.

That's when I became aware of Seth again. He was with me, falling. His hand gripped mine tightly. Together we spun. I saw the moon and then the trees, the water again. A cabin. A single wooden cabin, with a light burning inside. Over and over we spun together, and it was wonderful and easily one of the scariest damn moments of my life.

The instant we hit the water, it was over. My body went under and then I was lying on solid ground again, Seth on top of me, the spell broken. But we'd gone somewhere, fallen into some other place. That was all that mattered.

"I saw it!" I shouted, clapping my hand on his back. "I saw the swamp. I saw the cabin from the painting!" I tried to roll Seth off me, but he didn't move.

"Seth?" I said. I thought for an instant that he might somehow have died during the fall, but that couldn't be right. His breath was on my face. Then I felt something else, his lips seeking mine. To be honest, I don't even think I understood what was happening. At least not at first. I thought he might be confused in the dark. "Seth," I said. "Get off me."

He made one more urgent effort to place his lips against mine, and I shoved him hard. The wonder I had felt an instant ago burned out inside me, replaced by an anger so righteous, I felt possessed.

The little faggot. The goddamn little faggot.

I swung at him in the darkness but missed. My fists hit the concrete walls, busting my knuckles open.

"I'm sorry . . . I didn't mean . . ." Seth trailed off. "Jesus, Walter. Please don't hate me."

I hardly heard him. "Open this damn hatch!"

"Walter . . ."

"Let me out of here, you queer."

Something creaked, and light and rain came into the shelter.

I started up the short ladder. When I reached the top, the hail and rain hit me hard. Then the wind. I lost my balance and almost fell back into the shelter, but I clung hard to the first rung of the ladder and managed to pull myself out. Just before the hatch swung shut, I heard Seth call my name and say something about the storm. I didn't care. He could say whatever he wanted to. I only wanted to get as far away from him as fast as possible.

I probably should have died that day. The storm leveled trees for miles. Six people lost their lives in the county, even more statewide. The next morning Mrs. Parker came over to our house. She was a widow with three grown boys who'd abandoned her as quick as they could get out of the woods. She banged on our front door until I woke up to see who it was.

Her hair was wild, her eyes even wilder. "Your daddy home?"

I knew better than to tell the truth. "No, ma'am."

"Well, you'll have to do. I need help getting the tree off my house."

Mrs. Parker had never been much for subtlety.

"Okay," I said. "Let me get my boots on."

She nodded. I turned to go look for them and ran into my father.

He held his palm flat against my chest. I could tell from the way it didn't yield that this wouldn't be pretty. "No," he said. "Go on back to bed."

"Preston," Mrs. Parker said. "I got to patch my roof before the next one comes." She looked up at the sky warily.

"Not my problem," he said, and moved to shut the door.

"I'll help her. I don't mind," I said.

"You may not mind," he said. "But I do."

Mrs. Parker began to cry. She wasn't loud about it. She didn't beg, and somehow that made it worse. She wiped a tear from her face and nodded.

"I can pay you," she said.

"How much?"

"I got eight dollars."

My father spit past her into the yard. "Keep it." He closed the door and turned back to me. "Don't look at me like that."

I said nothing.

"That woman cheated on her husband. She don't deserve our help."

He brushed past me roughly and went back into the bedroom. I stood there for a long time, wondering at how cruel the world could be. It was something I thought about a lot as I got older. Why some folks seemed so obsessed with their own lives, why they'd only help if the price was right. I guess, if I'm going to be honest about things, I made myself a promise right then and there. I promised that I'd always do my best to help out anybody no matter what their situation was, no matter what they'd done, no matter if the price was right or even if it was wrong. Didn't take me too many years to test that promise because the price is nearly always wrong.

Chapter Eleven

What happened that day in the shelter nearly did me in. Before that day, I'd felt pretty confident in what I knew to be true. The world was a solid place. Boys liked girls and a storm shelter was a storm shelter. Nothing else. I hadn't been happy by any means, but I'd been comfortable, secure. Then everything changed. It was like somebody had pulled back a veil on the world. Everything was more complicated and when you peeled back one layer, there were always two more.

Eventually, I got over the doubts I felt after Seth's attempted kiss. But in the days and weeks that followed it, I agonized over stuff, spending long hours trying to convince myself that I didn't like boys. Thinking on it now, it seems like a curiosity to me, but then it was real, a near-burning blast of confusion at the worst possible time in my life. Fourteen is confusing enough for a boy without having to go through that.

The other thing—the glimpse of the swamp—that was what was hardest. I wanted it to be real, for it to be more than a dream or my imagination, but with each passing day, it got easier to believe it hadn't happened, to think somehow I'd made it up.

None of those things excused what I did next, though.

It happened in the restroom at school, between fifth and sixth periods. I was there, stealing a smoke, a habit I'd almost quit since Jake and Ronnie dropped me back in the summer. Lately, I'd been feeling the urge again, probably because of all the stuff that happened with Seth.

Ronnie came in and nodded at me. Jake hadn't so much as looked at me without a scowl on his face all school year, but sometimes when Ronnie was by himself, he still treated me like a human being.

I nodded back.

"Got an extra?" he said.

"Sure." I placed my last cigarette in his palm. He held it up and used mine to light it. It was hard not to like Ronnie. When he was by himself, he was okay. It was Jake's influence that made him do the things he did. Plus, I'd always felt bad for him. A couple of years back, his older brother, Bobby, had been hunting in the mountains north of here and some guys beat him to death. They took his guns and ammo and left his body naked in the middle of the woods. His brother had been an okay guy too, from what I could remember. I knew the loss had hit Ronnie pretty hard.

"You still hanging out with that queer?" he said, after he blew some smoke toward the open bathroom window.

I almost said, *He's not a queer,* but then I stopped myself. He *was* a queer. Wasn't he?

"Not anymore."

"Smart move. People were starting to talk."

I shrugged. "I never really wanted to hang out with him anyway. I just don't like to see somebody beat down in an unfair fight. Queer or not, nobody deserves to die."

Ronnie shrugged. "Who says?"

"You helped save him."

"That was before I knew him. I wouldn't save him again."

I didn't want to argue. "Okay."

"Seriously," he said. "I wouldn't. I don't think queers deserve to live."

He seemed to be getting angry. I held up my hands. "I'm not queer, Ronnie."

Ronnie leaned against the sink, backing off a little. "But you do admit he's a faggot, right?"

I could have said, *I don't know,* or *No way,* or I could have said nothing at all. Instead, I said the words I would regret for the rest of my life.

"He tried to kiss me. So yeah, I'd say he's a queer."

"See," Ronnie said, slapping the sink with his hand. "That's what they do. They can't, you know, control themselves." He shook his head, disgusted. "Did you sock him in the mouth?"

"No," I said, already regretting telling him. Whatever was said to Ronnie would go straight to Jake. It was guaranteed.

"You should have socked him."

I nodded, feeling ashamed. I wanted to take it back, to say I was just kidding. Despite all the anger I felt for Seth that day, despite the sick feeling in the pit of my stomach when I thought about his lips pressed against mine, I didn't want to see him hurt. I just didn't.

"Hey," I said. "Maybe you shouldn't tell Jake that. I mean—"

He wasn't listening. The bell rang to start sixth period, and he left at a good jog. I had no doubt what would happen after that.

December came and I hit a new low. Things were worse at home. Daddy had come in drunk one night and tried to jump on Mama, but this time she was waiting on him with a knife. She stuck it into his stomach and he bled a lot. He didn't die. He just lay in the hallway cursing and moaning. Mama went to bed, left him lying right there, the knife stuck in his gut. He pulled it out, eventually, and I helped apply pressure. Nearly a month passed before he was able to work again. On Christmas Day, neither of my parents got out of bed. I moped around the house the whole morning and afternoon, looking for something to eat. I went to bed that night hungry, alone, and in tears.

Sleep didn't come. I lay in bed night after night racked with guilt over betraying Seth. I went back and forth between hating him and thinking about what he'd shown me that day. How had he made me see those things? As much as I wanted to hate Seth, I couldn't deny the power of what I'd seen. It was the only thing I could remember in the fourteen years I'd been alive that seemed to matter. How had it happened? And what on earth did it mean? In light of those few seconds, I understood that the world was a much larger and more mysterious place. And I hoped, somewhere in the great mystery of it all, I might yet find some grace.

One of those sleepless nights, just after Christmas, I got up to piss. I walked down the hall toward the bathroom when I noticed a light on in the den. I kept walking and looked around the corner. The faint sound of a country and western song whispered across the room. Mama sat in front of the radio, her posture slumped, one hand brushing the hair off her forehead. In that single instant, I saw something that stunned me. Her gesture, the way she touched her hair, belonged to someone else. I'd wondered why Seth looked familiar to me, and now I saw the answer very clearly. My mother.

She looked up just then, and I saw he had her eyes. There was an instant where I didn't think she saw me. She seemed to look through me, but then she spoke. "Can't sleep?"

I shook my head.

"Come sit down," she said, patting the couch. I was amazed; she hadn't said more than two words to me in the last week.

I sat beside her on the couch. A twangy guitar started up on the radio. It was joined by the rasp of a cymbal and a voice that sounded like it was a million miles away and right in your ear all at once.

"Did you have a sister?" I said.

Mama's eyes—normally empty, distant—sharpened.

"No, only a brother."

"A brother?"

"Sure, you remember your uncle."

But I didn't remember. I tried to think about my earliest memories, the ones from way back when we'd been a happier family. I barely remembered when Daddy would still smile and sometimes pick me up and hug me. I'd smell the alcohol on him, and it didn't smell like anger yet. Hadn't there been another man once? A man with red hair? Jesus, when it hit me, I felt a cold chill. The reason Seth's father had reminded me of a family member was simple. He was my uncle.

"I think I do," I said. "Can you tell me about him?

Mama shook her head. "I don't want to talk about this."

I waited, knowing I'd have to go easy on her, coax it out of her.

"What was your mother like?" I said. "My grandmother."

"People said she was . . . was . . ." She seemed flustered trying to think of the right word.

I took a guess. "Crazy."

"Yes, crazy."

"Was she?"

She shrugged. "It's hard for me to remember. Everything about that time seemed crazy."

I waited, hoping if I was quiet, she might say more.

A new song started on the radio, its bass line fluid and long, peppered by a high-hat cymbal as a voice came through the tiny speakers.

"She died in the big tornado. Nineteen thirty-two. I don't remember because I was only a little girl, but they said I was playing at a friend's house and their family made it to the storm shelter. They took me with them. Only six people survived. Killed the whole town."

"What about your brother?"

"He lived. But wasn't never the same."

"Mama?" I said. "I think your brother is back. He's got a boy with him named Seth."

I waited for her reaction, but her eyes had already gone away, staring at the framed picture of her and my father getting married.

The turning point came in January, on my way home from school. I was walking along the highway when I heard voices off in the trees to my right. I slid down the embankment and moved in closer to see what was happening.

What I saw still makes my blood boil.

Ronnie, Jake, and five other boys formed a circle around Seth. The other boys' names don't matter. They were just wannabes, willing to do anything Jake said. They'd stripped off Seth's clothes and tied his feet together so he couldn't move. Each boy held a stick and they kept poking him and calling him names. Seth's eyes were closed and he seemed oblivious to their taunts. His flesh was torn up from where they'd prodded, scraped, and stuck him.

I experienced a moment of indecision so powerful I can still feel its hold on me. I wanted so badly to help. I wanted so badly to run away, to ignore what was happening, to save myself.

I think my mother swayed me. I'd seen her fail to act so many times, letting my father take advantage of her, turn her life into something less than human. She'd made the one desperate attempt with the knife, but that was too little, too late. I saw her sitting beside the window, listening to a radio program and slowly losing who she was, losing what mattered.

Mama had already lost the things that mattered—her dignity, her self-respect, her identity. Now, watching those boys kick the shit out of Seth, I had to make a decision about what mattered to me or, like Mama, risk losing myself. It was one of the first times I realized that the person you are is created by the actions you take, or, more importantly, fail to take.

I acted.

I was halfway there when I realized I couldn't take them all, and I held up, ducking behind a pine tree.

I had to help him. But how? I needed a gun. Dad had recently started locking his up, probably out of fear that if he didn't, Mama would use it on him.

Then I had it. In my mind's eye, I saw my mother sitting on the couch, her eyes empty, her mouth slack. Dad came in, fell on top of her, groped her like he always did when he was drunk. I saw the knife in her hand, the way she jabbed it hard into the fat of his stomach and then rolled him off onto the floor. I saw him struggle to get up, then walk three steps toward the hallway before collapsing again.

I ran home as fast as I could. My house was only a short ways through the woods. Even so, I knew I was taking a great risk. When I returned, Seth might be badly injured, or worse, dead. Still, I couldn't take them on unarmed. It was my only chance. When I got there, Mama was in her spot, on the couch, the radio on. She turned her head to see me. Her face stayed neutral. She seemed unconcerned with me and turned back to face her radio. Elvis Presley sang about heartbreak. I went into the kitchen and found the biggest knife in the drawer.

As I ran back, it was damn lucky I didn't trip and stab myself. When I returned, they were taking swings at him with their sticks, following through like Mickey Mantle. I found my target and broke through the trees.

Jake didn't see me coming until I was right on top of him. I could have killed him, would have killed him if he hadn't sidestepped at the last second. The knife nicked his shoulder. We fell to the ground, me on top of him.

I held the knife to his neck. His eyes were wide and filled with hate.

"This is over right now," I said. "Everybody goes home."

I felt Ronnie moving close. He was behind me. I couldn't see him, but I felt his presence.

"Ronnie, you can't go your whole life doing Jake's dirty work," I said.

He came closer.

"I'll kill him if you take one step closer. Do you think I won't?"

"Stop, Ronnie," Jake said. I heard fear in his voice.

"Now go home," I said. "All of you."

I turned my head to see that some of the boys had already left. Ronnie and a couple others glared at me.

I touched the knife to the skin of Jake's neck and said, "Tell them to go home and to stay the hell in their houses for the rest of the night. Tell them." I pushed the knife harder, drawing blood.

"Go home, guys," he said. "Stay inside for the rest of the night. This is over." He waited a beat before adding, "For now."

I pushed the knife harder, maybe too hard. He gasped. Blood was everywhere.

The other boys cleared out. Only Jake and Seth and me remained. Seth hadn't moved, and I thought he was probably dead. Thinking about him dying made one thing clear in my head. Queer or not, nobody deserved this. I'd done the right thing, and in doing so, I'd managed to save Seth and myself.

"Remember this knife, Jake. I'll always have it handy."

He smiled, thin lipped. "I told Ronnie you were still a queer. He said you had broken it off with your boyfriend, but I always say, once a queer always a queer."

"I should fucking kill you," I said. I was surprised by how calm I felt, how much I meant it, how easily I could see myself sticking the knife straight into his neck.

He spit at my face. I couldn't wipe it off without letting him free. I wasn't ready for that yet. I bore down on him instead, letting his own spit drip back onto his face.

He smiled. "Fucking queer. I'll bet you squeal like a little bitch when he gives it to you, don't you, Walter?"

I pulled the knife away from his throat and flung it out into the grass. I stood up. This was something that was long overdue. He got up, wiping the blood off his neck. He stepped back.

"It's just one on one now, Jake. Me and you."

He took another step backward. "You'll get yours."

"You're scared," I said. "I don't have a knife. Come hit me."

Jake continued backing up. That's when I realized we weren't alone anymore. I turned and saw Seth's father kneeling over him, his hand on Seth's bare shoulder. I honestly didn't know if Seth was alive or dead, and hated myself a little for not remembering him sooner. I got so caught up in my anger toward Jake that I forgot my friend. I ran over and knelt beside his father.

"He okay?"

His father didn't answer for a moment, and I thought he might be crying. He kept his head down, studying Seth's naked body, where the sticks had done their damage. He took his finger and ran it along a bad cut. Seth groaned in pain.

"This one is nice," he said.

"Huh?"

He looked up at me, like he just realized I was there.

"This one," he went on. "This one ain't nothing more than a surface wound. A scratch." He spit off into the grass, like such a small wound disgusted him.

"Shouldn't we get him to a doctor?"

He spit again, this time near me.

"Mr. Sykes? He needs a doctor."

"He don't need a doctor. He's fine." He grabbed Seth by the shoulders and shook him. "Get up. Come on. Get your ass up."

Seth stirred a little, groaning.

"I think maybe we should get him to the doctor. The boys . . . They had sticks . . . They—"

He shook his head, disgusted. "I was eight years old when the twister leveled these woods. Trapped in the cellar of our little cabin. Me and Mama. It had always been me and Mama, seemed like. There was my sister, of course. She was about six when it happened, but she was over at the neighbors' and didn't get stuck in the cellar with me and Mama. Daddy had run off, left us all. Mama was already crazy by then, talking about quicksand and godforsaken swamps. People thought she was the devil incarnate back then. A lot—" He hesitated. "A lot of bad things happened, leading up to me and Mama being in that cellar. It didn't make much sense to me 'cause I was so little, but sometimes, I think on it and realize all of it had to have happened for a reason." He was staring off into the trees now, as if seeing it all on some invisible television screen. "We didn't eat for a long time. See, the door was jammed. A big tree had fallen right across it. Mama said it was going to be okay, that we'd get out soon enough, that somebody would come looking for us. I believed her but nobody came. I got so hungry, boy. So goddamned hungry that I stopped being hungry at all. I just lost my energy and lay on the floor of the cellar. She drank the water that leaked in and that must have been what made her sick. Whatever it was, it took her fast. When she got near the end, she talked about all that stuff. Said she could see it from where she was and it was beautiful. Then she was gone. Talking one minute and dead the next. I rolled her body over so I didn't have to see her face. After that, I must have died myself because the whole damned shelter started rolling like the world had turned into a giant wheel, and then I saw her there in the swamp."

He paused. His eyes had lost their focus. They were dead and unseeing. It was like he had entered a kind of dream state.

"I'd give anything to go back there again," he whispered.

I shuddered.

"But you can't, right?"

He turned on me suddenly, remembering I was there. His eyes flashed with anger very briefly and then went away again. "When that sheriff from town finally found us, he said my eyes were all wild and I couldn't even sit up straight. Said I was near starved, and damned lucky to be alive."

I nodded, but he didn't even look at me. He had forgotten I was even there.

He stared off into the trees for a long time, like someone was there speaking to him. Once or twice he even nodded. Then he shuddered so hard I could hear his teeth clicking together. After that, he slumped over, his eyes barely open.

Seth groaned again, and that seemed to bring him back completely.

"Damn it, boy. Get up." He turned back to me. "You know, when I first met you, I was willing to give you the benefit of the doubt. You didn't seem like a queer. But I should have known, considering the people you come from." He stuck his finger in my face. "My boy ain't going to be queer forever. I'm going to beat it clean out of him." He looked back at Seth, who was struggling to get to his feet. "Them boys didn't do nothing compared to what I'm going to put on him. I see you near my boy again, I'll put it on you too, son. Something you'll remember the rest of your natural-born days. Now git on home."

I went. It was one thing standing up to Jake and his cronies, but something else to face an adult, especially one like Mr. Sykes. I saw now what Seth meant. I had seen the real man. His eyes, the way he touched his son's wounds, not with love, but with cold fascination. He was like a hunter evaluating a gun or an auto mechanic lifting the hood to check for an oil leak. And the spell that he'd fallen under when talking about his mother's death. It made me shudder when I thought about it.

That night, I cried myself to sleep. I could lie and say that I cried for Seth, but mostly I cried for myself. I'd made a decision, one that I thought was right. Now I would have to live with it. For a long time I let myself go. After it was over, I just lay there, listening to the music coming from the den where my mother suffered her own demons in silence.

Chapter Twelve

DANNY

Mom and Anna disappeared last September. A summer storm had blown in that afternoon. Anna had her earplugs in, so the storm hadn't yet caused her to get upset. I was on the couch, eating a piece of fried chicken and watching reruns of sitcoms, something I did only when it was raining and I had no book to read. Anna loved the sitcoms, especially *The Brady Bunch*, which she could quote so well that sometimes it actually frightened me. When the theme song came on each afternoon at three o'clock, she would convulse with delight, her hands involuntarily flying up over her head like ecstatic birds.

On the day they disappeared, she kept the earplugs in as the theme song played. I missed her voice singing along. More than that, I missed the battery of directives I always had to endure during the commercials: "Danny, say 'Brady.'"

"Brady," I would say.

She would giggle, her eyes almost rolling white. She'd shake her hands emphatically, as she anticipated the rest. "Say 'Brady *Bunch*,'" she said, her voice barely able to contain her delight.

"Brady *Bun-ch*," I said, stressing the last two letters in exaggerated fashion. I never knew why she loved this so much.

She'd be rocking by this point, positively shuddering with pleasure. "Again. Say it again, Danny."

So I would say it again. And again. As many times as I could take before I told her I'd had enough. There were days when I didn't want to participate in what seemed like mindless games. Lots of days, actually. But that was before she vanished. After, I understood how precious those interactions had been, how fleeting. Suddenly, the meaningless had become fraught with meaning.

On the day she disappeared, though, there were no silly games. She was *in a way*, as Mom liked to call it. She'd woken with bad dreams about the man again ("He grabs me, Mama. He grabs me and he won't let go," she always said). The storm came just as she was beginning to forget the dreams, a brutal storm with jagged lightning touching down in the yard. But the thunder was the thing that always got Anna. On that day, it was relentless, one loud booming shudder after the next. The earplugs helped only until the thunder began in earnest. By then they were worthless because the entire house shook with each deep rumble. Dishes dropped inside cabinets and shattered. Outside, a stray dog howled desperately with each concussive blast. Anna sat, eyes closed, earplugs in, rocking back and forth. There was no consoling her when she was like this. Mom, sensing, perhaps, that Anna was headed for one of her freak-outs, had already retreated to her bedroom and locked the door. I tried to concentrate on Marcia Brady and her troubles with the school bully.

After that things get blurred together. At some point the phone rang, and I rose to answer it, but Mom's door opened and she called down the stairs for me to leave it alone. I shrugged and sat back down. Mom raced past me to get to the phone in the kitchen.

I heard her say hello, but that was it. Our phone cord would stretch all the way to the back porch and if you wanted to talk in private, that's where you went. I heard the back door open and knew that was where she'd gone. I didn't think very much of it at the time.

I think a lot of it now.

When she came back in, *The Brady Bunch* had ended, and I was watching the Fonz hitting a jukebox with his fist, and imagining how cool it would be to be able to have two girls, one for each arm.

"Danny, I've got to step out for a few minutes. Can you watch your sister?"

"Seriously? Mom, it's about to storm. She's about two seconds from a freak-out."

Mom looked at Anna, and I looked at Mom. If I was honest with myself then, I might have admitted she didn't appear normal. Her eyes were bloodshot, her cheeks sallow, and most disturbingly, she looked drugged. Like she couldn't focus, like she needed to lie down and take a long nap.

But I wasn't honest with myself then. I ignored all of this and instead acted like an insolent brat.

"You know I can't deal with her when she freaks."

"Only Mama Anna," Anna said.

My mother's real name was Susannah, but Anna managed to always ignore the beginning of her name and focus on the part that sounded exactly like hers. So, Susannah became Mama Anna, at least to my sister. Mom and Dad always thought it was cute and would never have dreamed of discouraging it. And sometimes it seemed like Anna clung to this similarity in name more fervently than even she had a right to. It may have been Anna's odd obsession with the sound of words, the way she loved certain sounds more than she loved any of us, but whatever the reason, Mom was special to Anna. Mom was the only person who could calm Anna down when she was upset, the only person Anna would follow anywhere. Anna tolerated Dad and me, but she truly loved Mom.

Mom touched Anna's brow and pushed her hair back.

"Mama Anna wants you to stay with brother Danny."

Anna looked at me suspiciously. "Say 'Potsie,' Danny."

"Shut up, Anna."

"Don't talk to your sister like that."

"Mom . . . don't leave her with me. Where are you going anyway?" We had only one car, which Dad had taken to work. Her options were pretty limited.

I don't know how Mom would have answered my question. I think about that a lot these days. She never got the chance. Thunder, low and menacing, vibrated the roof.

And then it happened. Meltdown.

Anna stood up, ripped the earplugs from her ears, and screamed. The scream was terrible because it wasn't very loud. It was like hearing somebody scream who didn't have lungs or vocal cords or whatever was needed to produce a real, full-fledged scream.

"Goddamn it, Danny! You did this!"

She reached for Anna's shoulders. Mom was the only one who could calm her when she was like this. Gently, she massaged Anna's back and whispered softly to her.

After what seemed like a long time, Anna stopped shaking.

"Okay," Mom said. "I am leaving. Watch your sister."

As soon as she let go of Anna's shoulders, she screamed again.

Mom exploded. "Goddamn you!" she screamed. "Goddamn you both!"

She took Anna's hand and led her to the door. I was dumbfounded.

She opened the door, and the wind almost took it off its hinges. Anna started shaking her head and murmuring "no" over and over.

"Fine," Mom said. "You stay with your brother."

"Nooooo!" she wailed as soon as Mom let go of her hand.

I thought for an instant Mom was going to slap her. Then her face softened. The transformation was so sudden, I missed the calculation in it. I don't miss it anymore.

"Anna, if you can't stay here with your brother, then you have to go with me."

Anna began to sing *The Brady Bunch* theme song.

Mom stood up. Anna was still singing. She had both fingers in her ears.

Watch her, Mom mouthed. She slipped out the door and into the storm.

Anna stopped singing and began to scream.

———————

I'm not sure why I didn't watch her. Maybe it was because I was angry at Mom. She'd never cursed me before, and I was reeling from it as if she'd struck me in the face. Or maybe I was just fourteen and irresponsible. Maybe it wouldn't have mattered even if I did. When Anna was determined to do something, she did it. She was a lot like my mother in that regard.

It happened like this. She screamed. I tried to comfort her. I tried to massage her shoulders, just like I'd seen Mom do so many times before. It only seemed to make things worse. My thing wasn't comforting Anna. It never had been. Instead, I was Anna's entertainment, a sounding board off which to bounce all the sounds that fascinated her. When the shoulders didn't work, I tried talking to her, pulling out the phrases she loved best: *Blueberry banana-rama-pumpkin pie, Brady Bunch, Sit on it, Ralph Malph,* and a dozen others she'd latched onto over the years.

None of them worked. She shook with fear, closed her eyes, and stuck her index fingers in her ears.

I finally went upstairs. There, I lay in my bed and watched the big oak tree in the front yard as the rain and wind rattled it like a tambourine. It groaned under the pressure, and I imagined it snapping and rocketing toward our house, obliterating it once and for all.

Then I saw her. She didn't walk as much as float, blown on the high wind. Anna, heading toward the woods, her fingers still in her ears, her eyes squinting into the wind.

I went after her, taking the steps in a single bound. I would have caught her too, I feel certain, if a limb hadn't snapped off the oak tree and flown at the front door, blocking my exit momentarily. I got it pushed aside and started down the steps. I braced myself against the wind and held my hand against my brow to shield the hard rain. Looking toward the woods, I knew I only needed to spot her before she disappeared and I'd be able to chase her in and bring her back. But it was too late. She'd already vanished.

I tried to follow her. But you don't follow someone who has vanished. There's no trail, nothing left to follow. The storm subsided as I made my way through the woods, calling her name. There was no answer except the wind in the trees, and sometimes I still find myself believing that's the only answer, no matter how far you search or how hard you listen. Just the shaking of leaves, the swish and shudder of dry limbs, mysteries in the sky that keep secrets older than memory.

What do you mean they took off in the storm?" Dad said. I was sitting on the porch steps. He stood over me, not particularly impressed by my tears, looking out onto the wreckage that was our front yard. Oak tree limbs, trash, a piece of roof. This and more. Debris scattered everywhere. The aftermath was so much more potent than the storm.

"First Mom, and then Anna. Mom told me to watch her, but she slipped out." I pointed vaguely at the door. "It was crazy. As scared as she is of storms . . ."

"And your mother? Where did she go?"

I shook my head. For some reason, it never dawned on me to mention the phone call. Or maybe it did. Maybe, if I'm honest, I just stopped thinking about it.

I was afraid Dad was going to get mad. He had every right. Coming home to this: a son, but no wife or daughter. Most men would lose their cool, especially upon hearing that their fourteen-year-old boy stood by and watched as his mother and sister charged headfirst into a deadly thunderstorm, but Dad was different then. He stuck out a hand and helped me up. Then he put his arm around me, holding me steady. I smelled sweat and oil on him from work. He said, "Point which way they went."

I pointed toward the trees, the general direction Anna was headed before I lost her, not mentioning I had no clue which direction Mom had gone.

He headed off into the woods across the drive. Thirty minutes later, he came back.

When he saw me, he shrugged. "Let's get you cleaned up."

After my shower, Dad and I ate a frozen pizza. He seemed to be trying not to panic. He kept talking about possibilities: A neighbor had picked them up, they'd gone down to the gas station and waited the storm out, and now they were waiting for the old man who worked there to give them a ride home. I didn't bother telling Dad that neither of these made much sense. Instead, I let him talk and nodded along.

After we finished, Dad stood up. "Come on. You're okay, aren't you?"

"Sure," I said, though all I wanted was to fall into the bed and wake tomorrow and realize this had all been a bad dream. I followed him as he went outside and headed back for the woods.

This time both Dad and I shouted for them, our voices echoing back to us from the hollows. We went deeper, all the way back to the little shack, the one I later learned belonged to Pike. I remember Dad clearing the kudzu away from the door and going inside. He emerged a few minutes later, his face so burdened with emotion that

I half believed he'd found their dead bodies. Instead, he'd simply found the end of his own rope.

"I think it may be time to call the police."

Back at the house, Dad reached Deputy Jack Barnes, who was underwhelmed by the news of a missing woman and child.

Dad got angry with him, almost shouting over the phone, before he pulled back, reining himself in. "Listen, my daughter is autistic. They just walked away. None of this makes sense. Could you just try to put yourself in my place?"

Barnes said he'd send a cruiser by and put out an all-points bulletin.

"Too early to get worried," Dad had said to himself after hanging up. He looked relieved somehow.

That night, I barely slept. Each time I began to drift off, I was awakened by a noise, some sound that I imagined to be Mom and Anna returning. "We had to wait out the storm at Cliff's place," Mom would say. "And then we just stayed for dinner."

I'd rush downstairs to hug them, and Dad—who'd never even attempted to go to sleep—would put in two frozen pizzas and we'd sit around the table laughing and talking about what a close call it had been, about how we'd been to the precipice and almost fallen, until some hand, some high and lonesome hand, had reached for ours and pulled us back and made us a family again. In the vision, I saw us sitting on a mountaintop somewhere, all four of us, happy and content. Most of all, together. This was the vision that would drive me when I started to doubt Pike's sanity, or even my own. This image of us together. The way it should be. The way it will be, I told myself over and over again.

At some point I did sleep, only to be awakened again by a noise. Something downstairs, a sound like a door opening. My dream was true. Rushing down the steps, I found Dad standing at the door, holding it open with both hands, staring out into the hot night.

This was my night, over and over again, until at some point, very deep in the morning hours, I came to a realization. Mom and Anna weren't coming back, and the dream of the mountaintop was just that, a dream.

Chapter Thirteen

Y ou're not to leave this house."

I stood, staring in utter disbelief at Mr. Banks. He sat at a mahogany desk, his glasses halfway down his nose, hands clasped together as if in prayer.

"This is your father's wish," he said. "I've been in touch with his attorney, who will be acting as a liaison in this difficult situation. And though I do have some doubts about following your father's wishes, I have decided that in this case, at least, it is the right thing to do. Furthermore, he has expressed very clearly that he wants you to stay away from Walter Pike. I agree on that count too. Pike has mental problems. I know it's hard for you boys to understand, but he has a history of violence in this town. And coming back now, it just looks suspicious." He spread his hands out. "Besides, Daniel. It's not so bad. You'll have the run of the house. Your best friend is already here. Where could you possibly need to go?"

He was right in a way. If it hadn't been for the burning need I felt to visit Pike again, he might have been completely right. So I tried to hide my shock and displeasure and nodded solemnly.

"Good then. So we understand each other." He nodded at me curtly and turned back to the papers he had been perusing on his desk. I had been dismissed.

"What was that about?" Cliff asked me later in his room.

"My dad doesn't want me to leave the house, and your dad is backing him up on it."

Cliff smiled. "Big deal."

"Big deal? What do you mean, 'big deal'?"

"You think my dad has ever paid attention to me?"

"Huh?"

"You've been here, what, three days? How many times have you seen either of my parents?"

I thought about it. "Well, today . . ."

"And that's it. They do their own thing. They've built this vast . . . empire for me to hang out in and it's like they think it's enough. Screw that. We'll come and go as we please."

So we did. But most of the time, we didn't go far, just out back to the pool or down the road to the little gas station where Cliff bought some comics. Nobody seemed to notice or if they did, they didn't seem to care.

On one of our trips to the gas station, I mentioned to Cliff that I wanted to pay another visit to Pike's cabin.

He stopped walking. "What?"

"Think about it," I said. "There's no logical explanation for what happened. People don't just vanish. So when the illogical happens, you have to start looking for illogical explanations."

122

He said nothing. His silence said it all.

"I'm not asking you to go with me," I said. "I just wanted you to know."

"Before, when I said you should go see that man, I didn't know he was going to be crazy."

"Crazy?"

"Danny, he told us that your mom and sister had disappeared from this world. As if there's some other world to disappear from."

"He might not have literally meant it like that, Cliff."

"Yeah, right."

"I just want to hear him out."

"I think you should stay. That guy gave me the creeps. He's not right in the head. I've heard people saying he was involved with the two girls."

"What? I thought you didn't believe all that stuff about the girls."

"It doesn't matter what I believe, Danny. He could be dangerous. That's the bottom line. Think for a minute. Try to understand the risk you are taking."

Strangely enough, I didn't get angry with Cliff. I could see that he honestly believed he had my best interest at heart.

I decided to let it drop and we continued to the gas station. It was Wednesday, the day the new comics came in.

I don't know how it might have ended up if we hadn't gone to the gas station that day. Maybe I would have eventually let Cliff convince me that it was foolish and dangerous to pursue Pike. Maybe I would have lived out the rest of my days pondering how two people can just disappear. Or maybe I would have grown older and the mysterious circumstances around my mother and sister's disappearance would have grown murkier and less important with each passing year.

When we walked into the gas station, Cliff made a beeline for the comics rack and didn't notice the man standing in line to check out. Walter Pike.

I almost didn't recognize him either. He looked . . . well, he looked sober. His hair had been washed and brushed. Though he was far from clean-cut, he looked alert and put together, more like a man than a red-eyed demon of the night.

I froze, unsure at first what to do.

"New Hulk is in," Cliff said.

Pike turned and saw me. His eyes scanned me quickly until recognition dawned on his face. He placed a six-pack of beer on the counter and reached into his back pocket for his wallet, while I stood frozen to the spot.

"Earth to Danny," Cliff said. "Don't you want the new Hulk?"

I shook my head. The only thing I wanted at that moment was for Pike to turn back around. Then I wanted him to tell me how to find my mother and sister.

"Howdy," the cashier said. He was an old-timer, Mr. Grayson or Granger or something. Most people just called him Cap, though I didn't know why. What I did know is that "howdy" was his standard greeting. He liked Red Man tobacco and was partial to overalls, and he wasn't particularly impressed with my or Cliff's love of what he called "funny books."

"Afternoon," Pike said, keeping his eyes down, his wallet ready in his hand, anxious to complete the transaction.

Cap rang up the beer and said, "Four dollars nineteen pennies, my friend."

Pike pulled out a ten.

Cap picked up his spit bottle and deposited a long brown strand of dip into it. "Got nineteen cents?"

Pike shook his head.

Cap nodded and took the ten. He opened the register and began to count out change. He was about to hand Pike his money when he stopped, pulling it back. "Wait a minute," he said. "I recognize you now. You're Preston Pike's boy."

Pike nodded and reached for his change.

Cap pulled it back. "Hell naw." He dropped the change back into the register and pulled Pike's ten out, flinging it at him. "We don't do business with your kind."

A thin smile creased Pike's face. "My kind?"

"I know about you. You might think people forget, but Cap don't never forget. You and that Sykes boy. Both of you disappearing like you did. I don't forget."

"You don't, huh?"

"Go on. Take your pretty ass on out of here. Don't care to do business with a queer."

"Queer?"

"You heard me. Go on."

Pike reached for the six-pack. Cap did the same, pulling it away from Pike just before he could get his hands on it.

That's when I saw a different side of Pike, a side that gave me pause.

He moved quick, grabbing Cap's shirt in both fists and pulling him across the counter. The old man grunted and made a face like he was in pain. Pike jerked him again, the old man's belly pressing against the counter. "Let's me and you get a few things straight. I don't care what Cap remembers. It don't make it true."

The old man tried to pull away, but Pike yanked him so hard, I heard Cap's T-shirt rip. "I'm going to drop this ten dollars on the counter"—Pike opened one fist and let the damp bill flutter to the countertop—"and I'm going to let go of you and take this beer. If you try to stop me, I'm going to give you something to remember, and this time, it won't be some made-up shit that none of you will ever understand. You got all that?"

Cap looked like he wanted to spit on Pike or hit him in the mouth or maybe even kill him dead, but all he did was nod, his face set in stone.

"Good."

Pike let go and took the beer. He said something under his breath and turned to walk out. "I hate you had to see that," he said as he walked past me and out the door.

I whirled around and saw from the look on Cliff's face as he stood by the comics rack that he had witnessed the whole thing.

"Don't do it," he said, but I was already moving.

When I got outside, Pike was getting into his truck. He stopped, the door half-open. "Come with me."

His voice was cold and hard but low enough to make me realize he didn't want anyone else to hear him.

"Only if you promise to tell me how to get my mother and sister back."

"No promises. Only a story I think you might be interested in."

————————

We all piled into the front of his pickup, me in the middle and Cliff by the window. I knew he was pissed, and scared, but he came with me. I'll always appreciate that because

I'm sure the whole thing seemed crazy to him, not to mention dangerous.

Nobody spoke for a long while. Instead, we just watched as the mid-July landscape coasted by on a cloud of dust. This had been my favorite time of year before they disappeared. I could play for hours in the hot sun and not even feel tired. But this year the heat seemed draining, glaring, like some great white light that sucked at your energy, sometimes even your soul.

Finally, Pike looked over at me, nodding in Cliff's direction. "You trust him?"

I didn't hesitate. "He's my best friend."

Pike nodded. "I heard they put your daddy in the jail. He got a lawyer?"

I told him he did.

"'Cause I know one if you—"

"I just want to know where my mom and sister are. Please."

"Fair enough." He made a hard right onto a mud-splattered path that I'd barely noticed before. "I should start by showing you something."

Chapter Fourteen

WALTER

After the beating Seth took at the hands of Jake and his cronies, it was nearly March before he showed up at school again. The rumor was that he came then only because Sheriff Branch drove out to his house to find out what was going on.

One thing was clear: He had been beaten badly. His nose was busted and his face was every color a bruise can be—brown, black, blue, even green. I was pretty sure his daddy had told the truth about giving him more when he got home.

I kept my distance. No matter how bad I felt for him, I had no desire to be seen with him at school. Knowing he was my cousin made it that much harder. I felt like I owed him something, but I just didn't have it in me at that point. My own life had been hard enough since I'd pulled the knife on Jake. He'd told anybody in the school who would listen that I was queer and that Seth was my boyfriend.

I don't know how many people believed him, but I do know that everyone avoided me like the plague.

For the most part, Ronnie and Jake avoided me too. Occasionally, I'd catch one of them staring at me in gym or secretly flipping me a bird during class change, but they didn't get in my face. That was fine with me. I knew my threat of always carrying a knife might have been behind this, but I also hoped the tension was beginning to ebb.

Turned out, that was just a daydream with no basis in reality. Retaliation was coming, and when it did, I knew I needed to be damn ready.

The next day I swiped three dollars from my mother's purse and left for school early. I walked out to County Road Seven and found the half-crippled black man we called Old Roy. Roy could always be found on County Road Seven pushing a grocery cart full of whatever knickknack you might need—cleaning supplies, clothing, snacks, paperback novels, and knives. I bought a switchblade for two dollars and kept the other dollar in my pocket. That switchblade didn't end up helping me much against Jake and his cronies, but it did play a role in the coming days. A bigger one than I'd ever imagined.

———————

April came on hard with storm after storm. For several days the cotton fields turned to mud and the men who worked them stayed home or used the time off as an excuse to head out to County Road Seven and spend their wages on moonshine and women.

Getting to school became dangerous. I remember running across the highway in the middle of pounding rain and seeing two trees in front of me get split in half by lightning. Another time a whole line of pines was uprooted and thrown into the pond. The same storm took down our old fort, collapsing the roof and leaving it a twisted snarl of wood and rusty nails.

Another storm was beginning to gather over the cotton fields, turning the sky a coal-dark color as I headed home from school one afternoon in mid-April. I kept an eye out for Jake and his gang—something I'd started to do out of habit. I didn't see anyone, so I slipped past the football practice field and toward the highway. Moving quickly because of the coming storm, I let down my guard. As I ran across the highway, I noticed that no less than four boys were on my tail. I kept going. I thought I had a big enough head start on them and might be able to lose them in the woods.

Halfway through the trees, two other boys stepped into my path. One of them was Ronnie. He had his arms crossed and wore a smirk on his face. "You fucked up," he said.

I changed direction and headed for the deeper woods. Behind me, I heard the two groups of boys meeting up, discussing where I had gone. I kept moving, thinking I could go past my house, almost out to the meadow right before County Road Seven and then double back home. Surely I would be safe there.

That's when I almost ran over Seth.

He was standing in a clearing in the deepest part of the woods, surrounded by five boys, including Jake. I pulled up, realizing I had nowhere else to run. I didn't recognize the exact spot, but I knew we were close to the storm shelter. The remains of an old building were just off to my right, one large piece of its tin roof flapping in the wind.

Jake grinned his most spiteful grin. "Well, look at what we have here. Me and these boys followed Seth. Ronnie and some others followed Walter, and imagine that, they end up in the same place. I wonder what for?" He elbowed the kid standing next to him—an older boy, maybe sixteen, who played football and grabbed girls' asses in the hallways at school. I think his name was Steve.

"I'm going to take a guess," Steve said. "Just a wild guess. Maybe to suck each other's dicks?"

The whole group laughed. I turned to see that we had been joined by the six boys who had been chasing me. That made eleven in all. I thought I was going to die, but I wouldn't die without a fight. That's when I remembered the switchblade.

I kept it in my boot, so I had to bend down to pull it out.

"Hey," Jake said. "Stand back up."

I ignored him, instead digging inside my boot for the small switchblade. I popped the blade out, leading with it as I stepped toward Jake.

To my surprise, he just laughed.

This shook me some, but I knew once the blade was in him, he wouldn't be laughing. I broke into a run, only to pull up suddenly when I saw what Ronnie was holding in his hand.

The biggest, blackest gun I have ever seen. It seemed to swallow his hand whole, and the muzzle was aimed right at my head.

"Drop the knife, Walter," Ronnie said.

I started to drop it, but just then the wind picked up. One of the boys' hats flew off and got twisted up in the branches of a live oak. He cursed and a low rumble of thunder touched our ears. Rain began to fall. I kept looking at the gun, its single eye trained on me. Until you've actually had a gun pointed at you, it's hard to imagine how breathtaking the experience is, how useless you feel.

Seth stepped up beside me. "He's not queer."

"Shut the fuck up," Jake snapped back. "Nobody asked you."

Seth took another step until he was in front of me, his full attention turned on Ronnie. "I tried to kiss him, but he pushed me away. He's not queer. I'm the only one. Let him go. Do whatever you have to do to me, Walter's not queer."

Another roll of thunder. This one was louder, more insistent. The rain fell in big, cold pellets.

Jake grinned. "Oh my God. This is true love, Ronnie. Just like you said. One of them is going to be the hero for the other one." He turned to me. "You okay with a faggot taking up for you, Pike? Hell, I used to think you were all right, but this shit beats all."

Seth turned and looked at me. He shrugged as if to say he'd tried. When he turned back to face Ronnie, he said, "So what are you going to do with us?"

I noticed that Ronnie's hand was beginning to shake a little bit.

Jake said, "We've got a plan, queerboys."

Ronnie let out a long breath.

"You remember the plan, right?" Jake said. "It's easy and nobody will know. We're out here far enough that nobody will even hear the shots, Ronnie."

The gun wavered.

"Jesus, Ronnie. You said you wanted this. You said you wanted this for your brother."

Suddenly, Ronnie spun around, aiming right at Jake. "Don't you bring up my brother. Leave him out of this. You hear me? Do you goddamned hear me, Jake?"

Jake held up his hands. "Yeah. Loud and clear. It's just that you said, you know, you wanted to take out some queers because of what happened."

Ronnie's eyes were wild, his whole body crooked beneath the weight of the gun.

Jake kept his eyes on Ronnie. "It's not me you want, Ronnie. It's them. The queers."

Ronnie was still. He stopped shaking. After a long time, he nodded and turned back around toward us.

At that moment, I firmly believed my life was about to end.

"Go on," Jake said. "Do it for Bob. Do it for the other kids that these two will buttfuck and kill when they get older. Being queer is a disease, man. Take it out."

His hand shook. His face was flush and slick with rain, and just before he pulled the trigger I could have sworn I saw regret in his eyes.

I still don't know which one happened first—the impossibly loud *thomp* of thunder or the gunshot. Maybe they happened at the same time. The sky cracked and out poured long strands of lightning, making everything flash like a strobe light.

Several guys screamed. I'm sure I was one of them. Seth was not. He grabbed my arm and shoved me toward the trees. I still had the knife in my hand and I closed the blade as we ran, slipping it into my back pocket. Another shot followed us. This one flew so near to my face, it scorched my cheek with gunpowder. I screamed again but kept running.

We didn't go far before Seth was on the ground, flipping open the storm shelter door. He pushed me down the ladder despite my protests. I told him we would die inside the shelter, we needed to run. He just kept shoving until I half climbed, half fell inside. A second later, the shelter went dark and I felt his hand on my arm.

"I've gotten better at it," he said.

"What?"

"We can stay this time. At least for a little while."

I felt confused. "Where are we going?" I said.

"To the swamp, of course."

He pushed me toward the back wall.

"What? How? There's nothing here but solid concrete."

"We're not going that way. We're going through the slip."

Chapter Fifteen

DANNY

We stopped in a little clearing that I guessed wasn't too far from his house. I was and am still amazed by the secret places that can be found in a forest. This one was beautiful, an almost perfect little meadow, surrounded on all sides by tall pines, its borders laced with sunburned kudzu and Spanish moss that seemed to drip from the sky.

"There's two shovels in the back of the truck," Pike said as he climbed out and stretched himself. "Damn, I wish I had a cigarette."

I looked at Cliff. He shrugged and opened the door. Together, we went around to the tailgate and retrieved the shovels. Pike had wandered over to the tree line and seemed to be trying to pace something off, counting his steps and cursing to himself. After a few paces, he kicked at the dirt with a heavy boot. "Damn it. Damn it all."

I waited for him to offer some explanation of what he was angry about, but he didn't look at me or Cliff. Instead, he went back to the tree line and started again.

"I told you he was a nut," Cliff said.

I ignored him. Despite the heat, a cold chill had come over me. Was he doing what I thought he was? No, he couldn't be. But what if Cliff was right? What if he was a nut? And what about Dad? Dad had said to stay clear.

I know where your mother and sister are.

Were we about to dig them up?

It is hard for me to imagine now the kind of courage it must have taken to stand there and wait for this man to point at the place for us to dig. This is a kind of courage I can no longer comprehend, lost in the years of taking precautions and paying bills and getting old.

"Here," he said at last. "Right here. Dig."

"What are we digging?" Cliff said.

Pike glared at me. His eyes seemed to be accusing me. *I thought you said we could trust him.*

"Hello?" Cliff said. "What are we digging up?"

Pike didn't answer. Instead, he took the shovel from Cliff and began to dig.

A few seconds later, I joined him.

———

I hit the box first. Instead of the pliable soil and the pleasing *schluff* I'd been used to for the last fifteen minutes, I felt a solid resistance and a *thunk*. Pike threw his shovel aside and knelt. I noticed for the first time that he was sweating profusely and his breathing was extremely labored.

"Do you need your oxygen?" I said.

He waved me away and reached into the hole we'd made. He grunted and heaved out a metal box about the size of a couple of boxes of cereal stacked on top of each other.

I felt a twinge of relief. There was no way to fit a body in that.

The box had a small lock on the side. Pike fished into his pocket and produced his keys. He quickly found a small silver one and inserted it into the keyhole. It popped open and Pike reached inside the box with one hand, touching whatever was inside. His eyes were full of wonder and light, and a deep fascination that sent a chill down my spine.

"What is it?" Cliff said.

Pike wiped at his eyes and tilted the box over, so that the contents slid out.

"It's proof."

Chapter Sixteen

There was a moment—brief and panic filled—when I saw something that wasn't there. I saw a skeleton, the bones long and white and gleaming in the sunlight. It rattled out of the box and hit the ground in a jumbled mess. I had already turned away and opened my mouth to scream when I heard Cliff.

"This is what you wanted to show us?"

I made myself look again, and what had at first been an intricate network of bones was now the white backs of photographs. They were old Polaroids. Pike picked them up and held them out for me.

There were five in all. The quality wasn't great, and the lighting in them even worse, but I don't think I've ever seen anything so fascinating.

The first one was of a kid I didn't recognize. He was standing in knee-deep water, grinning. Behind him was a collection of oaks so massive, they made the one in my front yard look like a joke. Moss hung from the branches, and above the branches a deep blue dusk lingered like a soulful kiss.

The next photograph was the same kid, different angle. In this shot, the water he's standing in stretches out for hundreds of yards before the trees begin. In this wider shot, a full moon was also visible in the background, illuminating the photo with a pallid beauty.

The next three photos were the ones that took my breath away.

A different kid, a different angle. A cabin in the background. I might have fixated on that detail if not for the expression on the kid's face. He wore a sly grin I'd seen somewhere before. I recognized it instantly but couldn't place it. At least not at first. Then it came to me, like a sudden blast of lightning. My body tingled with it.

Pike. It was Pike as a young boy.

I said nothing and slid the photo to the back of the pile, revealing the next one. Pike again, this time laughing.

The last one was the best. Neither boy was in it. Instead, it was a close-up of the cabin. In every way, it might have been Pike's cabin, except one. It was situated on the edge of the swamp, and it had a little ramshackle porch, barely wide enough to put a chair on.

"Where were these taken?" I said.

Pike cleared his throat. "Not far from where we are now."

"That's impossible."

Pike looked at the sky. "I told you," he said to someone only he could see.

"Do you expect us to believe these were taken here? In these woods?"

Pike focused on me again with his good eye. "I don't expect you to believe anything. All I can tell you is the truth, and try to convince you to think rationally."

"Rationally?" Cliff said, taking the photos out of my hand. "You show us these photos of some place that's obviously miles from these woods—" He paused to flip through them quickly. "I'd say by the looks of those trees, we're talking at least a hundred miles south of here. This is the opposite of rational."

Pike shook his head. "Then explain how me and Seth got to this swamp a hundred miles from home. Seth's family didn't even own a car, and the one we had wouldn't make it ten miles without overheating. We were poor. Hell, poorer than poor. We had to steal the damn camera from the school just to take the pictures."

I was sure he was crazy, but I didn't want to give up. Not yet. Maybe I'd gone a little crazy myself. I said, "So if this place is in the woods, take us to it."

"Not yet," he said.

"Why? I'm ready to get them back."

"Don't be too sure. You're not going anywhere until I tell you my story."

"Damn the story," I said, "I want to go now."

Pike smiled, showing his yellow teeth. The resemblance to the boy in the photos I'd just seen was striking. "Maybe you will do," he said.

"What does that mean?"

"It means my instincts were right about you. Just like they were right about Seth so many years ago."

"Seth?"

"It's part of the story I need to tell you."

"Well, tell it already."

He shook his head and reached for the photos. Cliff let him take them, and Pike placed them back in the box, which he locked and dropped back into the hole.

"You're burying them again?"

"You always ask dumb questions?"

He took the shovel and began covering the box with dirt.

"None of this makes any sense," Cliff said.

"Ain't that the truth." Pike said, still shoveling the dirt back into the hole.

"So what do you do?" Cliff asked. "When things don't make sense."

Pike smirked. "You put those things in a box somewhere, bury them deep. Try not to think about them. It's easier than you might imagine. It's the remembering that's the hard part."

Chapter Seventeen

WALTER

*S*lip.

That was the only time I heard Seth give it a name. I'm not sure why he called it that, but later, when I had time to think on all the stuff that happened after I took his hand, it made sense. It fit.

But at that moment, I didn't know what to think.

"Trust me," he said. "It's what friends do."

He grabbed my hand. I tried to pull away, remembering how he'd tried to kiss me, but he held on tight.

"Just for a second," he said.

I relaxed. I might have closed my eyes. It's hard to remember. I do remember being excited. I wanted to go back, to prove to myself that it had happened. If it hadn't, we would both be in a world of hurt. I could hear the boys outside, the groaning of the hatch as somebody pulled it open. Then it got quiet, so quiet it almost seemed loud. That doesn't make sense, does it? No, I suppose it doesn't. Get used to it. From here on, forget sense. Toss it the hell out the window.

One minute I heard them rattling the shelter door and the next I heard the slow lapping of water against an invisible bank, the call of a whippoorwill, the chittering of the cicadas at dusk.

My heart jumped. It felt like I was going to fly apart into about a dozen pieces. Like riding one of those loop-de-loops at the state fair or one of those rides that drops you into a free fall. My lungs filled up to bursting. And hell if I didn't feel like my body was being drawn and quartered. I was a beat away from death, a hiccup in my chest from falling into nothing and never coming back, and then I *was* falling again, spinning, the swamp flying up at me so fast it blurred my vision, made my eyes water. This time I did hit the swamp, and it was cold and dark and dirty. My nose filled up with it. I sucked that mess into my lungs. I thought I'd drown for sure. My eyes saw light— green and murky. It came from above me. I tried to flail upward.

Then it was over.

We were back in the storm shelter again.

"It didn't work," I said, panic rising in my voice. Jake and Ronnie and Steve would be on us any second.

Seth still held my hand. He squeezed it tightly. "It worked."

"No," I said. "Look around. It's the shelter still."

"Follow me. I'll show you."

He led me over to the ladder. I let go of his hand and cringed as he started up. I'd heard them at the door. Maybe they weren't inside yet, but they'd still be right there. I hissed at him. "No. Don't—" He ignored me and opened the hatch.

The light was different. I noticed that first. It was darker outside, almost like dusk. He climbed through the hatch. "Come on up, Walter."

Slowly, I climbed the ladder. When I reached the top, I saw the full moon first, hanging in a dusky sky. I pulled myself up and out, sure that suddenly I was in the midst of magic, not the hocus-pocus stuff you see in movies or that illusionary bullshit of light and shadow, but real magic. Somehow, Seth had brought me . . . where? I struggled to get my mind around it. Somewhere *else*. And this time we were really there. No fleeting glimpses that could so easily be dismissed. This time it was solid ground, dirty water, gorgeous sky, and a light misting rain. We'd slipped—that was Seth's word—right out of our world into another one.

It wasn't until I stood up that I saw the cabin, its single light burning inside.

"Watch it," he said, tugging me back toward the bank. A snake, as thick as my arm and twice as long, skimmed across the water.

"Whoa."

"Yeah, they're everywhere." He pointed at the sky, maybe the moon, maybe the stars beyond. In the west, I could see lingering strains of red.

"Can we go in the cabin?" I asked.

"We could, but I like to stay close to the hatch. It's easier to find that way."

I turned around, thinking it would be right beside me, but it wasn't. I was standing in water now, at least two feet of it. The hatch was gone.

"Don't worry. It should be around here somewhere. This place is easier to get to than to get out of, but I've had some practice."

I felt panic coming over me. "But it was here a second ago. How could it just move?"

Seth laughed. "Listen to yourself, Walter. You want things to be so rational. The world we see may be rational, but the real one is not."

"The real one? What's that mean?"

"Just that this place doesn't follow the ordinary rules."

"I'll say."

"Let's go ahead and look for it. Might take us a while to find it, and I can tell it makes you anxious, not knowing a way out."

I nodded. He was right. Seth was nothing if not perceptive. It was uncanny, really.

It seemed like an eternity, us slogging through the water, looking for the hatch. Of course, it was mostly Seth who was looking. I was too distracted by where I was—a swamp, an honest-to-God swamp— to be much help. While we looked, Seth told me about one time when he couldn't find it.

"What did you do?"

"I freaked out a little. Started thinking about how I could live here. I realized it wouldn't be the worst thing in the world, you know? It's not like my life back in the real world is such great shakes."

I laughed at this. "True enough."

"But I still wanted to go home. After I gave up on finding the hatch, I started to explore the swamp because I figured there had to be more than one way out. I was right."

"Well, what are we waiting for?" I said. "Let's go that way."

"Trust me. This way is better."

Before I could ask him what the other way was, I spotted the hatch. The top of it was sticking out of the swamp water. "There," I said.

Seth put a hand on my back and patted me. "Good eyes. Ready to swim?"

The next part is the hardest part to describe. We swam down into the hatch. The whole shelter was filled with water, so we went right past the ladder without even touching it. We went down, down, down, so deep my lungs felt like they would burst from the pressure, but just before they did, we reached the bottom. The world did its wheel thing, and all the water drained away into the sky. I lay there at the bottom of the storm shelter, soaked to the bone, just breathing. And that's when a strange thought hit me. I was happy. I was exhausted, confused, my bones ached and my head was still spinning, but damned if I wasn't happy.

Chapter Eighteen

DANNY

We drove back to Pike's house in silence. He led us inside and told us to wait in the main room while he went to the bedroom to get something.

"What do you think?" I said to Cliff.

"I think those photos are weird, but there's definitely an explanation."

"Ditto on the weird part."

"I hope my dad hasn't noticed that we've been gone."

"You said that wasn't an issue."

He shrugged. "It shouldn't be. It's just that we've missed lunch and he sometimes asks me about lunch. You know, what did you eat, that sort of thing. He's obsessed with food."

I couldn't bring myself to even feel the least bit anxious about Cliff's father right now. "You can go back if you want," I said.

"We *both* need to go, Danny."

Before I could answer, Pike came back carrying a large framed painting. He leaned it against the wall and stepped back, waving us over.

It was a painting of a swamp at dusk. A full moon hung over a little cabin perched on the edge of the swamp water. High grass and slicks of mud helped complete the landscape, which faded near the edges into dark and luxurious trees. The light rippled through both the clouds and swamp water, setting the image aglow. The cabin, situated on the left of the scene, had a single warm light burning inside the window. Moonshine illuminated the tin roof and tiny, almost imperceptible silver streaks of rain fell on the cabin. Across the water stood three great trees—oaks or elms or something equally stately.

There was something enchanting about the oil painting. Something comforting. And disturbing. The disturbing part was that I was sure I knew the place, had even been there before, but the details were slippery, half-remembered.

Frustrated, I dismissed the feeling, deciding it was just the enchantment of the painting, the exhilaration of the moment, of feeling like I was finally making some progress toward finding my mother and Anna. I don't know. Maybe it was just the idea that such a place, so pure and so elegant, might have once existed. That somebody had thought to paint that very moment when the swamp was settling into itself, making peace with the dusk and the long night to follow. Like the moon had stationed itself in that particular spot on that particular evening because the night was too perfect to allow it to fade away unobserved.

"I don't know if your mother and sister are alive or if they're dead," Pike said, gesturing to the painting. "But if they are alive, I think this is where they are."

"It's the same cabin that was in the photos," Cliff said.

"Yep. My friend Seth, the other boy in the photos. He painted this. There was a time when he moved away from these woods, and he painted this to help him remember. Remembering is important. There's not much else in this world that matters in the end besides your memories."

"So, how did my mother and sister get to this place? How did you and Seth get there?" I asked.

"Let me get some more cigarettes and I'll tell you."

He left us as he went in the back again. When he came back, he had a cigarette between his lips. He sat down in a chair near his oxygen tank.

"How old are you?" he said.

Cliff and I both answered, "Fourteen."

Pike looked at Cliff with suspicion, as if he had not expected the boy to still be here. Then he shrugged and blew out a stream of smoke. "Isn't that something?"

"Isn't what something?" I said.

He looked at the couch across from him. "Sit down. Hell, you're not planning on standing through the whole thing, are you?"

Cliff and I sat.

"I remember fourteen. Best and worst year of my life. Best because I learned to be a man. Worst because I forgot how to be a boy."

I glanced at Cliff. He was gazing at the painting, his usual impatience stymied for the time being. Pike had already pulled us in. I should have been terribly impatient. I should have been angry, but I sensed something deep and mysterious in the tale Pike was already beginning to relate. I sensed that Pike could not hurry because if he did the whole structure would crumble to the ground. More than anything, though, I sensed that Pike was going slow because he had to convince himself again.

He began by telling us about the boy from the photo, about the boy named Seth.

Chapter Nineteen

WALTER

Lying there in the dark silence of the storm shelter, I felt as peaceful as I could ever remember feeling. I could be anywhere, and part of me wanted to believe I was in heaven. If it could be this peaceful, this fulfilling, I think I'd want to go. Then I heard a voice that made it clear this was not heaven:

"Where the hell did they go?"

It was Jake, and he sounded angry, a little dazed, maybe even frightened. His voice was coming from somewhere above us, a faraway sound. I sat up and remembered why we'd slipped in the first place. No, this definitely wasn't heaven.

"We did it," Seth said, his voice barely a whisper. "We showed those bastards."

He slapped my shoulder.

"We showed them. Yes, sir, we did. You okay?"

"I think so." I tried opening my eyes just a little. Seth had moved away, to the other side of the shelter. I heard him scratching at the ground, digging.

A light appeared from the other side. Seth held up a lantern.

He came back over, his face lit by the lantern. He was smiling so big. "That was the coolest thing ever. I wish I could have seen the look on their faces."

"So while we were there in the . . . swamp, Jake and his friends came in here? And we weren't here?" I couldn't get my mind around it.

"That's about how it works. Pretty cool, huh?"

"Cool. Jesus, Seth. That's the most incredible thing that has ever happened to me."

Seth started laughing. I'd never heard him laugh like that before. It was loud and obnoxious. The kind of laughter that came from the heart. I started laughing too, thinking about Jake and his buddies finally getting in and finding nothing. Just an empty storm shelter. We laughed so hard, I began to worry they might still be around and hear us, but when I tried to stop laughing I thought about Jake's face if he *did* hear us laughing and that was funny too, so I kept right on.

We sat in the storm shelter for a long time after that. When we finally decided to leave, the batteries in Seth's lantern had started to die and the darkness was creeping over us. Most of time, Seth talked and I listened.

He told me about his mother trying to leave his father when he had been younger. "That was a mistake. She paid for that one."

"Paid?"

In the dim light, he shook his head. "You saw my bruises."

"What's wrong with him?" I asked.

"My father?"

"Yeah."

"I can't explain it." He swallowed hard, and an awkward silence passed.

Maybe I should have pushed the issue, but I let it drop because it was obviously painful for Seth.

"Don't you even want to hear about how it works?"

I sat up. Of course I did. This was probably the only thing that could distract me from Seth's father.

"When my mother . . . her disappearance. After she was . . ." He hesitated, like he was searching for the right word. Finally, he shook his head in frustration and went on. "After my mother went away. That's the first time I actually slipped. I was so upset one day that I was determined to come out here and lose myself in these woods. I wanted to find a place so hidden from the rest of the world that nobody'd ever find me. I found this storm shelter. I came down here and just sat for a long time. I think I was close to giving up that day. You know, ending it.

"But this place. I liked it instantly. It was dark, and I could be alone here. I came almost every day after that, and eventually, I began to realize I was going away. I mean, I'd always been able to go away in my mind, but this was different. This was real."

"Going away? You mean slipping?"

"Sort of. But not quite. At first, I just saw the place, as if from a distance. I wanted to go there. So one day I came down during a storm. I'd been here no more than a few minutes when it happened.

The first time was just a glimpse like your first time, but the door had been opened. I started staying longer and longer."

I shook my head. "I still don't understand how you do it."

"I'm not really doing anything. It's already there. I just found it. This place is so close to our woods. It's the same place, really. Think of it like a book. The other world is on the front side of the page. This one is on the back. What separates the two is as thin as a sheet of paper."

"How did you know it would work? I mean, how did you know that by touching me, I would go too?"

"I experimented. I took objects with me. I brought things back. Want to know something I learned?"

"What?"

"The swamp has special powers."

"Special powers? You're kidding me, right?"

"I took a dead rabbit once. I wanted to see what would happen. It came alive again. In a way. I mean, it was all shady and dark like a shadow, but I could touch it. So I brought it back. Then it was dead again."

"Whoa. Did you take it back again?"

"Yeah. He's gone now."

"Gone?"

Seth shrugged. "Moved on, I guess. That's what dead things do, right?"

I had no answer for this.

"He seemed so normal."

"Who?"

"Your dad."

"He's not normal at all, Walter. He's evil."

I remembered the way he'd examined Seth's injuries. "Maybe. But he knows about slipping."

"What did you say?"

"The day you were hurt, the day he came to take you home, he talked to me about being in the cellar with your grandmother. He told me he'd been nearly starved, and he started to see visions. He saw the swamp."

Seth said nothing for a long time. The lantern was almost dead. I was still reeling from what had happened. My senses were overloaded, and suddenly I wanted nothing more than to be home in my own bed.

"I think you're right," Seth said quietly. "He told me the same story. It's one of the things that scares me most. I thought I'd finally found a place to get away from him, but then I find out he's been there before me, and if he's been there once, he could go again."

I thought about the swamp, how beautiful and special the place seemed. It was hard to imagine Seth's father there. "Maybe," I said, "he lost the ability to go. Maybe it's only something you can do when you're young."

The lantern went out. We were in utter darkness again.

"Maybe," Seth said. "And if that's true, one of these days I'm going to go there and never come back."

That was the point where Seth and I didn't agree. As much as I liked visiting the swamp, I didn't want to stay. Each time we went, Seth wanted to stay longer. Each time, I had to talk him into coming back.

I'd say we went at least once a day for a solid month. We explored everything—the cabin, the outer reaches of a swamp that seemed to go on forever. We learned that time never really moves there. It's always the same. Dusk, a light mist of rain. The same moon in the same sky.

Eventually, Seth got his hands on one of those Polaroid cameras, and we took photos. There were others besides the ones I showed you, but they're gone now. Sometimes, thinking of those photos is like thinking of a dream, and sometimes I believe that's all it was. The slip was a special place, but it's also a burden that I'll carry as long as I live.

Still, those days of going to the swamp with Seth were probably the best of my entire life. I wanted them to last forever, but I don't need to tell you boys that nothing lasts forever, do I?

See, I couldn't stop thinking about Seth's father, Mr. Sykes. Seth wasn't telling me everything. I knew that. Every time I'd bring up the subject of his dad, he'd tell me to quit ruining his day. "I come to the swamp to forget him, so please stop bringing him up," he'd say.

The more I thought about Mr. Sykes, the more sure I became: He was the one behind those girls going missing. I knew it. I knew Seth knew too, but he was too afraid to tell me. What's more, I decided I had to do something about it.

Chapter Twenty

One warm spring day I skipped school and walked the three miles to the police station.

Back then we only had the chief—his name was Wyatt Branch—and one deputy. You've seen *Andy Griffith*, right? Imagine that, and you'll just about have it nailed. Except there was one difference. Chief Branch was a dark, brooding, and cold man who did not suffer fools. It was well known that he didn't like kids, and when he saw me coming toward his desk that morning, he held his hand up.

"Hold it. I don't have time for bullshit today."

I stopped a few feet away from his desk. He had his feet up and a cup of coffee in his hand. A newspaper lay open on his desk.

"Just turn around and go home. Better yet, go back to school. I'm sure whatever it is that brought you in today will take care of itself eventually."

"I got something important."

"Of course you do." He blew on his coffee and took a swallow.

"It's about the missing girls."

He put his coffee down. "You'd better not be shitting me, boy."

"I'm not. I know who took them."

"You got a name, Sherlock?"

"Last name is Sykes." I realized I didn't know his first.

"Hell, there's a whole clan of Sykes round these parts. Which one are you talking about?"

"He lives out by the cotton fields, across the highway, not too far from the apple orchard."

"I think I know who you're talking about. Paid them a visit not too long ago. Boy wasn't going to school." He put his coffee down and looked me over. "You Preston Pike's boy?"

"Yes, sir."

"Tell your daddy if I catch him publicly intoxicated again, I'm going give him something worse than a hangover." With that, Branch stood up and put on his hat.

"I'll tell him."

"Good. You can tell me why you think this Sykes is the one on the way."

———

Don't think I haven't realized the similarities. Seems I'm always destined to be the bearer of unbelievable news. As we rode in that police car, I had no idea I'd be trying to convince people nearly thirty-six years later of something even harder to believe. Not that convincing Branch was going to be easy.

We made a turn by the gas station and saw them—twenty or so

men—all shirtless, bent over, their backs shining with sweat in the morning sun.

Branch parked the car along the side of the road and started to get out.

"Don't tell him it was me," I said.

He looked at me as a smile spread across his face. "You're a dumb kid," he said.

He left me in the car and walked through the cotton until he found Jim Reynolds, the foreman. It was a nice day and the men moved easily with smiles on their faces, enjoying the breeze.

He and Jim spoke for a moment and I saw Jim looking over toward the police car, shading his eyes as if trying to make me out. I slumped down in my seat, laying my head against the leather. I lay there for a long time, thinking all sorts of dangerous thoughts. What if Branch brought Seth's dad back over? What if he marked me next? I tried to think of the swamp, the twilight, and the full moon. The cabin. I thought of the way the water stirred just against the bank, the snakes and birds and maybe even an alligator slipping off into the swamp. I wanted to go there, but it wasn't happening. Even if I'd been in the storm shelter, I doubted I could go without Seth.

Branch finally came back to the car and sat down in the seat heavily. He wiped a line of sweat from his brow. He cranked up the cruiser and waited for a truck to pass before pulling back on the highway.

"You never told me why you thought it was him," he said.

"I just know. Why didn't you arrest him?"

"Son, I can't just go arresting folks because some kid walks into my office and says he just 'knows.' Jesus Christ almighty. You got to have some reason for making such an asinine accusation."

I almost told him about Seth, but I stopped myself.

"If you don't tell me something else, son, I'm going to start thinking you might have something to do with the missing girls. This Sykes fellow ain't the one. I talked to Jim Reynolds. Jim vouched for him, said he knows him from way back. Said he was one of the survivors from the storm in thirty-two. Bottom line, I trust Jim, which means you must be full of shit. Besides, I talked to him myself. Rodney's his name. Nice guy. Couldn't quite get his head around why some kid would accuse him. He did say his son has some . . . difficulties. You know, personality or whatnot since his mama left a few years ago. Said maybe his boy had started some foolish rumors. That the case?"

I said nothing. I knew implicating Seth now would be bad news for him later.

"Anyway, I've been at this policing business for going on twenty-five years now, and I'd like to think experience has taught me a few things. One, I know the kind of man who commits crimes. Hell, I can smell it on them. Rodney Sykes ain't that kind."

I turned on him. "You don't know him. You don't know what he's done, what he's capable of. He beats his son. Doesn't that count for anything?"

"The boy been to the hospital?"

I sighed. "No, but—"

"Then I call it discipline."

"You didn't see him!" I felt angry, helpless.

Branch studied me for a beat or two before nodding. "You feel pretty strongly about this, don't you, boy? I was going to say—before you interrupted—that the other thing I've learned in twenty-five years is that where there's smoke, there's usually fire. I'll keep an eye on him. My gut tells me he ain't the one, but I got nothing else right now."

We were coming up on the school now, and he said, "I reckon you should be in school." He pulled into the parking lot and eased up to the front door near the office. "You know," he said, "if you'd tell me why you're so suspicious, it might help me get to the bottom of this."

"I already tried," I said, and got out of the car.

Chapter Twenty-one

Keep your head down and keep moving," I said as we started along the narrow dirt road that ran past the field. It was spring, nearly May, and the eighth graders had been invited to football spring training with the varsity. They practiced out on the big field behind the school. Seth and I had to pass the field every day on our way home. Most of the time we tried to leave at different times because being together seemed to attract more attention, but today was one of those beautiful Alabama spring days when it was possible to forget your problems. We'd both been in a good mood, laughing and talking, and had come up on the practice field before we realized where we were. Once we were that close, it only made it worse to turn around.

We were no more than halfway to the main road when the coach blew his whistle and called for a water break. The whole football team came trotting over to the water hoses near the fence, just a few feet from where Seth and I were.

"Let's go," I said, breaking into a trot.

Seth grabbed my arm. "Don't run. That's what they want."

"Look at these two," one of the players said. I kept my eyes straight ahead, my speed slow and deliberate. Seth was right. Running from these guys wouldn't help.

"What I wonder," another voice said, "is who gets to be on top? I mean, somebody's got to be the man and somebody's got to squeal like a bitch." The voice sounded familiar. Jake.

Seth stopped. I kept walking, hoping he'd follow me, but he didn't. I turned to see him making his way over to the fence.

"I think she likes you, Jake," one of the players said.

Sighing, I joined Seth near the fence. I couldn't do anything else.

Jake and Ronnie and a couple of other guys walked over to meet us.

"I never thought you'd turn queer," Ronnie said to me.

"We're not queer," I said. "Why don't you just drink your damn water and leave us the hell alone."

Jake laughed. "I got a score to settle with you two fudge-packers." Some of the guys laughed.

Seth said, "Jake, take off the pads and come over the fence. One on one. Me and you."

Jake nearly spit on himself laughing.

"I'm serious," Seth said.

"Go on," one of the other players said. "Kick his pansy ass."

Jake looked around. The coaches were downfield, standing in a loose circle, deep in conversation.

"Seth," I said. "We should go."

"No. Not until I find out if Jake is a pussy or not."

That sealed it. With everybody watching, Jake couldn't refuse, and he couldn't bring Ronnie with him either. Seth's boldness was a stroke of brilliance, or so it seemed. What he didn't understand was that Jake wouldn't forget. No matter what happened today with all these players watching, Jake would try again when the odds were stacked in his favor.

Jake shrugged off his shoulder pads and left them lying on the ground with his helmet. He climbed over the fence easily, in a way that reminded me he was an athlete and Seth clearly was not.

"I'm going to beat the faggot right out of you, Sethie. No storm shelter to hide in today, you little pussy."

He lunged at Seth, leading with his fist. Seth moved aside and Jake ran into a bank of kudzu on the other side of the dirt road. The players laughed. I didn't. I knew this would only upset Jake even more. He came for Seth again. This time, Seth tried to stop him with a punch, but it was weak—a glancing blow off Jake's forehead. Jake shrugged it off and grabbed Seth's shirt with one hand to hold him still. With the other hand, he swung in a long, arching motion. His fist hit Seth's face. A tooth flew from his mouth and landed at my feet. Seth fell back against the fence. He gripped it with both hands to keep from falling. I couldn't wait any longer. Rushing Jake, I grabbed him from behind. I was about to hit him when I heard a shrill whistle coming from the field.

I stopped; we all stopped and watched as Coach Dave Nutley parted the throng of players like Moses parting the Red Sea. He stopped at the fence and surveyed us—Jake in front, me standing right behind him, Seth leaning against the fence, bleeding. He whistled again, this time low, almost to himself.

"You got some sort of beef with these boys, Jake?"

Jake lowered his gaze.

"You hear me, son? Answer me."

He cocked a thumb in Seth's direction. "He's a queer, Coach."

Some of the boys laughed. Coach Nutley walked along the fence until he came to Seth, who had managed to stand up straight and wipe the blood off his face. His bangs covered his eyes and he kept his face hidden as Nutley looked him over. For a moment nobody made a sound. It was so quiet, I heard something slither through the kudzu behind me. A king snake, if I had to guess. Good for killing rattlers. I hoped and prayed Coach Nutley was a king snake and not just another rattler.

He took a deep breath and began to speak. I can still hear his words just as clear as if he were standing right here beside me:

"Boys, there's a lesson to be learned here."

I perked up, sure that he was going to punish his players and tell them how wrong they'd been.

"There's a time and a place for everything. The football field is a place for football. For hitting, but not with fists. On the football field, you hit by tackling. It's where you prove your manhood. Prove beyond a shadow of a doubt that you're not queer or soft or just plain pussy." Here, he made sure to look at me. He'd approached me a couple of weeks ago and asked me to play. I wasn't interested, and I told him so. I could see now, from the look on his face, he hadn't forgotten that.

"See, if you boys had any sense, you'd handle this off school grounds, not on the practice field." The other coaches had joined him now. Both were a little younger than Nutley. I recognized one from school—Coach Harris. The other coach I didn't recognize. He was heavy and had a face like a small child, all rounded and mischievous with great splashes of red on either side of his nose. He paced alongside Nutley, spitting his dip on the ground in dirty strands.

"As it stands now, I could get in trouble with my boss, Principal Haynes. So, the way I see it, you boys are going to owe me some sprints."

Everybody groaned. The heavyset coach—who must have been a volunteer because I'd never seen him at the school—kept pacing and spitting.

Nutley cocked his head back at him. "Did you want to say something, Stan?"

"Yes, sir," he said. "Yes, sir, I do." He spat again and kept pacing. "Best way to handle a queer, gentlemen, is to kick him in the testicles. Yes, sir"—he let some more dip juice run from his mouth and kicked the dirt around it with his foot—"there was a couple of queer boys—we called them homos—at my school growing up. One of my buddies, ole Jim Dawson, caught them holding hands in the bathroom. We kicked 'em in the nuts every chance we got. We must have kicked them boys until their testicles crawled back up their asses, because we healed 'em. Them boys weren't never queer no more." He spit again and looked me and Seth over. "It ain't you boys's fault, though. You didn't ask to be babied. You, with the hair: How long did your mama let you suck on her tit?"

Seth pulled his hair out of his eyes and said, "Don't talk about my mama."

"See," the heavyset coach said. "He's got a damn complex because his mama babied him too long." He walked over to the fence near where I was standing. He put his full weight on it, and a board popped loose and fell to the ground. Nobody paid it any mind. All eyes were on me and the man Coach Nutley had called Stan.

"You like boys?" he said.

I shook my head. Why had I believed the coaches might help us? How stupid I was.

"If you don't like boys, you need to quit encouraging this one by hanging out with him. Go over and kick him in the balls. Hard. That'll be a good start to breaking the spell his mama put on him with her babying and tit feeding."

When I didn't move, he said, "Go on. Just kick him square in the nutsack. It'll do him—"

Coach Stan never got the rest of his sentence out because his mouth was suddenly full of splinters from the piece of wood in Seth's hands. Seth hit him solid and for a moment nobody said anything; we all just watched as the coach reached up to his mouth and wiped away blood. His meaty hands covered his mouth for a second like a man might do who was about to throw up. When he moved them, I couldn't see his mouth or his chin anymore. It was all blood. He tried to say something and Seth hit him again.

"I told you not to talk about my mama."

Then everything happened so fast, I couldn't keep it straight. I remember Coach Nutley coming over the fence and punching Seth. I remember Seth swinging the board but missing. I remember the heavyset coach trying to shout, but there was only groaning and bubbles of blood bursting. I remember hands on me and pain as my head hit a rock on the gravel and seeing the sky—a perfect blue, like blown glass—and then there was nothing at all.

Chapter Twenty-two

Sheriff Branch came by the house a few days after the fight at football practice. Dad wasn't home, and Branch seemed relieved. Mama and I were in the den, messing with the radio, trying to pick up the Grand Ole Opry but not getting much of anything except static.

Branch stood in the doorway, scratching the back of his neck and wincing in that fake way he had. Mama cut the radio off and asked if he needed something.

"I'm afraid your boy has got hisself wrapped up in a mess."

"A mess?"

"Fair to big one too."

Mama had seen my face, the black eye, the cut on the back of my head. I told her me and some other boys were throwing rocks down by the lake and one hit me by accident. I told her I was fine. She didn't believe me, but Mama never minded pretending.

Mama tried to act concerned. I didn't buy it, but Branch might have. It was hard to read him, sometimes.

"Seems he and another boy disrupted football practice the other day. They started jawing at some of the boys on their water break. Way they tell it was the other boy had a grudge against another boy on the team and started shouting some stuff over the fence. Some of the coaches came down to break it up, and—"

"That's a lie," I said.

Branch held up a hand. "You hold your tongue, boy. You ain't in a position to say a damned word."

"They lied to you."

Branch shook his head and winced like he was so disappointed in me, but I could tell that underneath he wanted this all along. He wanted me to lose control in front of my mother, so he could say, *See, ma'am, this is what happened out at the field. The boy just can't control himself.*

It hurt, I mean, physically hurt, because at that moment I hated Sheriff Branch and all those damn coaches. I bit my lip and didn't say another word.

He looked at my mother. "We've got numerous witnesses. The good news is the coach in question doesn't want to pursue charges, at least not toward Walter."

Relief flooded over me. But . . . wait. He'd said toward me. What about Seth?

"You might want to stay clear of your little buddy. He's going to go to trial for this one, and I ain't so sure he's in the clear for them girls either."

169

"The girls? What? Seth had nothing to do with those girls going missing."

Branch shrugged. "Time will tell."

"What are you talking about?" Before I even realized what I was doing, I charged forward, getting in Branch's personal space. I wasn't planning on hitting him or even touching him, but he must have seen it differently.

"Just back the hell up, kid." His eyes went hard and his voice was no longer sarcastic country-boy. Now it was fierce, ugly, hateful. "You really don't want to do something you're going to regret."

I stepped back. "Why," I said, almost in tears, "do you think Seth is involved in that stuff?"

Branch wiped his forehead with the back of his hand. "That's police business, but my advice to you is to stay clear of that boy. He ain't right in the head." He turned to my mother. "This boy, Seth. We've spoken to the father. Nothing but trouble everywhere he's been. You'd do well to keep your boy clear of him, he's a homosexual." Up until this last part, my mother had barely seemed awake. But suddenly she seemed to straighten up, a look of concern dawning on her face.

Branch seemed encouraged by this. "Yeah, his daddy says the boy ain't never been right, that he's always been a pervert." My mother seemed to realize that she was encouraging him and dropped the look of concern almost as quickly as it had come. Branch shrugged and turned to leave but stopped and put his hand on my shoulder. "You got lucky this time, son. My experience with luck is that it always runs out." Then he winked and left my mother and me in a silence that seemed as big as the whole sky.

We watched him drive away. I waited a beat or two to see if she was going to say anything. When she didn't, I said, "So you don't care about me getting in trouble with the law, but when he mentions that Seth's a queer, you suddenly give a shit?" I hadn't realized the anger that was inside me, the anger that had been building over this kind of attitude, the same attitude I had once held not too long ago.

She shook her head. "No," she said softly. "It's not that. I don't care about that. It's . . ." She hesitated as if she couldn't find the right words.

"It's what?"

"It's you hanging out with him. Please stop."

"I thought you said you didn't care if he was qu—"

"I don't. It's his father. My brother."

"Exactly. We're blood. Cousins, Mama. We have to stick together."

"His father is dangerous."

"What do you mean?"

She sat down on the couch and turned the radio back on, twisting the knob to pick up the station out of Birmingham. Hank Williams was singing about a whippoorwill and the kind of loneliness that burns the soul from the inside out.

"I don't guess I ever told you much about Broken Branch, did I?"

"No."

"You ever heard of it?"

I thought about Seth and the shelter in the woods. "Yeah. It was where you grew up, right?"

She ignored the question, her eyes focusing on the big maple tree right outside the window. The late-afternoon light died on it, turning the leaves bronze. "I was so little when the tornado came. I can only remember being scared. It's the feeling, you know? Nothing but the feeling right in my gut. I remember it to this day."

I said nothing. I knew these spells were rare. Anything could break it.

"Rodney wasn't a bad boy at first. He was quiet, though. Some said he'd been cursed at birth, stricken dumb. I think the first time he said a word, he must have taken everybody by surprise." She smiled and her face looked ten, maybe twenty years younger. I saw Seth again in her eyes, the way she held her chin. "He was really sad too, I remember that. He wanted Mama back so bad. He wanted Broken Branch back too, but it was gone. Mama was gone. Daddy had disappeared a few days before the big storm. I don't remember him that well because even before he disappeared, he had already, well, sort of disappeared. I mean, he only came home to sleep. He and Mama didn't see eye to eye on things. I was too little to understand it, but it was a feeling even a little girl couldn't miss." She hesitated, as if trying to find her place in a very long book. When she spoke again, the smile was gone. "I was thirteen, I think, the first time I remember thinking there was something bad wrong with him. Rodney, that is. We were living out near County Road Seven in a house with four other kids. Our parents—if you could call them that—took us in only because they needed help in their garden. Anyway, one day in the fields, Rodney and me found a kitten that seemed lost. We petted it and played with it and that night we snuck it back to the house. When the man—we called him Jim because he only let his 'real' kids call him Daddy—saw it, he got angry and said he wouldn't waste his money on feeding a damn cat. He kicked it . . ."

She stopped, her voice almost ready to crack. Swallowing loudly, she met my eyes and continued. "He kicked it so hard the poor thing died. Rodney took it real hard. It was almost like something in him snapped that day. He got angry and mean. He talked about hurting people a lot, which wasn't Rodney, you know? I mean, he'd always been different and sad, but he only wanted to fit in, to find his place."

Another pause, this time for a deep breath. Her lips were trembling.

"Jim told us to take it out and throw it in the quicksand, but Rodney wouldn't do it. He took the kitten and ran off into the woods. In a few days I forgot all about it.

"Then I stumbled upon Rodney's 'spot' in the woods. He had a place under some big trees that he'd dug out and encircled with stones. A fire pit, I guess is the best way to describe it. I came up on him without him knowing and saw him playing with something. As I got closer, I saw it was the dead kitten. He was talking to it like it was alive, playing with it like it was a toy."

She closed her eyes.

"It only got worse. He got worse."

She opened her eyes and looked at me. "I know I ain't worth much as a mother, but I do love you, Walter. I love you even if I don't know what to do about it most of the time. But this time, I know. I got to tell you, cousin or no cousin, don't have nothing to do with that boy because his father will hurt you."

I sat quietly, thinking of all the questions I could ask her. In the end, I only asked one.

"You said he only got worse. What else did he do?"

But the moment was gone. I knew it when I looked at Mama and her eyelids were beginning to droop. She had that look she got most evenings. It was almost the look of a drunk, even though I never saw her touch a drop of alcohol. Whatever else the look meant, I was sure it signaled the end to our conversation, and with that, another window to understanding my mother was shut right in my face.

Seth's trial was set for the second week in May. There was some debate about whether he should be allowed to come back to school in the meantime, but in the end they let him. Kids were horrible to him. They called him queer to his face now, without worrying about consequences from teachers. Hell, the teachers went after him too. Mr. Bell, our math teacher, made him sit in the back of the room, facing the wall, because he couldn't stand to look at him. I know that's hard to believe now, but in 1961 rural Alabama, that's the way it was. Mrs. Benedict gave us a long talk about the Bible and what it said about homosexuals and how it was a sin, and how no man should hold another man despicable for trying to instruct another in the ways of God. I wanted to ask her where it said in the Bible that you should kick somebody in the balls if they were gay.

That was the other thing that had started since the incident. People would come up to Seth between classes and kick him in the balls. Really kick him. Sometimes they'd punch him there too, leaving him doubled over in pain. He never told any of the teachers—not that it would have mattered if he did. He never fought back. He just took it.

Once when I was walking beside him in the hall, some guys came by and spit on us. Another time, I was suspended for fighting back after a tenth grader slapped me and Seth in the balls. Seth told me to let it go, but I went after the guy and slammed his head into a locker. My luck hadn't run out yet, because nobody pressed criminal charges. I was only suspended.

I guess in a way I was always lucky. Even in Vietnam when I watched a friend try to dig a bullet out of his neck with his bare hands. Even at the Hanoi Hilton when they tried to make me wish to be dead, I kept hope. Even now with the emphysema and weak heart and all the alcohol, I feel pretty lucky.

Anyway, maybe it all balances out because I've got guilt, the kind that gnaws at you, until you wake up one day and feel your soul has been half eaten and you know the gnawing won't be done until it eats it all or you do something about it.

A few days before Seth's court date, I had an encounter with my father that has continued to haunt me to this very day.

I climbed out of bed to go pee. Our bathroom door was locked, so I figured my mother had it occupied. She'd taken to spending a lot of time in there. I'd hear her go in, lock the door, and run a bath. It might be an hour or more before she came out. I was afraid one night she wouldn't come out at all.

I considered knocking, but the thought of her not replying was too much. Instead, I did what I had gotten used to doing: I went outside.

It was a clear, cool night, and every star in the universe was shining. No moon, but the starlight alone let me see where I was going.

I went around back of our house to the shed and started my business. I was just finishing up when I heard someone singing. I froze and saw my father coming through the trees, headed back to his house, drunk as usual.

Wasted like he was, I knew he wouldn't see me as long as I could stay still in the shadows. I studied him, feeling suddenly like this might be my one true chance to see who my father really was. I can't explain it. What I saw in him that night shook me to my core. He was me. I saw it clearly for the first time. In this moment of unguarded drunkenness, I saw myself, not my father at all. I looked away and then back again, trying to shatter the illusion. It was still me. I was there in his walk, the tilt of his head, even the silly way he ended the lines he had forgotten with words that didn't rhyme except when he pronounced them wrong. I saw in him the kid who didn't know how he ended up like he did. I wanted to call out to him, to stop him, to let him know I was there and that I understood. More than anything else, I wanted him to know I forgave him. He wasn't mean or hateful or selfish or anything I'd once thought. He'd only lost his way. I understood that now. I opened my mouth to speak, but I couldn't. That would break the spell, and as long as the spell was unbroken, he was innocent, and as long as I could see him like that, I loved him.

So I watched him, wishing the moment would last forever. He stumbled to the porch, still singing, his face turned bright by happiness. After he'd gone inside, I stayed in the shadows for a long time, thinking about how I could make my life different than his.

Chapter Twenty-three

DANNY

Pike paused to take some oxygen. He'd been talking for a long time while Cliff and I listened in absolute silence. It was getting dark outside, and the trees swayed in the evening breeze. Way out on the highway, I heard a horn blow and the squeal of brakes, but the sounds didn't seem real. All I could think about was the painting, this strange and brave boy named Seth, and if that little cabin held my mother and sister.

Pike lit a gas lantern, and the flickering flames threw shadows across the walls. I slid closer to the chair where he had leaned the painting. Looking closely, I could just make out the shadows inside the window, distorted wisps against the pale moonlight.

He stood. "Piss break," Pike said, and stepped through the front door.

I looked at Cliff, who appeared to be half-asleep. "I'm going in. I'm going to slip and bring them back."

Cliff opened his eyes wide enough to stare at me. I couldn't tell if he was worried or just felt sorry for me.

A few minutes later, Pike came back in and lit a cigarette.

"There's still a good bit more."

I nodded. "I'm listening."

Pike smoked the cigarette. Full night had fallen outside, and I was amazed at how dark it got back here with no power, no moon or stars to break through the interlocking branches of oak, pine, and elm. Like being in the storm shelter, I thought.

I closed my eyes and tried to imagine being there, up against the back wall in total darkness. I tried to imagine moving through the wall, just phasing through it like I was Kitty Pryde from the X-Men, and coming out on the other side to a swamp at dusk and a little cabin and Mom and Anna.

Pike cleared his throat and began to speak.

Chapter Twenty-four

WALTER

A couple of days later, I walked over to Seth's, hoping to find him at home and his father gone. What I found was the exact opposite.

I knew something was wrong when I saw the blue lights through the trees as I drew closer to his house. Sheriff Branch's car was in the yard and Mr. Sykes stood on the porch talking to Branch. I didn't see Seth.

Confused, I stepped out of the trees. Mr. Sykes saw me and pointed. Branch turned around. "You, boy."

I froze.

"Get over here."

I debated bolting for the trees, but my curiosity got the better of me.

I walked slowly to the porch. "What's going on?"

"I'll ask the questions," Branch said.

I nodded and stood with my arms wrapped around myself.

"You seen Seth?" Mr. Sykes said. His voice was firm and he looked at me like I might be the one responsible for all of his problems.

"No."

"This is his little boyfriend," Mr. Sykes said to Branch. "If anybody knows where he is, this one does."

"I'm not his boyfriend," I said.

"Now I don't care which way you sit in the saddle, son, I just want to know about Seth. When did you see him last?"

"I'm not answering any questions until you tell me what's going on."

Branch shook his head and tipped his hat back. "How about this? How about you answer my questions or I take you in for obstructing justice?"

I held out my hands, wrists together. "Okay."

Branch cursed and spat on the ground. "You're dumber than you look. Get in the car." He pointed to the backseat.

He turned back to Mr. Sykes, and I bolted, full speed, back into the trees.

"Son of a bitch," I heard Branch say. I didn't turn around to see if he was following me.

I headed straight for the shelter hoping to find Seth there. Even if I didn't, I knew I could hide underground until I figured out what to do.

I climbed down the ladder and pulled the hatch shut above me. I crawled on my hands and knees to the back wall, to the place to where Seth and I had slipped before. He wasn't there. I was alone.

Leaning back against the wall of the shelter, I closed my eyes and tried to think of the place, the swamp, the moon, the little cabin with the orange lamplight burning inside. I had the place in my mind pretty well, when I realized I might be doing it wrong. Was it the painting Seth imagined or the actual place? Shit, I didn't know. I tried both. Neither worked. I was still in the dark twenty minutes later when my hand fell on the paper.

As soon as I touched it, I knew Seth was gone for good. It was his note, not a suicide note, but a good-bye note. It was too dark in the shelter to make any of it out, so I tucked it in my back pocket and thought about where I could go. I knew Branch would talk to my parents and I'd have to deal with him if I went back home. I didn't have anywhere to go, so I stayed put, hoping that maybe Seth would come back. He didn't. I fell asleep, leaning against the back wall.

When I woke, I didn't know where I was. I'd have similar experiences in Vietnam when we were thrown into mudholes for days at the time, that feeling of dislocation, of being quite sure that your life had ended and this was what was waiting for you—just darkness and confusion. Fear is the best name for it, really. You'd get your head screwed on a little tighter and latch on to something solid. Might have been the ground itself, just a handful of hard-packed earth or some clumps of grass or once even a piece of feces gone brittle. Then you were back in the world, at least enough to carry on.

That day when I woke up in the shelter, I didn't have a clue about Vietnam. It was still years away. What I did know was a darkness that might not ever let go. I pulled out the note from my pocket and ran my fingers over it, trying to touch the pen strokes to make out Seth's words. I wanted to believe it said he was going away for a while, to the swamp, but just until things cooled down. He'd be back and we'd carry on as friends because we were best friends and that is what best friends did. They stuck together. I savored this vision for a while, letting my hands caress the page before climbing the ladder into the light.

I found a warm morning, birds singing in the trees, the smell of wood smoke coming from either my house or Seth's; I couldn't tell. I plopped down on the ground and opened the letter up. It was printed in Seth's handwriting on a piece of yellow legal paper:

Walter,

Gone for good. You'll be able to get on better without me, I think. By now you know my father is evil. You know what he did. I hope you're wise enough to keep clear of him. Please, Walter. Do that for me. Stay away from my father.

By the time you read this, I will have done what I can to make it right. You'll probably want to go to the authorities about this. Don't. He's too dangerous. What's done is done. Like I said, I have tried to make it right.

I've decided the swamp is the best place for me. I'm finally going to do it. My only regret is that you're not here with me.

Seth

The paper, wet with my tears, wilted between my hands. I read it again, over and over, wishing it said something different. Finally,

I crumpled it into a tiny ball. As soon as I did this, I regretted it and tried to straighten it out, but it was ruined. Still crying, I opened the hatch and climbed back into the shelter. I went to the back wall and beat my fists against it, hard and then harder, hoping somehow on the other side, Seth would hear me.

Chapter Twenty-five

It never really crossed my mind to follow Seth's advice and stay away from his father. Part of me hoped I could prove his guilt and somehow Seth would know and come back. Another part of me was just angry. For Seth, for those two girls.

I'm afraid that one of the reasons Seth slipped when he did was for me. Sure, he was bound to do it eventually, and maybe it was his court date that pushed him to go when he did, maybe he left to avoid what would almost certainly be an unsympathetic judge, but I think it was more than that. Seth was the kind of person who always thought of others. This is part of my guilt too. It should have been me trying to protect him, but instead it was the other way around.

The next day, Sheriff Branch picked me up at school. He made me sit in the back of the cruiser and he took me down to the station. I'd had some time to think about things and had something resembling a plan, even though I suspected it would be a miracle if it worked.

He sat down at his desk and pointed at the chair for me.

"I know you know where he is."

I stayed quiet. I wanted to play this just right.

"Son, this ain't playtime. This boy has skipped out on a court date. His father has reason to suspect he might have been involved with those girls." He leaned forward, his leather chair creaking. "You tell me the goddamn truth or I'm going to lock your ass up."

I didn't say a word.

"You ever been in our jail before, boy? It's only one cell, so if you're there and we bring in somebody else, say a drunk, or God forbid one of them perverts from up on the mountain, you'll be sharing the toilet with him. So tell me."

"I'm scared," I said in a weak voice.

"Scared? Just tell the truth. The only thing you've got to fear is that jail cell."

"No, that's not true. I have someone else to fear."

"You talking about Seth's daddy?"

I nodded.

"You think he's out to hurt you?"

"Yeah."

"Why would he do that?"

"Seth said he killed those girls."

"We've been down this road and I think that's a bunch of bullshit."

I shook my head. "That's not all."

Branch drummed his fingers on the desk, waiting.

"He killed Seth too."

"Now, this is just ridiculous. I—"

"You wait," I said. "Seth isn't coming back. He's dead."

I must have convinced him because Branch didn't speak for a moment. He only looked at me, studying my face. Finally, he stood up. "Get the hell out of here. He'll come back and when he does, I'm going to nail your ass to the wall."

I started toward the door, but paused right before going out. "You'll see. He's gone."

The thing that ate at me the most was the part of Seth's note that said he was going to do what he could "to make it right." What did that even mean? Would he come back and kill his father himself? That was the only conclusion I could draw, and if that was what Seth had meant, I wanted to make sure he wouldn't face his father alone.

I began to watch him. What I found, while crouching in the trees near his house, disappointed me. He was a boring man who went to work every day and came home every evening. At dusk, I watched him through the kitchen window as he cooked his supper. He didn't drink, at least not that I could see. Of course, when he moved away from the kitchen windows into the deeper parts of the house, he might have been doing anything.

A week of this got me exactly nowhere. Seth was still gone, and the kids at school still hated me. My father still hated me. My mother was still a lost soul who locked herself in the bathroom for hours at a time. Maybe Seth did have the right idea. I started spending time in the shelter, just sitting in the dark, trying to go there, to tell him he was right to get out of this godforsaken world once and for all.

But I didn't have whatever Seth had. Maybe it was imagination, maybe it was just that my life wasn't as desperate as his, but I couldn't do it.

Soon I was sleeping there and not going to school at all. I'd sneak into my house for some food late at night and then slip back out to the shelter. It was on one of these nights that I finally found the proof I was looking for.

It happened by accident. I couldn't sleep and had decided to wander over to Seth's house to see if his dad was still awake. In the darkness, I must have taken a wrong turn because the woods grew thicker and soon I was lost. Despite the lantern I carried, I got confused and I couldn't find my bearings, something that's easy to do in these woods.

Then I saw something. It was up ahead, a hulking shadow covered in kudzu, just a shape in the dark. It was a little hunting cabin that was almost invisible to the naked eye except from the back, which just happened to be the direction I'd come from. It must have been the same one Seth had mentioned before, which meant I wasn't very far from the storm shelter.

I probably don't even need to say that the cabin, the one I found that night, is this same cabin. Rebuilt by Seth's father, my uncle, it looks basically the same, minus a few vines of kudzu, as it did in 1961.

I stopped a dozen or so feet short, studying the place for any signs of life. A few moments passed and I saw nothing. I crept a little closer.

I paused to listen at the back window—the one in the room right down that hallway. There were no sounds other than the crickets and bullfrogs down by the pond. I took a deep breath and pressed my face against the glass. It seemed empty. Abandoned.

Circling the cabin, I looked for a way in. The door on the front was locked. I went back to the window and tried to open it, but it was stuck in place. I tried again, this time putting everything I had into lifting it, but I wasn't strong enough. I'm not really sure why I felt it was so urgent to get inside, but I did.

I cast around for a rock or heavy stick to break the glass with. Waving my light around, I spotted a fallen tree limb, picked it up, and swung it like a baseball bat. It would do. Back over at the window, it took me three swings to break through the glass and another few swipes to knock loose the shards so I could pull myself up and through.

I tumbled inside, just managing to get my hands up before I hit the floor face-first. I was lucky I didn't land on any of the glass. Other than a few pieces of half-finished furniture, the room seemed empty. I made my way into the short, narrow corridor that led to the back, holding my light out in front of me, feeling like I'd found the very answer to all my problems right here in this cabin, but I had to just unwrap it, you know? I was close, so damned close, but not there yet.

If my light hadn't gone out, I might never have found the cellar. It was an old oil lantern I'd swiped from Daddy's shed, and I hadn't bothered to get more fuel for it. I watched in dismay as it dimmed, casting flickering shadows against the wall, and then went completely dark. I set it down and reached out blindly, determined to keep searching.

In the hallway, I stubbed my toe on something. I sprawled forward and hit the wall. I lay on the floor for a moment, shivering. It was like I'd crawled into some monster, and a false move would wake it up, and once that happened he'd swallow me forever. I touched my head to see if it was bleeding. Only a little. I sat up. The moon was rising and its light filtered through the cracked glass. I saw what I'd tripped on.

There was a rug, a big throw rug embroidered with every animal imaginable—deer, elk, wild turkeys. In the center was a tiny rise, like a bump in the floor. I pulled the rug away and saw that I'd stubbed my toe on a metal latch that led to a trapdoor in the hardwood floor. I didn't even think about it. I opened it up and saw a ladder leading to a cellar. I was halfway down it when I noticed the ladder seemed encrusted in a dried, flaking substance. The smell of copper and rust and something deeper, older, invaded my senses and I knew it was blood.

I kept going.

A beam of moonlight filtered through the hole and as I neared the bottom. I let myself drop. I landed on my feet but was almost knocked over by the overpowering stench of blood and waste as I covered my mouth, trying to keep from vomiting. It came anyway. Thankfully, only dry heaves because I had nothing in my belly to expel. Once my stomach stopped seizing, I turned around slowly, letting my eyes adjust to the deep black of the cellar.

Nothing came clear—some shapes slouching into themselves, the swirl of odors too strong to comprehend—until I saw them standing there against the back wall, two girls glowing in the dark, so bright I thought I'd go blind.

They were dead, ghosts or something even less than ghosts—afterimages, photonegatives burned like heat into the cellar wall.

For an instant, they were everything. I lost sight of why I was there, what I was doing, who I was, even. I felt a sadness cinch so tight in my gut that I doubled over, dry-heaving again, my cheek cold against the dirt floor.

Then they were gone.

The afterimages stayed in my vision like those floaters you get from staring into the sun too long, but the girls were gone and if I'd wanted to (and part of me did, believe me) I could have forgotten them, pretended they never showed themselves, written it off as my mind playing cruel tricks on my soul. But I refused to do that.

I pulled myself up and slid carefully to the back wall. The wall was sticky to the touch. I felt around some more until my hand landed on something else, a leather strap attached to the wall. After some investigation, my heart sank when I realized what it was—a shackle. Two sets. The same crusty blood clung here and had been smeared against the back wall. For an instant I saw them again—or heard them—this time moaning, begging for mercy, but Sykes wouldn't give them any. There were shouts and cries, and deep moans, things that I never heard before or since, not even in Vietnam, and I understood then what Seth had meant about his father being evil. I clamped my ears with both hands, but the sounds wouldn't go away. Instead, I heard new ones, dripping in the hollows, the empty spaces of the screams, flesh being torn away, bones cracking, and all the while the cries for mercy. But Sykes wouldn't give them any. Not even a drop.

When it finally ended, a long silence remained. It was like wind had come through and blown everything away. I couldn't even smell the blood.

I didn't need to. I'd experienced everything I needed. I clenched and unclenched my fists, trying to keep my lungs working evenly, trying to feel the anger as it seeped out into my fingers and toes.

I was halfway back to the ladder, a plan formulating in my head about a visit to Sheriff Branch's office, when the cabin door slammed shut somewhere above me. I slipped back toward the back wall, pressing myself flat against the place where he'd shackled the girls. I reached into my pocket for my switchblade and waited. I prayed he didn't have a light.

That was one prayer that didn't get answered. I saw the light bending into the cellar as he drew nearer. He was whistling. Damn if that didn't almost do me in right there. That whistling. I still hear it in my nightmares sometimes. I wanted to rush him, run at the ladder, climbing up it as I swung at him, but I held on. I had to make this count.

For Seth. For those girls. But mostly for me. Up until that point, I had been just sort of drifting. Now I had a purpose, something I knew was right, something I knew that I could do. A man could do a lot worse than that feeling.

My hand itched to pop that blade.

He stopped whistling, and I knew he'd noticed the cellar door was open. There was another long silence. I heard my own heart thudding against my rib cage, the sound of my breath coming out in a stifled wheeze.

One more step, the floorboards groaning. Another, this one not as loud. He stopped again. His boots creaked as he settled his weight right above me. I looked up, wondering how strong the barrier between us was, and if I could stick a knife through it.

"Somebody down there?" he called out. His voice sounded pleasant. Almost jovial.

I didn't breathe.

"Well, I don't suppose," he said, "that this door opened itself."

The floorboards above me groaned as he took another step.

"Did you like what you found down there?" he said. His voice changed to a falsetto. "I didn't mean to kill them. Just happens sometimes when you're trying to get them to do right."

I clenched the knife in my sweaty palm, determined not to let him bait me.

"Not a talker, huh? Or maybe you think I'm a damned enough fool to come down there." He laughed and began to whistle again. The light moved, the floorboards talked, there was a loud slam, and I was completely in the dark.

I was in the cellar for a long time. Because of the darkness, I can't say exactly how long. Four days is my best guess, but it might have been more as each moment bled into the next. I was hungry, but not frightened. That might sound strange, even hard to believe, but no part of me was afraid, not anymore. When you're as hungry as I was, fear will always take a backseat.

There were bugs, creepy crawlies that I managed to put my hands on in the dark. I ate them as reflex, not even considering what they were, popping them inside my mouth like candy, sometimes swallowing them whole, feeling them squirm down my throat. I trapped a rat in the corner of the cellar using an empty jar. At my lowest moments, I wanted to eat it alive too, but I'd heard about the diseases they carried. Still, I kept it under the jar, ready if I got desperate enough.

Luckily, it never came to that.

Rats and bugs weren't the only things I shared that space with. The past lived in that cellar. As I began to slide in and out of consciousness in my weakened state, I saw the girls again, their dresses shining in the dark, their hair like silken coal. They were unaware of me, and time and time again I listened to them moan for help.

When they finally stopped, there was only a moment's worth of silence and absolute dark before I heard the small boy crying. Then I saw him, not two feet from where I lay, hunched over the body of his mother. What kind of ghosts were these? The boy was Sykes, and Sykes wasn't even dead yet.

Yet.

At some point, the door above me creaked open, and when it did, I was lying huddled in the corner, still gripping my switchblade tightly. My eyes were closed, but I opened them just enough to watch as Seth's father came down, first a heavy boot and then another, until his whole body was inside.

I watched him, so smug as he stepped off the ladder and swung his lantern around, just missing me, against the far wall. He had a knife in his hand, and I knew I'd only get one chance.

It was hard—no, impossible—for me to square the man who stood next to me with the crying boy that I'd spent the last several hours with. They were two different people, and that, I think, is all you need to know about growing old.

He swung the lantern light out again, this time in a wider arc. I felt the light moving over my body, and I wondered what I must have looked like lying there, half-starved, unmoving. I hoped I looked dead.

That's when I heard him gasp.

I stayed still, barely opening one eye to see. He'd moved past me and was examining the blood spots on the back wall. Was it possible he wasn't aware that the girls were gone? And if this was true, who had taken them, and why?

He swung back around violently. "Where are they?"

I continued to play dead or at least passed out, holding the knife under my shirt, the cold casing next to my empty belly. He drew back with his foot and kicked me hard in the ribs.

"I asked you a question, boy."

I bit my lip, holding it all in. I wanted to scream. Damn, did I ever. His boots were steel-toed, and my ribs felt like they'd been knocked right into my lungs.

I heard his boots creak and he knelt next to me. I opened my eyes just enough to see his outline, blurry in the lantern light. He was holding the knife out, ready to prod my face with it.

Slowly—while his attention was focused on my face—I slid the switchblade out of my shirt. His blade touched my face. He used the tip to pry at my right eyelid, trying to force it open.

Without a sound, I put the switchblade inches away from his midsection. His blade was so near my eye now, and that was when I realized what he meant to do.

With a shriek, I popped the blade and thrust it into his midsection. His hand jerked and slashed my eye good. Instantly, I felt blood running down my cheek like tears. I released the switchblade, leaving it in his stomach, and grabbed his arm with both of my hands. I shoved him off me, and his knife fell onto the cellar floor.

I touched my eye, sure that I'd find only an empty socket. But it was still there. For now.

Half-blinded, I fought him, tumbling on the ground. He cursed me, beating at me with his big fists. I absorbed the pain because none of it hurt as bad as the knife in my eye. Somehow, I managed to work my way onto his back. He stood up, trying to spin around and fling me off. My hands clawed at his face, his eyes.

He kicked over his lantern and there was a sudden explosion of flame as the oil caught. I didn't let go. Madness had come over me and I only wanted to claw out his eyes, to pay him back twofold for the one he'd taken of mine.

I rode him like a bucking bronco around the cellar. He pummeled me against the walls and tried to toss me off into the fire, but I held on to him with everything I had. I worked a hand inside his mouth and ripped his right cheek hard and then harder, screaming for all I was worth. He flailed back at me with his fists, striking the spot he'd kicked.

He twisted his body around, so that my head collided with the ladder, knocking it loose from its moorings and making me momentarily woozy. Still, I held on.

He staggered into the darkness, tossing me like a bull flings a cowboy, but I wouldn't let go. My eye had gone numb and blind from where he'd cut me, but I continued to twist at his cheek, stretching it until it bled over my fingers. He must have spun himself dizzy because eventually, he fell. He was still spinning on the way down, which explains how I ended up landing on the knife. It sliced into my leg. The puncture was deep and hurt like nothing I'd ever felt before, but when I reached for the knife, it slid out of me as easy as pulling a toothpick through melted butter.

Then he was on top of me.

I slammed the knife into his side and twisted. He moaned and cursed. He told me he'd see me in hell.

I kept twisting and he kept talking. I was surprised he knew who I was. Had he gotten a look at me at all? I didn't think so. He just knew.

Then the thing that haunts my dreams still: He spoke of the swamp. "I see it," he said. "I see the swamp. I see them."

Believe me, I've lain awake so many nights debating what he saw,

who he saw. Despite all those sleepless nights, I don't have answers.
Just a bushel full of doubts and bad lungs from all the cigarettes I
smoked sitting upright in my bed beside the open window.

Finally, he stopped talking and went still. I let go of the knife and
tried to push him off. Unfortunately, my energy was running out of
my leg. I settled for sliding out from under his weight. When I stood,
I felt light-headed. I couldn't think. The pain wasn't so bad. It was
more that I felt different, not all there, woozy. I was covered with
blood, slick and warm. My stomach lurched, but nothing came up
other than bile. I coughed it out, there on the floor. My hand fell
back to my thigh, and I plugged the bleeding by pressing my fingers
into the cut. I stood, took a faltering step, still keeping my hand on
the cut, and began to stumble toward the ladder.

There was pain, but I ignored it. Somehow, I worked my bleeding
body up the ladder and into the cabin. It was daylight, and I had to
fight the overwhelming urge to just lie down and fall asleep in the
sunlight shining through the cracked windows. If I'd done that, I'm
certain I would have died right there. So I forced myself to ignore
what my body wanted and I dragged myself through the woods, trail-
ing blood along the way to my house. Mama was in the bathroom.
We didn't have a phone in those days, so I would need her to drive
me to the hospital or go get help or something. I collapsed against
the door, and I didn't remember anything else until the next day.

Chapter Twenty-six

I woke in a room and saw both my parents sitting next to me. My good eye fell on my father first. He held my gaze long enough for me to know that he was sober or as close as he would ever get to it. This small sacrifice touched me. Maybe he cared about me. It's still a debate I have in my head to this day.

Mama's eyes were more vacant, but when she saw me awake, she leaned in and hugged me. "Thank God," she whispered. "Thank Jesus."

Dad stood. "The sheriff is wanting to talk to you." He was fidgeting with his collar, pacing now. He was ready to go have a drink, and I knew his encounter with sobriety was about to end. I nodded at him.

He started to leave and stopped. "You all right?"

I didn't have a clue. I knew that something was wrong with my eye. It still felt numb all around the socket, and no matter how hard I tried to open that eyelid, it refused to budge. I told him I was fine.

He considered leaving again but stopped short. His mouth opened to say something else. He was about to speak, and God only knows what he might have said. I think about that all the time, far too often for an old man whose daddy's been gone for nearly twenty years. He opened his mouth to speak, but then thought better of it. He shook his head and left.

I like to imagine he was about to say something encouraging. Something that might have gone a long way toward erasing some of the hate I had for him. Maybe he thought it, and maybe that's enough. I go back and forth about that too.

S heriff Branch came into the room and asked my mother if she would give him some time alone with me.

When she left, he sat down heavily in her chair. He didn't ask how I was feeling or anything like that. Instead, he just looked at me for a long moment. I looked back, meeting his eyes.

"We followed your blood to the hunting cabin."

"There was someone down there. The girls, I think. Are they—?"

He shook his head. "Easy. Don't get all excited. The doctors say they'll kick me out if I rile you up." He took a deep breath. "You know something about the missing girls?"

"I think he kept them down there. There were shackles on the wall. I—"

"We found the shackles, but we figured those were for you."

"No, sir. I went there looking for the girls. The cabin was empty when I got there—"

"Hold it. You telling me he didn't kidnap you? That you went there under your own will?"

"Yes, I was looking for the girls. Seth told me that his father killed them."

"Back up. To what you said before about going there on your own. One more time. I want to be clear," he said. I couldn't be sure, but I believed I saw pleasure on his face.

"I went to find the girls. More than your dumb ass has been able to do." I realized the instant I'd said it that it was a mistake; everything I'd said had been a mistake. Branch didn't like me, and before he'd talked to me, he'd believed that I'd been right. That Sykes had kidnapped me and therefore had probably done the same to the girls and Seth too. It had seemed pretty clear. Now, I'd managed to give him an out.

He took a deep breath and barely hid a smile. "Did you find them, boy? 'Cause if you did, I'd like to know about it."

"No," I said. "I didn't find them."

"You didn't find them, huh? But you did manage to trespass on a man's private property and kill him? That about right, dumbass?"

"What about the shackles?" I said, sure that there would be nothing he could come up with to explain that away.

"What about them? Ain't no crime to hang shackles on his wall. For all I know, he used them to discipline his boy." Branch nodded thoughtfully. "Can't say it helped much."

"You're an idiot," I said.

He patted my knee, smiling. "How old are you?"

I was silent.

"I'm going to guess fourteen, maybe fifteen. Either way, old enough for a jury to convict you as an adult for trespassing on another man's property and killing him in cold blood. Now, I may be an idiot, but you're a damn fool if you think you're getting out of this one, son."

"Look at me," I said, on the verge of tears. "He tried to kill me."

"A man's got to defend himself. Especially when somebody comes trespassing on his property." He stood up. "Get better soon. I'll be checking on you."

A few days later I left the hospital. I waited until the place was dead quiet, and I just got up out of my bed and walked out. I hiked home and, without waking my parents, packed a bag of clothes. Then I left again, walking out to the highway, where I cocked my thumb in the air and waited for no more than thirty minutes before a grizzled old coot in a Ford picked me up. He asked me where I was going (he didn't ask about the patch on my eye, and I took this as a good sign). I told him anywhere. He nodded as if he understood and began to drive. He let me off somewhere in Tennessee.

I spent the next four months living hand to mouth in the foothills of the Smoky Mountains. I rummaged for food. I begged for it. I stole. Sometimes I found work, but I never found a place to call home until I met a man who hired me to clean out his barn. After it was apparent I had no place to go, he allowed me to live there in exchange for keeping up the place and helping out with his cows and horses.

I was pretty happy there, but there was something growing inside me. Call it a darkness or doubt, or maybe it was just confusion, but I felt like I needed to move on to something . . . I don't know . . . more dangerous. I suppose if I was honest, I'd tell you I never quite got over my death wish, but I think that was only part of it. I also had a desire to go back to the slip, to find a way back to that magic, to prove to myself that it had really happened, that there was something more to this life.

Chapter Twenty-seven

After I got back from the war, a time came when I had convinced myself I was nothing more than a crazy drunk. That the things I remembered from my boyhood were hallucinations brought on by the alcohol, or maybe I was shell-shocked. If I had any real sense, I'd let them go and get on with life, but my life was a wreck. Three failed marriages, two addictions, and the inability to tell anybody—including the three wives—what was bothering me. No matter how hard I tried, I couldn't let go of the past. So eventually, I came back home.

At first I camped for several months near the storm shelter. For a while, I was afraid to go inside. I'm not sure why. Probably had to do with finding something there that might actually prove my crazy fantasies true, because as much as I obsessed over Seth and the slipping and the swamp, I wasn't actually convinced I wanted any of it to be real. But eventually, I had to go in. I had to see.

Nothing happened. I sat there for days waiting for some vision, some flash of the swamp, but there was nothing.

I was almost ready to move on, to forget that part of my life altogether, when I made a last stop by the ruins of Seth's old house. Like I said, the place had burned down sometime while I was away, but picking through the rubble I found a couple of things that made me realize I couldn't take the easy way out. I couldn't forget.

I found them in a large metal box near the back. Someone had put them there, almost as if he was expecting the house to burn down. Inside the box, I found the canvas of Seth's painting, the one I showed you earlier. But more important than that, I found the photos we took. I looked at them just like you did. Wasn't there some explanation? Sure seemed like there had to be, but the more I thought about it, the less I could convince myself that anything besides slipping could explain those photographs. Before I went to Tennessee, I'd never been out of the county, yet there I was standing knee-deep in a swamp.

The next day, I put five of the photos in the box that you saw and buried it in the meadow, being sure to count off the paces, so that one day when I doubted again, I could come out and dig it back up. I kept the painting for myself.

Nearly ten years passed. During that time, I lived off the grid, so to speak. Sometimes I came back here, but mostly I roamed the Southeast, working odd jobs for cash. I stopped paying taxes, receiving mail. I didn't even have an address. Most days I wondered if I had a purpose, but I held on anyway. Now that I've met you, Danny, I see that after all these years I was meant to do something.

Chapter Twenty-eight

DANNY

When something really traumatic happens to you, the world starts to looks a little different. I'm not talking about how it looks when your dog just died or you discovered that you won't be getting into medical school after all. I'm talking about finding out you have cancer or losing your kid to some stranger with a candy bar in a Honda Civic. I'm talking about watching your mother and little sister walk out into some storm-ravaged landscape and never return.

You begin to notice the shadows. Before they were just a nuisance, a distraction from the sunlight. But when there's a turning point, like what happened with Mom and Anna, the shadows cast a spell. You feel it when you try to remember and when you try to forget, omnipresent, sticky, and so cloying you try to make your mind go blank just to live a moment without them.

After a while, the melancholy becomes so commonplace that you grow numb. You find that you are forgetting now without even trying. The shadows become more inconspicuous, just trees, bare and cold, lurking on the periphery of your vision. All of which seems good, except by then you're so used to the heartache that when it fades away, you're left with nothing but emptiness. You're face-to-face at last with the bottom, and it stares at you, unrelenting, calm, ageless.

Even at fourteen—especially at fourteen—the bottom is a scary place.

I went through all of this in the months that Mom and Anna were gone, and even though I came face-to-face with utter hopelessness, I never bottomed out completely. I always held a spark of hope—sometimes nothing more than a sputtering flame—that my mother and sister lived. I believe if I'd been older, wiser to the way the world has of knocking you in the mouth repeatedly, I would have dismissed Walter Pike's story with a cynical shake of my head. I would have walked away from his place numb, and content in my numbness because the ache of hope hurt too damn much to mess with again.

Nowadays, I think a lot about what it means to slip. About the ways a person can slip, because it's really something we do all the time. You go along, thinking everything is fine, and ignore all the tiny slips, the glimpses of what your life could be. It's easy to ignore because you come back so quickly, until you really slip, you fall off the path and spin and tumble and hit the water much too fast. You find yourself in another world, a disorienting one, and no matter how many times you look for the exit, it just keeps moving, until the only way out is too painful to even consider.

I didn't know then if I believed Pike's story. I know I wanted to. Now, I'm no better off. Doubt still dogs my every step, but there is one thing I do know, one thing that I've learned.

We all slip. In one way or another.

And when we do, very few of us ever find our way back to the surface.

Sometimes you get lucky, though. At fourteen, I still had hope. Just the smallest sliver, but I clung to it like a man clinging to his very last match in a world without light.

H e told us just a little more.

"When I came back this last time, a few weeks ago, I decided I was going to stay. I came here, to this cabin."

I opened my mouth to speak, but Cliff beat me to it. "This is where you killed Sykes."

Pike nodded. "And don't forget, it's where those girls died too."

"And it's where Sykes was with his mother when she died."

Pike pointed at me. He seemed pleased I had been listening so closely.

"Yeah, that's something to remember. Seth believed that the storm shelter was the way, but somehow the cellar right below us is important too."

Suddenly, the darkness seemed oppressive. I wanted a bright light to shine in every corner of this place.

"I came here because I began to wonder if this cabin could connect me to the swamp." He was silent for a moment, and it was weird to see him sitting still, no cigarette, no oxygen, just him, and it made him seem naked, vulnerable beyond all telling. "I've been having other dreams about the swamp. Hell, I don't even know if they're dreams. It's almost like I go there, but I'm helpless, just an eye in the sky, watching."

"What do you see?" I asked. "Are the girls still there?"

He nodded. "Yeah. And somebody else."

I said, "Sykes."

"Bingo."

"But how?" Cliff said.

Pike shrugged, and the spell of his stillness was broken. He patted his shirt pocket for a cigarette. "Seth always worried that he'd find a way in." Pike lit the cigarette, and in the glow of ash, I saw pain etched into the creases of his face. "I worry that maybe I killed him in the wrong place. I worry that somehow, it's my fault."

"It can't be," I said, amazed by the outrage in my voice. "Don't even think like that. The note Seth left. He said he was going to make it right. That meant he was going to take the girls' remains to the swamp, right? Like the rabbit."

Pike grinned around his cigarette. "Hell, now how did you figure out in a couple of hours what it took me years to get ahold of?"

I blushed in the darkness, thankful that Cliff couldn't see. "It just makes sense. But it proves that killing somebody in the cellar doesn't take them there. Sykes must have found another way in. Maybe it's genetic. I mean, your grandmother saw it first, then Sykes, and finally, Seth and you."

"This is ridiculous," Cliff said suddenly. "Listen to yourself, Danny."

I looked at Pike. He nodded. "Maybe he's right, Danny-boy. Maybe it is ridiculous. Hell, I know he's right. It is ridiculous, and if we could tape-record our voices and listen to them again, we'd probably commit ourselves to Bryce Hospital over there in Tuscaloosa, but, and this is a big God-blamed *but*, that don't mean it isn't the truth."

He was talking to both of us, but his eyes were on me. He blew out a stream of smoke. "Sometimes you got to take a chance. Sometimes, that's all you have left. A crazy, ridiculous chance."

He laughed, and the laugh turned into a cough. When he finally cleared the smoke from his lungs, he leaned forward. "What do you say, Danny-boy? Take a chance? Get your mother and sister back?"

These days, I might try to fool myself and pretend I agonized over the decision, but that would be a lie. I was desperate for something, and when I saw it, I grabbed it with everything I had.

I opened my mouth to speak, but Cliff interrupted me.

"What's that?"

Far away, I heard the sound of an engine.

Pike held his hand up for silence.

"Sounds like a—" Cliff began.

"Shhh!" Pike shot him a look.

The sound got closer. It was a car. Coming this way.

"You boys had better go in the back."

Cliff and I sat there.

"You heard me. Get in the back. Don't come out until I tell you to."

We both got up and went down the darkened corridor to the back room, the same room where we'd found him in his own vomit the other day. I'd been nervous then, full of something like dread at what I'd find. I felt the same way now as I stumbled forward, hands outstretched into the utter darkness.

Shapes—dark and undefined—floated in front of me. I reached

for one and felt a softness. The bed. Pulling myself around, I settled down on the floor on the other side. I heard Cliff join me, his breathing rapid and shallow.

Other than that, the cabin was quiet.

A car door slammed outside, and I heard Pike rising from his chair, the hardwood floor creaking under his feet with each step. I imagined him walking over to the window and peering out.

"Who do you think it is?" Cliff whispered.

I had no idea, but for some reason I was frightened. There had been something in Pike's voice when he told us to go to the back, something that suggested he had been expecting the visit. That put me on edge.

"Don't know," I said, my voice barely even a whisper.

There was a knock on the door. Three of them. I heard Pike clear his throat and say, "Come on in."

The door swung open with a long creak. I leaned forward, frantic to hear something, anything that would tell me who it was.

A moment of agonizing silence passed. Then Pike spoke.

"Help you?"

"Are you Walter Pike?"

"That's right."

"I'm Deputy Sims from the county sheriff's department. We received a call about thirty minutes ago from a Eugene Banks. Know him?"

Cliff pinched me hard. His dad had called the police. I shook my head, willing him to be silent.

"Don't recognize the name."

No one spoke, but I heard movement, saw a shadow down the corridor, and I pictured Sims—in my opinion the biggest buffoon in the department—taking his hat off, walking over to look out the window, rolling his neck, posturing like he always did when Dad had to deal with him.

"I'm going to shoot straight, Walter."

"Mr. Pike."

"Say again."

"You called me Walter. Seems a little too familiar for my taste. My friends call me that. You can call me Mr. Pike."

"I don't think you quite have a handle on the situation here, Walter. You picked a hell of a time to come back. Sheriff is dying to pin this shit on somebody, with the election coming next spring and all. You, though? Heh. A known queer that was a major suspect in the last mystery these woods have seen that shows up when you did *and* immediately starts messing with young boys? Hell, man, this town will burn you at the fucking stake."

"You plan on arresting me?"

"I'll ask the fucking questions."

Pike said nothing.

"Now, the way I figure it, you got the bodies somewhere on these premises . . ." I heard the floorboards creak as Sims moved across the room again.

"What's back here, old man?" Sims's voice was closer. I could feel Cliff tense up beside me.

"Don't go back there."

"I'll go wherever I like. Sheriff warned me you didn't have a bit of respect for the law."

"I respect the law, just not the lawmen around here," Pike said. "I'm telling you to stop."

"How about this, old man? How about you stick one thumb in your mouth and the other in your ass and shut up?"

I heard Cliff draw a sharp breath as the footsteps echoed toward us. I was looking for a back window to escape out of when it happened.

At first I thought the whole cabin was coming down, that something had fallen from the sky and landed on the roof. The very air shook with it. Cliff shrieked and I clamped my hand over his mouth. He nodded quickly, to show he understood, and finally, I did too. Somebody had fired a shot. Since I hadn't seen a gun in the cabin, I could only assume . . .

I came out of the corridor on the run. I almost collided with Sims, who was standing at the end of the hall, his hands up, his back to me.

Pike stood across the room from him, the lantern burning bright at his feet, holding a sawed-off shotgun to his shoulder. The double barrel was pointing right at Sims's face.

"I told you not to go back there."

Very slowly, I slid back down the hall into the darkness of Pike's room. Cliff grabbed me.

I put my hand over his mouth again.

"You going to shoot a lawman?" Sims said.

"They told you some shit about me," Pike said, and his voice was ragged, full of sharp edges and menace. "But they must have left out the most important parts. I'm a crazy motherfucker. I spent nearly three years in the Hanoi Hilton letting Charlie pour sand down my throat. I've killed before, and it ain't nothing for me to kill again."

Sims was silent.

"Now I'm going to step out of this doorway and you're going to walk out of this cabin and get back into your cruiser. You're going to drive all the way back to the sheriff's office and tell them what a crazy, murderous bastard Walter Pike is."

I heard footsteps, shuffling. The door groaned opened.

"Tell your sheriff if he wants me, he better send more than Deputy Sims next time."

"Oh, we'll be back."

"Bring the whole damn force next time."

The door slammed. Cliff tried to get up. I held him down. I wanted to wait until I heard the cruiser pull away.

A few minutes later, it did.

Chapter Twenty-nine

When we came from the back, Pike was seated, using his oxygen tank. He looked pale in the lantern light. The shadows around him had lengthened and he seemed to have become lost inside them.

"We got work to do," he said. "This is going to happen sooner than I planned."

"Okay," I said. "The sooner the better. Just tell me what to do."

Pike chuckled softly. "So you're not scared? I mean after what just happened, you still trust me?"

I thought about this for a second. I knew that I shouldn't trust him, and my parents had raised me to stay away from men like Walter Pike. He was obviously not playing with a full deck. He was a beaten, broken man, prone to outbursts of violence and masochism, and maybe some of that would have mattered if I hadn't been so sure that he was telling the truth. At fourteen, I believed the truth was in someone's voice, the tone of it, and for the most part this belief did not fail me. I only wish this ability had followed me into adulthood. But like so many things that change when you get older, determining who was telling the truth and who wasn't became akin to navigating an endless series of switchbacks and dead-end roads in a blinding snowstorm. All you could do was close your eyes and guess.

Not at fourteen. At fourteen, I knew.

"I trust you." I had no more gotten the words out of my mouth when Cliff elbowed me.

"What?"

"Can we talk? Alone?"

I looked at Pike. He nodded. "Better make it quick. We're about to have police all over the these woods looking for me and you."

Cliff and I walked outside. The air was humid, the way it gets before rain. It was quiet out here, except for the sound of bullfrogs down by the pond, the drone of their voices broken only occasionally by the night sounds: a branch breaking, the hoot of an owl, the low rustle of wind sweeping through the leaves.

Cliff grabbed my arm. "What are you thinking?" His voice was fierce, urgent.

"What do you mean, what am I thinking? You heard his story too. Don't you believe him?"

Cliff let go of me and stepped back. He put his hand over his face. For a second I thought he was about to start crying. "It doesn't matter if I believe him or not. It can't be true. It just can't."

"Why not?"

He laughed then, but it wasn't the kind of laugh that someone does when something is funny. It was the exasperated, I-don't-know-what-else-to-do kind of laugh. There was an edge to it, and I knew then Cliff had already had about as much of this as he could take.

"Why not? You are absolutely kidding me, right, Danny? Well, let's just see. Well, why don't we start at the beginning? He says they threw Seth into the quicksand. I've told you a hundred times, quicksand doesn't work like that. People don't sink into it like they sink into water. That's just the movies. This simple point puts his whole narrative in doubt."

"Narrative—what?—you're kidding, right? You're willing to believe that somebody can slip into another world, but you question drowning in quicksand?"

"I never said I accepted the slipping. The quicksand was first, so I started with that. He's lying. Let me take that back. He's delusional. Shell-shocked. Probably not quite the same as lying, but the effect is the same."

"And what's the effect?"

"The effect is trouble for you if you go along with him." He put his hand on my shoulder. "Let's go, Danny. Right now. Let's get out of here. He shot at a police officer, for God's sake."

"Sims had it coming. He's an asshole."

Cliff sighed. "Let me repeat. He shot at a police officer. Asshole or not, that's a huge deal."

I was about to speak, to try to explain that *asshole* didn't quite do Sims justice, when we heard it. A siren.

Pike's door swung open. "Time to shit or get off the can," Pike said. "You coming with me or not?"

I knew he was speaking to me and me only.

"Depends," I said. "Are we going to get my mother and sister back?"

Pike stepped out of the cabin. He was smoking a cigarette. "Is there anywhere else?"

"Then, yes, I'm coming."

Cliff shook his head in disgust but offered his hand. I took it and squeezed. When I let go of his hand, I knew our relationship would never be the same again.

Everything went to hell after that. Apparently, a squad car had been sent out ahead. It pulled up way before the one with the siren arrived. Cliff had just disappeared into the woods heading back home while Pike and I were caught in the headlights.

We ducked into the trees just as an officer on the car's loudspeaker told us to freeze.

"We need to split up," he said.

I tried to reply, but he was already walking away. "Meet me at the storm shelter. One hour," he said, and then he was gone.

I took one more look at the police car—two men were getting out now—and then took off as fast as I could run in the other direction.

For a long time I just ran. Branches beat at my arms, neck, and face. The woods seemed endless, and I was lost. Panic started deep in my gut and crept outward. I didn't know where I was going. Every time I thought about slowing my pace, I thought about the sheriff's car and the policeman. Had they seen Pike and me? Or were they searching the cabin right now, disgusted that it was empty?

I kept running.

I didn't stop until I came out of the trees and saw my house looming in the distance. I stopped hard, skidding my Keds across the gravel drive. Rocks flew up, bouncing off my pants leg. Sheriff Martin was standing near my front stoop, under the big oak tree, not too far from where Pike had stood just a few weeks ago. Martin was talking to one of his deputies in the glow of his headlights. The deputy pointed in my direction, and Martin swung around. I wished I could evaporate back into the woods, but I knew there were several dozen feet before I could make the trees again.

"Hey, boy!" Martin called. "Danny! Come on over. We've been looking for you."

I didn't answer. Instead, I took a couple of tentative steps back before turning and running full tilt for the trees. Martin shouted at me once, and then I heard car doors slam shut.

In my rush I failed to find a proper opening in the foliage to escape through and found myself nearly at a standstill, fighting through a thick drapery of kudzu and creepers. Behind me, the cruiser crunched and spit gravel as it closed in on me. I plowed on through, the vines breaking open wet on my arms, lashing my face. Some bent for interminable lengths of time, and then bent more, and only broke when I'd tunneled deep enough to bind myself with other vines, no end in sight.

There was a chirp from the road and then Sheriff Martin speaking through his loudspeaker: "If you can hear me, Danny, please stop running. I want you to listen." There was a pause, and to my surprise I stopped fighting through the vines. I was in so deep, I felt confident they wouldn't find me, at least not at night unless I gave myself away by making too much noise. I also realized I wanted to hear what the sheriff was going to say. I wanted to hear something about Dad.

"This man you've been with. Walter Pike is his name. He may have told you something different, but he's a deeply disturbed individual. Danny, let me repeat. He is deeply disturbed. I know you're angry about your father. I know you're in a place right now . . . a, hell, a vulnerable place, but you have to think things through, son." There was a squawk and I heard the cruiser pulling closer. "You have to know that this man may be responsible for killing your mother and sister. Even more, he might have killed those girls thirty years ago."

I started fighting through the vines again. The sheriff continued to talk—he must have sensed I hadn't gone far—but I didn't listen anymore. If he believed my mother and sister were dead, he didn't have anything to say that I wanted to hear.

Sometime later, after the loudspeaker had at long last fallen silent and the pounding in my heart had subsided and my journey through the vines had become more about steady, deliberate clearing than headlong crashing, I reached the end and broke through to open air and space. I had no idea what time it was. I only had the vaguest of notions of how to find Pike, but what was worse was the tiny, tiny seed of doubt I felt growing inside the pit of my stomach.

I decided to ignore it and broke into a steady jog, aiming as best I could for the center of the woods and the place I hoped would take me out of this world and into the next.

I heard the dogs before I reached the shelter. Their bleating filled the night from one horizon to the other. With every step I took toward what I hoped would be the storm shelter, I heard the sounds come closer.

When I finally reached the shelter, I was so tired I could barely breathe. I stood there, outside the hatch, marveling at how I'd been here just a few days earlier, during the storm, and not had a clue in the world that I'd be coming back again with a purpose.

I opened the hatch and went inside.

Taking the ladder slowly, I made it to the bottom and held my hands out in front of me to ward off the darkness. "Mr. Pike?" I said.

There was no answer.

I stepped closer to what would be the back wall, ducking my head a little for fear of scraping it against the concrete top, and called his name again.

Nothing.

I was alone. The hatch was still open, and I could hear the dogs baying through it. They were coming this way. Hands out again, I made my way back to the ladder. I was halfway up when I heard him call for me.

His voice sounded like a deep moan from hell.

I didn't hesitate. Springing out of the hatch, I took off at a dead run. It had started raining, and thunder cracked the sky open, letting out hail and huge, hard pellets of rain.

He was still hollering my name. I ran blindly toward his voice, ignoring the other voice—the one inside my head—that told me it was foolish to run toward the dogs.

When I found him, he was on the ground, lying in the mud. His breathing was labored, and he couldn't seem to stop cursing.

"My oxygen," he managed. "Left it. Goddamn it all to hell."

I knelt beside him. The dogs were impossibly close, maybe only a minute or two away.

"I tried to throw them off, but I nearly killed myself doing it." He grimaced and reached for my hand. "We aren't far, are we?"

I looked at him blankly. He squeezed my hand so hard it hurt. "Damn it, Danny. Wake up. How far are we from the shelter?"

"I don't know. Maybe two hundred yards."

"Drag me."

"What?"

He kicked my shin.

"Ow!"

"Drag me. Let's go."

Before I could answer, a streak of lightning jumped out of the sky and struck a nearby tree, momentarily lighting the night up like one of those disco strobes. The world seemed to splinter between light and dark, frozen in a split-second burst of blinding, soundless white.

The dogs howled. I got Pike under both his shoulders and dragged him through the mud.

We'd made it no more than a couple dozen yards when he let loose a series of hacking coughs that made me wonder if he didn't have rocks in his lungs.

"Let's rest," I said.

He shook his head. "Those dogs aren't resting. Besides, this storm is going to be a big one. We rest too long, we'll die out here. The real storm ain't even here yet."

Something told me that Pike's real problems weren't here yet either. Something told me he was only going to get worse.

I got him going again, trying to keep his body off the rocks and sticks, Pike cursing under his breath, me just trying to find the leg strength to keep moving forward. It went like this for another hundred feet before I collapsed.

"Shit," he moaned. "Shit."

I started to get under his arms again, to lift him for one last heroic pull, but he felt heavier this time, and my muscles quivered as I strained to get him up. The dogs were even closer now, having clearly locked onto our scent.

We made it three more steps before his weight became too much for me, and we fell.

This time I just lay there. What was the point? I'd only get him up again and then fall again. I was so tired.

The dogs drew closer, their throaty calls increasing in intensity and fervor. I wondered what Sheriff Martin would think when he found me here, lying in the mud next to Pike.

"And where exactly were you and that old fool headed?" he might ask.

"To the slip, sir."

"The slip?"

"Yes, sir. It's where my mother and sister are."

I saw him laughing then, his mouth first forming a half-open, slack-jawed look of incredulity and then opening wide into a belly laugh.

And at that point, I'm ashamed to admit, I think I might have been done. The rain was coming down so hard it felt like someone was spraying us with a hose. The dogs were so close, I couldn't imagine outrunning them, and the faith that I had held so dear for so long was beginning to feel like a fantasy after all.

Then I heard Pike grunt. He kicked me. I sat up not because I was ready to move but because he kicked the shit out of my knee and it hurt.

"Goddamn it. I thought you wanted your mother and sister. I thought you were going to do anything to get them. Well, this is it, son. Get your ass up and take my hands and drag me over to the storm shelter."

I stood up, getting my legs back under me. They hurt so badly. Then I took his hands and pulled. He groaned, and so did I, but I didn't stop. If I slowed even the slightest bit, he shouted at me to pull harder, cajoling me with gasping taunts about being weak, about being just like all those other bastards who didn't believe. Whether it was because he made me angry or because he made me believe again, I can't say, but I began to pull harder, closing my eyes and driving my legs.

At some point, Pike said, "Stop," and I opened my eyes. I was standing in just about the same place I had been standing the day I saw Anna. The shelter was close now. I let go of Pike's hands and went to find it.

Chapter Thirty

In the dark of the shelter, there were three sounds that nagged at me—the booms of thunder outside; Pike's labored breathing, which was so bad that I tensed before each intake, cringing at the sawing sound that came back up; and the baying of the dogs. They'd obviously tracked us to the shelter. It was only a matter of time before the police discovered the hatch.

Despite this, I felt it was imperative for Pike to rest. I'd never heard someone die before, but if I had to guess, Pike was coming pretty damn close to what it might sound like.

But he refused to rest. "It's now or never, Danny-boy," he gasped.

"What do we do?" I asked him in the dark.

"Just be still. Wait. Hold my hand."

I found his hand in the darkness. It felt cold.

"Now, just close your eyes, Danny-boy. Just close your eyes and wait."

We waited. For a long time nothing happened. Pike talked in between labored breaths. He talked about cigarettes. He told me how if he had his oxygen, he'd put about four in his mouth right now and smoke them all. He told me that addiction is one of the ways we curse ourselves, and he had a double dose of it, what with the cigarettes and the whiskey, but he reckoned if he could have only one, it would be cigarettes. He felt the need for them in his bones, he said. "A deep need, the kind that kills you." He laughed then, obviously amused by the irony of his situation.

"Listen," he said suddenly. "Hear that?"

"What?" All I heard were the concussive blasts of thunder, so frequent they blended into each other, creating one long drumroll of booms.

"The dogs. They've gone quiet."

He was right. I realized it had been several minutes since I'd heard them.

"Good and bad," he said.

"What do you mean?"

"I mean they're gone. That's the good news."

"And the bad?"

"Think about why they left, Danny."

I shrugged. "I don't know. They gave up."

"Dogs don't give up, not when they had us dead to rights. The storm. They must have gotten word it's going to be a hell of a thing. Either that or the dogs just got spooked. I'm betting the latter. Dogs know before people."

I said nothing. At least we were in the safest place for a storm.

Another long silence passed. His hand, once cold, was sweaty in mine. I kept trying to imagine the swamp, trying to make it happen, but nothing did.

Pike groaned loudly.

"What?"

He tried to speak, but all that came out was another hacking cough. His grip loosened on mine.

"Mr. Pike?" I said.

"Shit," he groaned.

"You're dying," I said.

"Not yet."

"But soon. Real soon if you don't get your oxygen."

"Too many cigarettes," he said weakly. He started to laugh, but it got stuck in his throat.

"That's it. I'm going back for your tank."

His hand gripped mine again. "Don't go nowhere. I'll be fine. We . . . we gotta stay right here."

I shook my head. "No. You're dying. I'm going to get help. Or at least your tank."

He gripped my hand again, this time softer, with less urgency, and I knew it was because he couldn't get air.

"No. Look, damn you. You made it here. You beat them damn dogs, the police, the doubts. You beat them all. Now, you just got to stay put. And when it happens, you go in and bring them back."

I pulled away from him. "No. You've got to get help." I stood up, backing away, stumbling over my feet and landing in a heap next to the ladder.

"Your family or me?" he rasped. "Think, you damned idiot. You go out there into that storm, there ain't no guarantee you'll come back."

I did think. Right there in the pitch dark, the only thing that was in my mind was having them both. My family and Pike. I could get the tank and still go to the swamp for my mother and sister.

"I'll be back," I said. "With the oxygen. Just hang on, okay? Hang on."

He muttered something else, but I couldn't hear it. Once I was to the top of the ladder, I flung open the hatch and was hit hard by a blast of wind and rain. My head was forced back, and I couldn't see for all the rain and debris flying at me. It was morning. It didn't seem possible that so much time had passed, but the sun was up—at least dimly—and when the wind wasn't making me squint, I could see the devastation from a night's worth of storming. The storm showed no signs of abating with the morning. Trees creaked and threatened to splinter, straining themselves all the way down to their roots, as straight-line winds attacked the woods with such force I could only imagine what they'd do to me. Still, I ducked my head and pulled myself up and out of the shelter.

The wind made it difficult to do anything, even to keep my body aimed in the right direction, but I stayed low to the ground and set off in a straight line for Pike's cabin. A fox shot past me toward the pond and clearer land, and it occurred to me that all sensible creatures would be doing the same. As if to underline this thought, a blast of wind cut through the trees to my left and lifted me off the ground, tossing me up like a paper airplane. I must have flown six or seven yards before a big elm stopped me. The impact into the tree wasn't so bad, but when I tumbled to the ground, I twisted my ankle.

I wiggled it, testing the range of movement, and decided it hurt, but it wasn't going to stop me.

I waited, pinned against the elm, while tree limbs all around me snapped like dry matchsticks. Pieces of them flew in my direction, and I made myself into a tiny ball at the base of the elm and closed my eyes.

For a while, I just sat there, shivering, thankful to be braced against the one tree that would not snap. A lull ensued and I opened my eyes to view a wasteland of lumber and vegetation and something else, dark and exploded all over the ground. I tested my ankle and got my bearings again and started toward Pike's place. That's when I saw what the dark stuff on the ground was. The wind had ripped the roof of the cabin off savagely, twisting it and grinding it into the tiny pieces that lay all over the forest floor.

Down the dirt road, no more than twenty or thirty yards, a sheriff's cruiser was stopped, a huge pine laid across the hood. The driver was out, trying to roll it off without much success. Another officer—Sheriff Martin, from the looks of his pear-shaped profile—climbed out of the passenger side and looked directly at me. For a second, we both froze—me all locked up with indecision about whether to go on for the oxygen tank or try to enlist their help for Pike; Martin, I'm sure, just shocked to see me.

I think he hollered at me. His mouth moved, I'm sure of that, but with all the commotion, I couldn't hear anything. I wonder how long they'd been stuck like that, how they'd managed to survive aboveground.

I shook my head in frustration. It didn't matter. Time was wasting. I slipped inside the now roofless cabin.

Somehow, being inside felt even more dangerous, especially with the roof gone. The place was destroyed. Water stood on the floor at least three inches deep. The furniture was missing—some of it tangled in the tree branches above me. I paused long enough to sort out my bearings—a difficult task in the midst of such disarray. We'd sat in this room, but there was no couch now, no bookshelf. Pike's ashtray lay against the far wall, on top of a pile of dishes and splintered boards. Digging through the debris, I spotted what I'd come for. I picked it up, making sure the tubes were still connected.

I was just heading out the back, hoping to avoid Martin and his deputy, when I heard his voice.

"Daniel, slow down there, pardner."

I stopped and turned. Martin stood in the doorway with the deputy—a slim, clean-shaven man that I knew from the D.A.R.E. rallies at our school. Neither held a weapon. Both wore long black rain slickers but still appeared to be soaked to the bone. A gust of wind blasted them, and Martin had to hold on to the deputy in order to keep from falling over.

There was a moment—albeit brief—when I believed it was over. Pike had been right. I was a fool to leave. They would take me back to the squad car, finish moving the fallen limb, and take me to the police station, where I would wait for Mr. Banks to come pick me up and Mom and Anna would still be trapped inside a damned swamp that might or might not exist. And Pike, Pike would die alone inside the very storm shelter that had wrecked his life. That was the kicker, thinking of him lying there, not being able to breathe.

I rushed them.

Sheriff Martin had just managed to squeeze his beer gut through the door frame and shake his head slowly.

"You know, we almost died last night trying to help you. What I don't understand is your fascination with the old coot. He's plainly—"

But I never heard the rest. I hit him running full speed. He was big, over six feet, and probably approaching three hundred pounds, but I led with the oxygen tank to his midsection, and he stumbled backward with a surprised *whoof.* I kept my momentum moving forward. The deputy reached out for me, but I twisted sideways, out of his grasp and through the door.

I'd made it maybe five yards, back toward the shelter, when I realized something was wrong. I stopped, putting on the brakes so abruptly I almost lost my balance.

Tornado survivors typically talk about an eerie calm just before the storm hits. They describe the sky as turning a putrid shade of green. The wind dies down and the animals fall so silent they might as well be dead. That's why I stopped. It was suddenly silent, calmer than any day had a right to be, but there was something on my skin, in the air, a smell I could almost recognize. I knew it well enough to realize it spelled doom.

"Holy shit," I heard Martin say. "Will you look at that?"

I saw it too, a stack of darkness, churning and undulating in the sky to our west. It was probably somewhere over the cotton fields, but there was little doubt it would soon be here.

Then the silence was gobbled up, eradicated so thoroughly, I was never able to remember it properly because my mind always wanted to jump from hitting Martin with the oxygen tank to the sound of it coming. Oh, the sound. There are certain things in life that do not make good stories because they are so unbelievable. I think the volume of this tornado is one of those. In the years after it happened, I'd catch myself trying to describe it at a party or on a date and

229

realize how futile it was. In the end, I stopped trying because most people just looked at me blankly as if I were making it up, or at the very least, being overly dramatic.

I'd also always heard that tornadoes sounded like freight trains, and the thought of this was enough to give me bad dreams as a kid about running away from funnel clouds bearing down on me with the ferocity of runaway locomotives, but in reality, this one was more like an earthquake. It sounded like a deep, guttural moan from the atmosphere bolstered by the breaking of trees and a thousand tiny explosions, that I later realized had to be the snapping of power lines out by the highway. It was like God himself had decided to expel a bad meal all over this particular corner of northern Alabama.

I tried to make my feet move again, but that's when I saw it, and the raw power of the thing held me in place.

This was the tornado, breaking free of the stack of clouds over the cotton fields, defining itself, charging straight for us, the god of all other tornadoes that kept growing bigger by the second until I lost the sky somewhere behind it, and the whole world was twisting and shaking and about to shred apart.

Trees lifted off the ground, roots and all, and vanished into the swirling folds of the twister. Somehow, one particularly large tree escaped the pull of the twister and shot past me, traveling on a trajectory so straight it might have been a missile. It collided with the front wall of Pike's cabin, leveling it and sending Martin and his deputy running.

With this my paralysis broke and I started trying to find the storm shelter—no easy task considering the way the storm had already changed the whole area.

Years later, the change would be the thing I would remember

most. It was as if the tornado were slowly ripping apart the woods, razing them, only to put something else in their place. At the time, I didn't completely understand, but now, I think I might. Or maybe I don't. My thoughts on this—as well as everything else these days— vacillate.

Meanwhile, the twister continued to eat its way east. There was a great boom, like a stack of dynamite going off, and little pieces of painted wood and siding began to fall out of the sky. I knew that meant the storm had gotten a house, maybe mine, maybe one of the half dozen others scattered around these woods between the cotton fields and County Road Seven.

I kept looking for the shelter hatch.

I heard Martin and the deputy yelling at me. They'd made it back to their car and were now shouting at me to join them. I could only guess they were hoping the winds would lift the branch off and then they'd be able to make their escape, though I had no idea where they'd go.

I couldn't imagine them making it out alive, so I yelled back, trying to tell them about the storm shelter, but they waved me off and got inside the car.

The tornado was on me now. I watched helplessly as it lifted not only the branch from the squad car, but the car as well. My foot hit concrete and I knew I'd found the shelter. But before leaning down to open the door, I watched, mesmerized, as the police car shot upward, like it had been caught in some sort of supersonic tractor beam, and disappeared into the ever-growing swath of whirling darkness.

I dropped the oxygen tank inside and managed to get one foot on the ladder, when I felt it. The brute force of it picked me up, launching me out of the shelter like a rocket. I managed to hold on to the top rung of the ladder with one hand. My legs flew into the air and I was turned upside down. I stayed like that for what seemed like an eternity, my arm stretching and my hand aching with the pain of the abrasive steel step as it dug into my palm.

The wind shifted suddenly, and my body twisted. My hand slipped, and instead of flying away, I was driven down into the hatch.

Chapter Thirty-one

To this day I don't know what happened. I think I hit my head on either the ladder or the oxygen tank, maybe even the ground, or maybe I just passed out. Either way, the next part is indistinct in my memory, like the fragments of long-remembered dreams, images shaken out of a tree, hundreds of leaves falling at once. Only a few stand out.

Mom. Her face, filled with the sweetest light, sitting in the backyard, peeling a pear, her knuckles wet with the sticky juice. Me bounding across to her, so full of enthusiasm it hurts to remember it because the hard fact hits me: I won't ever be that enthusiastic again.

I buried my head in her lap, and she tousled my hair. Her hands in my hair. Jesus, I go back to that even now, even when I can no longer determine if the image was a real memory or just a dream. In the end it does not matter.

There's not an honest man anywhere who would deny the

sweetness of a memory like that. Even now, the emotion of that moment is a real thing. And it occurs to me that if all of life had to be reduced into one moment, one gesture, this is the one I'd put forward.

The second image is of Seth. He came to me in the darkness, the boy from the photograph, his face lit with a glow that illuminated his whole body. He knelt beside me, whispered in my ear. Told me things about the slip. I listened so close, but when I came to, I could barely remember any of it, just his presence, his soothing voice in my ear, a phrase that he kept repeating—*Sometimes you find your way when you stop looking so hard.*

The third was even more dreamlike, but somehow, it is the one that I go back to the most now, as if it really happened, as if I can place real meaning in the contours of its mysteries. It was Pike, standing over me, his white hair dangling around his neck and hanging down in my face. I could smell the scent of Wild Turkey and cigarettes on him (two smells I've continued to love even through adulthood). He shook me awake, pulling me up with both hands. "You've done too much believing to quit now," he said. "Besides, if you don't believe for yourself, nobody is going to do it for you. Seth and me got lucky and found something important. It wasn't a new world or a swamp or a little cabin in a picture at dusk. It was more. It was a piece of God. The piece that resides in us, that lets us be more than just dirt. It was a door and we opened it. Now you've just got to do the same."

I tried to tell him I couldn't open it without him, that I was still in the storm shelter, and that he was dead, and I didn't buy this shit about a piece of God. But every time I tried to stand up, he pushed me back down, telling me to wait, to rest. "You'll need your energy."

Overhead, rain continued to pelt the hatch, and I could hear it leaking through the cracks, splattering on the soil.

"Aren't you dead?" I asked him.

He nodded.

"What do the dead know?" I asked him.

"Nothing. We know nothing. But we see everything. You've got to *see*, Danny."

Then he was gone, and I was too.

The last thing that happened before I returned to full consciousness (though my therapist, Dwight, would suggest that I didn't ever really return to full consciousness until days later) was the falling.

Even while it happened, I remembered how Pike had described it and found myself amazed by how it was exactly like I'd imagined it. The wheel first. The world shifting, turning over like a great stone behemoth, and then the eerie dusk, the bottomless blue sky, the full moon, and—something I don't remember—the lightest touch of rain on my skin. The cabin flashed by, the water below, the giant oak trees, again and again until I slapped the water and sank to the bottom of a new world. Either that or an old dream.

When I woke some time later, it was to the sound of silence, and I knew the storm was over.

Dim light filtered through the opened hatch. I sat up, groggy. Hungry too. When had I last eaten? I tried to remember, but images got in the way—me pulling Pike through the mud, Sheriff Martin and his deputy running to get in their police car only to see it picked up like a plaything and tossed God knows where, the sound of Pike's labored breathing, that awful broken-glass sound.

"Pike." I scrambled across the storm shelter, feeling for him in the darkness, sure that when I touched his body I'd find it cold and lifeless.

But how could I imagine that I wouldn't touch it at all?

I walked the shelter over twice, and then twice more, before I allowed myself to believe it. He was gone.

But where? Better question: But why? He wouldn't leave me. Unless he'd been crazy all along. I dismissed that. There was no point in even considering such a thing.

He couldn't be gone. I searched again, this time on my hands and knees, but the shelter was empty.

The adult me finds this hard to believe now. It's one of those easy places where a skeptic will say, "You were groggy. It was dark. He was there, you just didn't find him. Hell, maybe you were still dreaming."

And maybe I was. Maybe, a part of me still is.

It doesn't matter, though. What matters is that I searched five times, and Walter Pike was gone.

Chapter Thirty-two

I've always thought the shadows were deepest at dusk when they lengthened and twisted themselves into ominous distortions. If you are caught walking at the moment when the sun dies and the woods go silent from birdsong, it can be disconcerting. The trees take on new, sometimes vulgar shapes, their vines casting out a more expansive web, the birds disappearing with sudden hushed eeriness, the very ground before you shifting and offering new contours, and sometimes a strange figure is glimpsed, flitting among the trees like a washed-out image from an old motion picture before disappearing in the periphery of your vision, blanketed by the oncoming night.

All of this might make a person disoriented, sure of themselves in the light of the day, but now—in the sudden dusk—leaving them groping for something familiar.

Sometimes I wonder if this is what happened to me when I came out of the shelter that day and saw the landscape changed, the very trees grown denser and more full of vines, the water on the ground, murky and knee-deep. Sometimes I wonder if stumbling out onto the flooded ground, I fell into a long, perilous delusion—a dream state brought on by the stress of the storm and Pike's disappearance.

Here's the thing: I've spent the last sixteen years trying to fashion the events I've been telling you about into pieces of a larger whole. But no matter how many times I try, no matter how thoroughly I analyze things, I can't make some of them fit. I get ideas, fleeting images; sometimes I wake in the morning with the maddening sense that I had it all figured out in my dream, but the dream is always gone, leaving me with the tantalizing feeling akin to having a name on the tip of my tongue, except this is not a name—this is my life.

When I become frustrated with this conundrum—pieces of a puzzle that never quite interlock—I tell it back to myself, much like Pike telling the story of his time with Seth not only for my benefit, but also for his own.

And when I tell it, this is how it goes.

I know what my therapist thinks. Dwight doesn't say it, but he thinks it. I can read his face. It's an easy face to read, lacking true guile. His face tells me that he believes I'm delusional. The way he hesitates, the way he parses his words just so, the way he scribbles on his pad to fill the uncomfortable silences, the silences he wants to cover up with words. But he doesn't. Not yet. He leads, mostly, and it's almost funny to watch him try to lead me to places I've already been, places I've already considered, turning them over like found things, artifacts from the imagination. I've touched them all.

When I told him the part about the story, about how it helps to tell it back to myself, he smiled. He tried to hide it, but I saw his lips break their flat line and crease ever so slightly. I saw something like the shine of satisfaction in his eyes.

"What?"

He shrugged. "Nothing. Continue."

"No, you were smiling."

He pushed his glasses up and looked at me directly then. His face turned smug, superior, and this was the only time I hated him. When he was so sure of himself, so unwilling to even consider for just a moment that there could be truth to my story. It must be how people who have seen ghosts or claim to have been abducted by aliens feel. It's a hateful, frustrating, alone way to be, and it makes me sympathize with every last one of the poor bastards who carry either the reality or the delusion of something the rest of the world won't accept.

"Why were you smiling?"

He shrugged. "It's just from my perspective, your words make it so clear."

"So clear?"

"What you're doing. How you're coping."

"Tell me."

"Maybe it would be better if you just continued. I think the discoveries you make on your own are the ones that will stick. Anything I say right now will be of lesser value."

I leaned forward, gritting my teeth to keep from raising my voice. "Tell me."

Dwight held out his hands, a gesture of supplication. "Sure, okay. You have a right to know where I'm coming from. It's just that the things you've told me are so unbelievable that you can't even justify them. Seriously, you can't. Instead you're using the storytelling, the narrative itself, as a kind of coping mechanism."

"Not following." I felt mean and ornery. Ready to snap.

"You don't believe what happened to you, but facing that means you'd have to accept some other things you're not ready to accept, so you cling to the story. The story as some magical boon—a tool, if you will—a tool capable of tying all these impossible things together. You lift the narrative above the fray, so to speak."

"So to speak?"

He grinned, this time his fake grin, the patronizing one.

"Maybe we should slow down. Not push things. Sound fair?"

I nodded despite myself.

"Please," he said, holding his hands out. "Continue."

So I did.

When I came out of the shelter, the woods were flooded. The water came up almost to my knees. That was the first thing I noticed. The second thing that struck me was that Pike's cabin was still standing. The roof was there, the structure still intact. No—I saw that this was different. This cabin had a porch, crooked and slanted, but a porch, nonetheless. The roof was pitched differently, and a warm orange light bloomed from one of the windows.

I stood for a moment, completely stunned, trying to make my mind understand how I could have been so confused. I turned, pacing back my steps to the shelter only to find more murky water.

These days, I wonder how I could have been so damn slow to

realize what had happened, but I think I forget how truly confusing a situation like that can be. To realize that another world, totally different from the one you've known your entire life, had emerged from the shadows, and that it had been there all along, *you just failed to see it*, is so disconcerting, it's a wonder I dealt with it as quickly as I did.

It was the trees, really. They were unharmed, not a one of them crippled by the straight-line winds and the tornado that was almost certainly an F5. They were the same trees too, but different. These were swarming with Spanish moss, cloaked in kudzu, their limbs grown out at odd angles, holding things in their shadows—perhaps the other woods, the ones I'd grown up playing in. Likely others too.

Then I remembered the photos of the cabin, the ones of Pike and Seth standing in the water. I must have stood there for a long time, staring at the cabin in front of me, mentally checking it against the one he'd showed us. It was like all truly great successes—at first I wouldn't allow myself to believe I was actually there. But there was no denying the cabin. It was real. Somehow, without even meaning to do it, I was here. If Pike was right, and I believed he was, Mom and Anna were here too. I'd check the cabin first. What if I found them inside with Pike? What if he smiled and said, "What took you so long, Danny-boy?"

I was overcome by the image and felt my legs go weak. I sat down right in the water and began to sob.

I'd slipped. I had started in another world, my world, and I'd found my way into this one. Now all I had to do was get them and go—

Suddenly I remembered what Pike had said about the hatch. *It moves. Getting in is the easy part. It's getting back out that can be a challenge.*

I took off on a run, sloshing the swamp water as I went. I kept my head up, surveying the swamp as I moved, looking for that hatch, knowing it had to be somewhere. That's when I nearly ran into them. And even if I hadn't, seeing them would have made me break my stride. They were breathtaking.

What I saw could only be properly called ghosts, but I think that's more a failure of the language than an apt description of what they were—evanescent sunbeams cutting through the dusk. I immediately thought of my earlier visits from Anna. Anna had been different, more like a vision or a trick of the shadows, a messenger from my subconscious. These girls were simultaneously not there, yet more present than anything I'd ever seen. Hadn't that been how Pike had described them? He was right. Damn, he was exactly right.

Their spirits burned and shone with a dim light, and when they moved, they left the scent of mossflower and the tinkling sound of tiny bells.

They watched me, their eyes wide with something—hope? I thought it was.

They wore dresses, old and pleated. Their shoes were leather and immune to the dirt and grime of the swamp because they floated, their toes dangling just inches above the silt. Each of their dresses was torn at the hem, and a single piece of fabric hung down, dragging the water and causing the tiniest of ripples, like anchors keeping them moored. Without these loose hems weighing them down, I could imagine the girls floating away or dissipating into the dusk, becoming one with the mist.

Neither spoke, and I wasn't sure if they could. I pointed to the cabin. "I'm here for my mother and sister. I want to help you too."

The girls didn't answer me, and for a moment I thought maybe they couldn't. Then I realized their attention was fixed on something just behind me. I started to turn when I heard him laugh.

It was a high hollow sound, like the scream of a bobcat that used to wake me up late at night.

"We got another one, girls," the voice said. "He's slipped down the rabbit hole and now he'll never climb back out."

I turned around slowly.

Sykes was different than I'd imagined him. Taller, his head a wilder shade of red than I'd pictured. His face was locked into a garish smile; his eyes carried the wide, bugged look of a madman. This didn't surprise me, but his presence did. Unlike the girls, he was completely here, as if his body had been hauled, wholly resurrected, out of the swamp. His feet were sunk into the water as deep as mine. His face was lined with scars, the skin of his cheeks and lips loose against his skull from where Pike had pulled on it for so long. He walked with a stoop, tilting toward me, and his feet stirred the water, causing the fish to scurry for more remote parts of the swamp.

Up to this point, I'd felt every emotion I could imagine: joy, despair, grief, blind hope. Every emotion, I realized, except fear. Not the brain-numbing kind anyway, not the *Oh shit, here comes pain in my face right now* kind of fear. I couldn't react. Finally, when he lunged at me, his face—God, I'll always see that face—contorted into that crooked grin, my paralysis broke.

I made it to the porch steps before he caught me, his hand falling on my calf and pulling me back. He lifted me in the air, dangling me face-first over the swamp water. He was strong. Sixteen years later, I still marvel at his strength.

One of the girls screamed, a high, pure note of misery. Sykes laughed.

I do not know why evil exists in the world. Like many other people before me, it's a question I've pondered on sleepless nights, and I've yet to find a satisfactory answer. But I know what evil is. Even today, I can see it in the faces of certain politicians, talk-show hosts, and those that seek power at the expense of others. I know it, and I think the moment I heard Sykes laugh at the girls' terror was when I learned what it looked and sounded like. It was a lesson I would not forget.

Filled with rage, I twisted my body and reached for him, grabbing his crotch and squeezing for everything I had. He groaned and let go of me. I dropped headfirst into the swamp, the world going from a shimmering haze to a dank, slick blackness in an instant. I might have been in the storm shelter again, it was so dark.

I pushed myself up in time to see Sykes lunging at me. I rolled over, making him fall into the water. My hand found the bank and I pulled myself to the porch steps for a second time, my determination growing inside me like a ball of ever-expanding energy. I was too close to stop. Inside my mind, I heard Pike's voice cajoling me on as he had on the way to the storm shelter.

Halfway up the steps onto the rickety porch, my ankle gave way and I fell in a heap.

Sykes was standing over me, the loose skin of his jowls hanging inches from his skull, swaying gelatinously.

He tightened the skin into a smile. His eyes were so damned big, and I noticed that he never blinked. Maybe Pike had ripped his eyelids off in the struggle.

"Do you really think you can go in there?" Sykes said.

I didn't answer; instead, I scooched myself away from the steps, away from Sykes.

"Go ahead," he said. "Try it."

Warily, I worked myself to my feet and reached for the door handle.

Somewhere out in the swamp, I heard bells and worried murmuring.

I reached for the door handle—an old, rusted knob. It turned easily in my hand. I pushed it.

The door wouldn't budge.

Sykes laughed, a wet cackle that rang out through the trees. Have you ever been walking in the woods, alone, around dusk, when one world starts to settle down and another begins to wake up? Have you ever heard a sound—some shrill and distant sound—that you don't recognize as a whippoorwill or a loon or anything else that would be in your woods? It had happened to me dozens of times before I visited the swamp and dozens since, and after hearing Sykes cackle like that, and having the benefit of sixteen years to mull it over, I think I understand that sometimes sounds—like people—slip through.

I was about to lunge at him, thinking my best shot was to bring the fight to him, when I heard a click behind me.

I turned to see the door open just a hair. I fell over trying to move so fast and hit my head against the door. Before I could get myself back to my feet, two things happened almost instantaneously—Sykes grabbed my ankles, trying to haul me back off the porch, and I reached for the door frame, clutching it with both hands.

For a moment, I felt like I'd be split in two, but Sykes won out.

He was too strong, and he ripped me away. However, in pulling me back, he lost his balance on the steps and tumbled backward. I hit the steps pretty hard, my knee colliding with the edge of one of the bottom ones, my chin against the top.

But I was free.

The door was still open, and I saw Anna there, just inside, and that was all I needed. I pulled myself to my feet and lunged inside. I hit the floor again and heard the door slam shut behind me.

Sykes began to bang on the door, shaking the entire cabin. He rattled the handle and must have thrown his body into it because it sounded like something big hit the door. None of it helped. I heard his footsteps clomping across the porch and back down the steps.

Then a silence, followed by the sweetest words I'd ever heard.

"Danny? Say 'Brady.'"

"Brady," I said, still lying on the floor, facedown.

Anna giggled. "Say 'Brady *Bunch.*'"

"Brady *Bun-ch*," I said, hitting the last *ch* hard like Anna liked. For the first time in nine months, I smiled the kind of smile that I felt deep inside, the kind of smile that a person can forget if he's not careful.

Chapter Thirty-three

W here's Mom?" I asked, standing up, brushing the mud off my jeans. If this was a dream, it didn't feel like any dream I'd ever had.

"Say 'Mama.'"

"Mama. Where is she, Anna?"

She giggled.

I wanted to embrace Anna, to squeeze her tightly and nuzzle her neck, but those weren't things you did with Anna. Another thing you didn't really do with Anna: ask her questions. Well, you could ask all the questions you wanted, as long as you didn't expect an answer.

I looked around. It was mostly bare here: a single half-finished wooden table, two chairs, a worn-out dirty couch.

I stepped past the table. There was a short hallway and then a back room. A rug lay in the hallway. It was red and green, and the image of a deer gazed back at me. I tried to remember if there had been a rug in Pike's cabin, and I couldn't. Didn't matter. Two sides of the same page. Isn't that how Walter said Seth explained it?

"Mom?" I said, stepping over the rug. I knocked lightly on the door.

I pushed the door open. The room was empty except for a single bed. A window on the other side of the room framed a cluster of shadowy trees, and through their weblike branches, the full moon.

I sat down on the bed.

Confused, I tried to think of some possible explanation. How could Anna be here without Mom? I don't know how long I sat there just thinking. I hadn't panicked yet, but I think it might have happened soon if Anna hadn't walked in.

"Danny?" She stood in the doorway, on top of the rug.

"Hey, Anna."

"Say 'dark.'"

"Dark."

"Say 'in the dark.'"

"In the dark. Jesus, Anna, where's Mom?"

"Dan-dan, say 'dark.'"

There was no stopping her sometimes. For this I both admired and hated her.

"Dark," I said with a sigh. I could sigh all I wanted. It wouldn't bother her in the least.

"Say 'in.'"

I stood up, planning on forcing her from the room. I used to do it all the time when we were younger. There was only so much a person could take.

"Say it, Dan-dan. Say 'in.'"

I swear if she hadn't been like she was, I would have socked her right in the arm. Hell, maybe I still should've. Maybe then she'd shut up and give me some peace.

"Say it, Dan-dan."

I yelled at her. "Shut up." Right in her face. She didn't even flinch. I wanted to keep yelling, but why? The message would be worthless, incomprehensible to her, and I'd only be inflicting my anger on her to no purpose. I shook my head and lay back on the bed, resigned to just play along until something else struck her fancy.

"Say it, Dan-dan."

"Say what?" I'd already forgotten.

"In. Say 'in.'"

I'd never heard that one. "In."

"Say 'the.'"

"The." *Brady Bunch*, my mind added automatically.

"Say 'dark.'"

"Huh?"

"Say 'dark,' Dan-dan."

"Dark."

The word was already out of my mouth when something clicked into place. It was more physical than mental. A leap in my gut. I sat up, not fully aware of why. Then it hit me. "Did you say 'in the dark'? As in Mom is in the dark?"

She giggled.

I stood up and walked quickly back out to the hallway. Kicking the rug away, I saw what I should have thought of before, another hatch.

I knelt down and tried to twist the little steel nub that held the door to the cellar shut. It was stuck. I twisted it harder. It barely

249

budged. I bore down, nearly cutting my fingers as I worked the nub, until I finally made it move and the door popped loose.

I turned to tell Anna I was going down, but she was already gone.

That was something I thought about a lot later. Anna. Her ability to come and go as she wanted. I think in the end that may have been the most important thing of all. More important than my belief, my hope; more important than Pike's brokenness that made him seek me out, more important even than Seth finding the place to begin with. In many ways, Anna is the bravest person I know. Or maybe she doesn't even understand what it means to be brave. Either way, she's a miracle.

Dwight asked me once why I thought she was a miracle. Why I believed she saved my mother.

I asked him if he had a better explanation. He paused for what seemed like a long time. His head was down, and he seemed to be studying the little pad where he wrote God only knows what about me. When he looked up, his face was solemn, like it hurt him to say the next part.

"Go on," I said. "I can take it."

"A better explanation? I'm not sure if it's better, as much as it's the only explanation. What happened to you was a kind of prolonged delirium, Dan. I've been hoping you'd come to this conclusion on your own, but I can see that's not happening."

I think what I said next surprised him. "I've thought about that. A lot."

"And?"

"I reject it."

Dwight shifted in his seat. Nodded. Picked up his pen to write something and then put it back down.

"I think it may be time to go back on the meds, Dan. I think—"

"No. No more meds."

For a brief moment, I thought Dwight might lose it. He looked genuinely frustrated with me. I can understand that. I don't expect anyone to believe me. Some days I don't even believe it myself. Those are the days I open up my cabinet and stare at the pills Dwight insisted I take. I stare at them and wonder if it might be easier just to give in, just to . . . slip back into a fog. I'd been there before. The first few months that I saw Dwight, I took the meds. I have to hand it to him. He knew exactly what to prescribe. Under the spell of the medication, I barely thought about anything except the day-to-day. I slept well, and felt good, but I didn't remember, and that ate at me like a cancer.

See, remembering is everything. A small miracle every time.

I went down the ladder. It wasn't unlike climbing into the storm shelter. Somehow, there was more light than there had been in the shelter, but other than that, I might have been climbing into that concrete bunker again. I was halfway down when I saw them.

Like an old film, I saw the girls, images against the dark wall, gauzy lace against a rust-blood wall. They burned and flickered and screamed silent, eternal screams, and I knew absolutely that this was why they hadn't left. This was why they were trapped. I watched, unable to tear my eyes away from their agony, mesmerized by their hurt, the sadness that seeped off them like blood from a deep cut.

I wanted to call out to them, to help them, to free them from the shackles where they hung, but when I took a step closer to them, they began to fade. Have you ever seen an old television? The kind that has to fade out when you turn it off? That was what it was like. They shrunk until there was only a single pinprick of light in the center of the wall. And then even that vanished.

The girls had just been afterimages, a kind of psychic residue. I was alone. Completely alone.

Or so I thought.

Gradually, I became aware of a presence behind me. A slow heaving, so slow it was barely detectable. I turned around and saw a dark shape in the corner.

I stepped over to her and knelt down. I waited for my eyes to adjust to the darkness. When they did, I saw her face.

I touched her hair. I kissed her forehead. It was as if she were in a coma. She didn't respond to my touch. She was asleep. She was in the dark.

Shaking her harder, I saw her eyes flutter. She looked at me. "Mom? It's Danny. I've come to take you home."

She shook her head. "No."

I shook her harder. Maybe she was still asleep. This didn't make any sense because I was here now and she was supposed to be happy to see me, and together along with Anna, we'd get out of here.

Later, Dwight would suggest that my mother's unwillingness to wake up was metaphorical, indicative of the fact that she didn't really want to come home.

I couldn't disagree. I mean, it wasn't something I thought about a lot. Mostly, I spent my time trying to get my head around the reality of it all. The swamp, the girls, and Sykes. Mom not wanting to come home was there, but it was hidden like a piece of glass that had been buried deep inside my heart, an aching part that I stayed away from once I realized how much it hurt to touch.

"She did," I told him. "She just didn't know it yet."

Dwight wasn't buying this. "So she wasn't ready?"

"I don't know. Maybe."

"So, how did this make you feel, Dan? To come all this way, to want her back so much and then to realize maybe she didn't want to come at all?"

"Like a million bucks. Happy as a jaybird. Shit, how do you think it made me feel?"

He held up his hands. "Dan, I mean no offense. This is all obviously very real to you. I want to respect that. It's just a question."

"It's more than real to me, okay? It's my life. What happened when I was fourteen—it defined me. It changed me, and for you to sit there and imply that none of it was real, that it was some psychotic episode brought on by hitting my head in the storm shelter—"

"Dan, I never said anything about a psychotic episode. What I'm trying to get you to understand is that your story is rife with meaning, with truths, even if it's not completely, literally true. Your mother, for instance. Wouldn't it be fair to say that her 'slipping' into the 'darkness' could be understood as metaphorical rather than literal?"

Of course it was fair. I hardly need a shrink to alert me to the metaphorical dimensions of what happened to me. It's easy for him to sit across from me and talk about metaphors. I have memories. Images that are vivid in my mind's eye. Still, there's a part of me that's reasonable enough to consider that people don't slip into literal darkness. That understands people slip all the time, and what a great metaphor my story is, but I refuse to see it as only that.

I refuse.

So what? What else is there?

The story. That's all I have in the end. Just the story. Pike's story. My story.

That's where the truth resides.

Chapter Thirty-four

I didn't know what to do about Mom. Not being able to make her wake up stumped me. I climbed out of the cellar to look for Anna. The house was empty. Wherever Anna had gone, she was there now, and Mom and I were alone.

Outside the window over the table, I saw the girls hovering near the trees. Pressing my face up against the window, I looked around for Sykes. Not seeing him, I decided to take a chance. I didn't know if it would help me with Mom or not, but I had a feeling it would help the girls.

I pushed open the front door carefully, just in case he was waiting outside. The swamp appeared deserted, silent save for the buzz of cicadas, the distant thrum of bullfrogs.

Walking quickly, I slogged through the swamp to where the girls floated.

Tina—she was the older one, right, the one Pike had had a crush on—moved to meet me. Again, I was struck by how present she was while at the same time it was like she was barely there at all.

"Why are you here?" she asked me.

"I came to help my mother and sister. I came to help you."

"You're a fool."

I stepped back as if slapped. I hadn't been expecting this.

"Why . . . ?"

"There's no leaving this place. You can come in, but look around you. Do you see a way out?"

"Maybe," I said. "If you'll trust me."

"Why should I trust you?" Tina asked.

"I know Walter. Walter Pike. He told me about Seth."

She said nothing. A wind blew, and the image of her wavered. There was the light tinkling sound of bells.

"Seth couldn't help us either," she said.

"What happened to him?"

"He's gone."

"Where?"

"He's dead." She said this as if there could be no question.

"Did he die here, in the swamp?"

She nodded. "He believed the quicksand near the creek was a way home. He believed a lot of things."

"Are you telling me Seth killed himself?"

"He was a good person. He brought us here to help us. He didn't know what would happen."

"What did happen?"

"We got stuck. He hated himself for it. He went to the quicksand."

"To kill himself?"

"What do you think?"

"I think he left. I just don't know why," I said.

"Why would he leave?" Tina said. "He had nothing to go back for."

"That's not true. He had Walter." It came to me then. I saw it all, and didn't even consider the possibility that I was wrong: Seth returning during the war, unable to even ask anyone where Walter was, but maybe guessing just the same. Seth going home and collecting the photos and the painting, putting them in the metal box and then burning the place to the ground. Where he might have gone after that was anyone's guess.

"You remind me of him," Tina said.

"Who, Seth?"

She nodded. "You believe things. You believed you could come here and save your mother and sister."

"I can save them. I think . . ." I hesitated, knowing I was heading toward rocky ground. "I think I can save you and Rachel too."

"You're a fool."

"Maybe so. But I have something I want you to see."

She said nothing, waiting.

"I think it could help us both out. It's something you may have forgotten."

———

Tina followed me inside. Rachel, whom I had not heard speak yet, stayed near the trees, the outline of her dress a gauzy shimmer among the leaves.

Tina began to shake as we neared the hall. By the time I'd pulled back the rug to reveal the trapdoor, she was like an old film hitting a bad spot, a shuddering image stuck on the screen.

"No," she said, and her voice was barely a whisper. "No, no, no, no. Why are you doing this to me?"

"Seth brought you here to make things right, but this is not where you belong. You have to go down. Go down and face it. And . . ." I chose my words carefully now. "Understand that he doesn't keep you here. Not anymore. You can move on."

For a long time, she didn't move. Her shaking stopped, and she seemed to be pulling her energy inward, causing the light that burned across her countenance to blaze brighter. I thought I had lost her, that she might implode from the misery of it all. It was as if her body had been frozen and no outward movement or expression was allowed. She pulled everything in, though, internalizing all of her anger and fear and despair. It was Anna who finally broke the spell. She must have come in behind us while I had all my attention focused on Tina.

"Tina," she said. "I came to the cabin just like you said. I came, Tina. Say 'We'll have fun in the cabin, Anna.' Say 'There's a place where it never thunders.' Say it, Tina."

The burning stopped and Tina looked me in the eye. "Okay," she said.

That has been one of the hard things. When I'm awake in the wee hours of the morning and the trees outside my window begin to take on shapes and I wonder if I'm insane or just blessed because of what I remember, this is one of the memories that I come back to, time and time again.

They had called to her. Bored, scared, alone, confused after Seth left, the girls promised Anna a place where it would never thunder. They invited her here. Somehow, Anna heard their voices. Somehow, Anna came.

Somehow. That seems to be the word I come back to a lot. Somehow.

There are nights I go to sleep with it on my tongue, repeating it like a prayer.

Tina reached for the trapdoor. Her hand flashed and then went dull, almost ashen, and she clutched the handle and pulled up. It had stuck for me, and I'd had to jiggle it, work it loose before it popped open. For her, there was no resistance, and I wondered if any place existed—in this world, or the next—that these girls couldn't access.

What surprised me was the thing she did next.

She turned to me and whispered that she was sorry. Then without so much as touching the ladder or the ground, she sank. Straight down into the gap, as if her physical being—once so light—were now a lead weight.

She was there for a long time. Anna stood behind me. She said nothing, as if waiting for something to happen. Nothing did. Until we heard the sobs rising like wisps of dusky smoke from below. I knew that she'd seen what she needed to see—the same image that had greeted me: Rachel and herself, chained in Sykes's cellar. She'd seen the very thing she'd been trying to forget, the very thing—I hoped—that would set her free. Going back to that cellar had caused her to remember, and remembering was what she had to do.

Chapter Thirty-five

After Tina came out of the cellar, it all happened very quickly. "Your mother is awake," she said, and then she was gone.

Anna giggled. "Houston, Texas," she said.

I went down.

I'm not here," Mom said. "You're not here."

"Mom, I don't know what has happened to you, but I'm going to help you." I reached for her hands. She clutched mine, limply.

"It's so dark."

"I know."

"He won't let me leave."

"Who won't let you?"

She didn't answer, but I knew. "He can't keep you, Mom. He's a liar. When you slip, you just have to get up again."

She smiled just a little then and put her hand in my hair. I closed my eyes, savoring the moment, which was wise because it didn't last long. She pulled her hand away and said, "I'm scared, Danny. Scared like I've never been scared in my life."

"He can't hurt you, Mom. Being afraid is the only power he has."

"It's not him I'm afraid of," she said.

I wrapped my arms around her and pulled her up, much as I had pulled Pike up from the mud. She was in a kind of mud too. Finally, I saw that she had slipped in more ways than one.

———

Dwight came back to this point time and time again during our talks. At first, I couldn't figure out why.

He'd always say, "Let's go back to that moment with your mother. The part where she said she wasn't afraid of Sykes. You said you wrapped your arms around her. Talk about that."

And I'd always tell it over again, not sure what he was driving at. After about the third or fourth day he did this, I finally asked him, "What do you want me to talk about? Why this part?"

He shrugged and peered at me over his bifocals. "It seems important."

I shook my head.

"How?"

"Let me see if I can be more specific. Your mother said it wasn't Sykes she was afraid of . . ."

"And?"

"It seems like her statement raises a question."

"You're saying I should have asked her what she was afraid of?"

"No, I'm not saying you should have asked her. I'm suggesting you consider the question. Maybe even contemplate the answer."

"No."

"No?"

"I don't need to."

He shifted in his chair and marked something in his notebook. He did this a lot. I think it was just for show, a way to create the long pauses that encouraged his patients to keep talking. I wasn't biting.

He cleared his throat. "Why don't you need to, Dan?"

"I already know."

"You know?"

"Yes."

"And what was she afraid of?"

"Herself. She was afraid of herself. She was afraid she might slip again. To get up, to pull yourself out of something, that takes courage, all right? Because you might fall again."

"So how did she 'slip,' Dan? How did it happen?"

"What do you mean?"

"It seems like an important question. You said she was afraid to slip again. Define *slipping*, because it doesn't sound like you're talking about the same kind of slipping Walter Pike told you about, the same kind of slipping you are claiming that you did when you were in the storm shelter."

Here, I was forced to hesitate. I realized he was right.

"I think . . ." I began, but then trailed off. What did I think?

Either she climbed into the storm shelter that day and slipped to the swamp or she ran off on her own. It was hard to imagine my mother going into the storm shelter for any reason . . .

It was almost as if Dwight read my mind. "Isn't the storm shelter the only way in? I mean, I've not heard you mention any other way . . ." He shifted in his chair and peered at me hard over his glasses.

"That's true, but maybe Anna went in first. Maybe she went in after Anna," I said, pleased at finding an explanation that actually made sense.

Dwight wasn't buying it, though. "Maybe," he said. "But it sounds like a stretch."

I said nothing.

Dwight bit his pen cap. "Maybe this is a good place to stop for the day. Maybe you need some time to process all this."

"Sure," I said. "I'll process."

I t wasn't easy getting her up the ladder. I had to stay behind her and keep her from falling back. Once I got her up, I sent her and Anna to the back room and shut the door.

My plan was forming. What Tina had done was crucial. It made me understand that nothing could keep them here. Nothing, really, could keep my mom and sister here either, except free will. If a person doesn't want to climb out of the morass, then you can't make them. You can only help a person so much, but Mom was coming around. She was awake now. That was a big step.

I left them and headed back to the front room, to the window to look for him. I knew I'd have to face Sykes, and only time would tell whether I believed my own rhetoric about there being nothing to fear. I was just pressing my face to the window when I heard it.

A knock on the front door.

Chapter Thirty-six

I suppose it could have been Rachel or Tina, but I can honestly say I never really believed it was. Besides the fact that it didn't seem like something the girls would do—knock—there was also something in the sound, something cold and removed. Something foreign in that knock, a lack of rhythm that still chills me to think about it. It was as if Sykes were announcing his presence, reminding us he was still out there. The nightmare was not yet over. Indeed, it might have just begun.

I sprinted back down the hallway and pushed the bedroom door open. "Don't come out until I come to get you." Mom, sitting on the bed, looked at me groggily.

"It's him, isn't it?"

"Yeah."

"He wants me."

"He's not going to get you. Just stay here until I come back." I looked at Anna. She was singing quietly, oblivious as always.

I paused, a thought I had not considered flitting through my mind: What if I didn't come back? What if Sykes got me before I ever had a chance?

I dismissed the thought. It wasn't a thought I could really afford to dismiss, but I couldn't afford to dwell on it either. It was time to act.

Closing the door, I walked carefully past the trapdoor that led to the cellar. It was still propped open against the wall like it had been since Tina came out. Once past the cellar opening, I moved quickly to the door. Timing would be key. I'd have to make sure I had enough time to get in position before he came in. *And what then?* a voice said. It was the voice of doubt, something I'd managed to keep at bay pretty well until now. But now . . . this was uncharted territory. This was a madman. No, the ghost of a madman, and I was running on pure instinct.

I tiptoed over to the window to look for him. If he'd stepped off the porch, I would be able to see him. Pressing my face against the glass, I scanned the swamp. He was out of sight, which probably meant he was still on the porch. I took a deep breath. There was still time to back out. I'd done nothing so far that couldn't be repaired, but once I opened that door . . .

My thoughts were interrupted as I saw Sykes step off the porch and back toward the water. *Like a snake,* I thought, *slithering back into the murk.*

You could catch a snake. It was hard and you had to be extremely careful because not only was their strike quick, it was often fatal. I'd escaped his grasp one time before. I knew this time I might not be so lucky. I walked over to the couch. This was important. I gripped the old thing on one armrest and slid it across the sawdust floor. Once I made it to the hallway, I stopped. Would the couch fit through the hall? Definitely not like this. I flipped it up on one side and pushed it through. It went with an inch or so to spare on each side. I pulled it back out and wondered if I should risk leaving it turned over. It would certainly save me some time, but I had to consider if seeing it overturned would give Sykes pause. In the end, I decided to leave it as it was. One way or another, Sykes was going to come past the cellar door. He had to do it if he wanted to find anybody.

Once I opened that front door, there would be no turning back. I'd have to make it to the cellar before he saw me or it wouldn't work. I checked the window again. Sykes was farther out in the swamp, his eyes turned toward the last streaks of red in what must have been the west. Those streaks never changed here, and more than anything else that was what made me do it. See, I had Mom and Anna, but staying here would mean I'd lose myself. I needed for this to end. I needed to rejoin the real world because that was the way real life worked. Even then, I sensed that one day this would all recede like a bad dream.

I strode quickly to the door. Purposefully. My hand fell on the door handle. I drew a sharp breath and let it out. Then I turned the handle and pulled the door back.

I didn't wait to see if he noticed. Instead, I bolted for the hall, for the ladder leading down to the cellar. I stopped halfway down the ladder, so that I was completely inside, hidden from view unless Sykes were to stand right over the opening and peer directly down at me. Still, I was close enough to the top that I'd be able to reach for him when he went past me. I meant to grab his ankle, his foot, and pull him inside the cellar. If things went perfectly, he'd fall to the ground while I stayed on the ladder, leaving me plenty of time to get out and shut the door before he could make it back up. Then I had to get the couch and shove it down the short hall and over the hatch.

It would be near impossible.

So I made myself think of something else. I thought of Dad, the look on his face when Mom and Anna came back. When I showed up at the jail with both of them. Sheriff Martin—providing he'd survived the storm—would piss himself. The papers, the news channels, they'd all have to write new stories about Mom and Anna and where they'd been. Scientists would want to investigate the storm shelter, the woods around our house. They'd want to see the painting, and I'd tell the whole story about Seth, and . . .

Who was I kidding? Even at fourteen, I had enough sense to know nobody would believe any of that.

So what would it be like? No idea. *One thing at a time, Danny. One thing at a—*

I heard a footstep near the front door. He'd be on the porch by now, stunned into a deep suspicion by the door being flung open wide. But the suspicion would not be enough to override his hunger (*He wants me*, Mom had said), and he would come down the hall anyway.

Something—likely the door—creaked and I heard his footsteps again. He was moving slowly, checking things out, surely wary of a trap.

I waited, my hands growing sweaty and weary around the ladder rungs.

He came closer, one slow footstep at a time.

Then I heard him stop. For a long time, the house was still. I pictured him beside the couch now, trying to puzzle out why it had been left there, turned over like it was. Time passed, and after a while, I began to count in my head to mark time. I made it to nearly three hundred before I lost track and gave up. My heart thudded in my chest. I heard Anna's voice, very faintly, from somewhere above me. She was saying one of her words, happy and carefree, and I allowed myself a brief moment of envy. At that moment, I might have traded my so-called normalcy for Anna's ability to be oblivious.

If Sykes heard the noise, he gave no indication. The cabin was quiet. Mom shushed Anna. There were other murmurs from the back. Surely he'd hear this and be unable to resist.

I removed my hands one at a time from the sweat-dampened ladder and wiped them on my shorts. Below me, the darkness seemed to simmer, and I thought I heard noises from there too.

I turned away from the cellar, choosing to focus on the dim light above me. Total focus. No distractions.

But Sykes was being still. Silent. Was it possible he'd abandoned the house, sensing a trap? No, he was still there, probably just a few feet from the ladder, waiting, trying to draw me out. Hadn't he done Pike the same way, so many years ago? I tightened my sweaty palms on the ladder rung. I wouldn't be tricked. I'd stay here as long as I needed to stay.

Time is a nonentity in the swamp. You wait and wait, and nothing changes, so you begin to question how long you've been waiting at all. When it doesn't get darker, when it's always dusk, this makes time seem slow, stuck, so to speak. So I waited as patiently as I could, long enough to become frustrated, to almost give up. I waited long enough that my feet hurt from standing on the ladder rung, long enough that my arms grew stiff and sore and I wanted to stretch them out, so I leaned back, extending them as far as they would go.

Even though the standoff seemed to last for an eternity, it shouldn't have mattered. I should have played it smart and waited as long as it took, but I began to believe no man could stay silent as long as he had. I truly believed he was gone.

I climbed slowly, peeking my head out over the lip of the cellar just enough to look down the hallway.

Do you know how it feels to realize you've made a critical mistake and it's too late to fix it? There's usually a rush of shock, an initial reaction to try to take it back, and then the realization that you can't. I've felt a similar phenomenon while driving. I once pulled out in front of a truck that I didn't see. Time slowed down. I wanted to throw the car in reverse and go back to where I was, but time wasn't that slow. All I could do was cope. I floored the car, trying to buy myself some time before impact. But the impact came. I'd guaranteed that by pulling out in front of the truck.

That's how I felt when I eased up out of the cellar and looked down the hallway. Sykes was standing there, his body perfectly still, a wicked, expectant grin plastered across his face. He saw me immediately and his smile grew larger, but otherwise he made no move, instead waiting to see what mine would be.

And I almost blew it. I'd already begun stepping down the ladder to retreat inside the cellar when I realized he'd only close the door on me and go take full advantage of Mom and Anna.

So I did the only other thing I could think of—I scrambled out of the cellar and up to the ground level to face him.

At least I was smart enough to position myself on the other side of the cellar from him. That still meant he'd have to cross the opening in order to reach me or anyone else.

He laughed when he saw me face him, my fists at my sides, ready.

"This is my house," he said, and took a step forward.

I tensed, readying my body to leap. A half-formed plan had wedged itself in my brain. I hadn't considered the consequences, which was just fine.

"Those two girls? Mine."

Another step.

"A man doesn't get much in this godforsaken world, and what's his is his. Your mama? Mine too. I've got plans for her. Plans for you too, although I wouldn't exactly call those plans long-term."

He was close to the edge now, and he had to look down at his feet to avoid falling in.

"This cellar? Mine too."

He stepped across the cellar opening.

Had I been thinking, there was no way I would have done what I did, but instead of thinking, I acted, launching myself toward him with an earsplitting scream. For a moment, the whole world slipped inside that scream. It was a battle cry, a call of ecstasy, a prayer. It was all of these things, and I felt it coursing through my veins and my veins pumping blood to my arms and legs and those arms and legs flying into action. I jumped from several feet away, laying my body out like a wide receiver lays out when he's trying to catch a pass. Halfway there, I realized I was going to go down with him. It wasn't a regret. Just a realization.

I hit him with a tackle my middle school football coach would be proud of. Lead with the shoulder, head up, arms out. I knocked him back and into the cellar.

I tried to grab the side, the ladder, something to avoid going down with him, but Sykes held on to me and together we tumbled inside.

Chapter Thirty-seven

There are parts of the journey that are so indelibly etched in my mind that I can go there in an instant, turn back the clock to the moment as if experiencing it again for the first time.

Going into the cellar with Sykes was one of those moments. Losing the dusk, the half-light of the cabin, my grip—however tenuous—on reality and disappearing into the full dark of the cellar. Slipping, actually. Slipping right into darkness.

The darkness was first. Second was the inability to breathe. He was squeezing my midsection, his two fists tight under my rib cage like some terrible version of the Heimlich. I smelled him. That was the third thing. His body reeked of the swamp, and all the dead, decomposing things—mildewed leaves, fish, the rotten corpses of a thousand dead animals.

I flailed my hands around in desperation, trying to beat at his shoulders and arms, but since he was under me and he held me so tight, there was little damage I could do to him. I reached for his face, only to have him bite my hand savagely. I felt the sickening crunch of his tooth grinding against my knuckle.

I still couldn't breathe.

My lungs squeezed shut. I had to cough. There was a moment when I became Seth drowning in quicksand, Jake reaching out to shove him under, except now it was Sykes, his iron grip around my midsection. I flailed and sputtered and felt like I was being burned slowly, from the inside out, like a bomb that was ticking toward detonation.

Then—and this is the part that is most clear—I heard a voice, calm and soothing. It was a voice that loosened the knot that I had frantically been cinching ever tighter in my desperation.

"Reach out for my hand."

The voice belonged to Pike. I had no doubt of it then or now. With my free hand, I reached blindly. I grazed his fingers and strained my back trying to touch them again. Finally, his hand enveloped mine. His grip was strong and firm, and I felt him pulling me away from Sykes. I flew through the air. My eyes were still shut, but images flashed before them like one of those time-lapse movies when the director speeds everything up really fast to show the passing of time. I saw a glimpse of Pike sitting in his cabin, the oxygen tubes in his nostrils; I saw him in the dark woods standing on the edge of a bright clearing, taking in the view; I saw him leaning over the counter, Cap's shirt bunched inside his fist; I saw this and more until they became a fluttering of images so fast that I couldn't make out a single one except the last: Pike smiling at me on a cloudy day in the woods—the real woods I'd grown up playing in—a fresh rain covering everything with a shiny polish. I didn't know it then, but this last image was one I would see again, and one I would always remember.

After the images stopped, I hit the cellar ground hard enough to force the breath out of me. I lay there for a second, trying to breathe normally. I couldn't see anything other than the top of the ladder above me but decided that would work both ways. Sykes wouldn't be able to see anything either.

I scrambled to my feet and lunged toward the ladder. I grabbed it and started going up. I was a rung from the top when I felt his hand on my ankle. He yanked hard, and both feet lost contact with the steps. Somehow, I managed to keep my hands on the ladder. I kicked backward with the foot he wasn't holding and landed a blow to what must have been his face. He gasped and let go of my ankle. I made it to the top and tried to pull my way out onto the plank floor.

Mom was there, staring at me, her mouth gaping.

I got my elbows up. And then my midsection. "Go," I gasped at Mom. "Go back to the room."

She shook her head and ran to me, kneeling beside the cellar opening, reaching for my arms, pulling me up.

Without her help, I probably wouldn't have made it because Sykes grabbed me again, this time around the thighs. Both of her arms wrapped around me and for a moment I was stretched between the darkness below and my mother. She pulled on me hard, but her hands were slipping, she was losing her grip on me.

When I realized she wasn't going to overpower him, I met her eyes. *Let go*, I mouthed.

She stared at me.

I nodded at her, and I hoped she could see my confidence in my face. She shook her head.

Trust me, I mouthed.

She let go.

I knew what would happen—or at least I thought I did. Turns out, I was right. Sykes had been pulling hard. When Mom let go, he pulled us both back in. This time, though, I landed on top of him as he hit his head on the dirt floor. His arms flailed up and I was free. I scrambled toward the ladder and made it up in seconds. Once clear of the hole, I slammed down the lid and leaned back against the hallway wall, trying to catch my breath.

Mom came over to me and hugged me hard. I buried my face against her shoulder and hugged her back.

I don't know how long I would have stood there with her if I hadn't heard the *thunk* of his feet and hands on the metal ladder below us.

"The couch," I said.

"What?" Mom let go of me.

"We've got to get the couch."

His fingers were on the underside of the door now. I could hear them, touching, probing, looking for the latch.

"Come on!" I sprinted down the hallway and jumped over the couch. Mom was right behind me, but I had to wait for her to get out of the way before I could slide it to the top of the door. She got on one side and together we pushed. As we pushed the couch closer, I saw the handle turn and the door begin to lift . . .

We shoved harder, forcing the couch over the door, and the weight of the couch made the door slam shut.

I heard a moan and then a *thunk* as he hit the bottom again.

Out of breath, I plopped down on top of the couch and felt the absurd desire to say that line from *The Wizard of Oz*. So I did.

"Ding dong," I whispered. "The witch is dead."

Chapter Thirty-eight

Except he wasn't. As far as I knew, he couldn't die. He could be hurt, maybe trapped (as I hoped I had done), but something told me he couldn't be killed. Pike had already done that once, and as far as killing went, I suspected once was enough.

He needs to move on, I thought. *Just like the girls. Just like us.*

No, not just like us. We would all be going different places. Or so I hoped.

"What now?" Mom said.

I pulled myself up. "Now, we need to go for a walk. Through the swamp. But we have to hurry."

Mom glanced at the couch and nodded. "He's not dead, is he?"

"No way."

"Danny?"

"Yeah?"

"I can't go. This place . . . it's a dream. I—I need to just go back to sleep."

I waved her off. "We can talk about that stuff later. Just trust me for now."

She did say one more thing, though. One more thing that I still think about a lot these days. "Okay," she said. "It's a deal. We'll talk about it when we get home."

She never lived up to her promise. We didn't ever talk about it again. Still, those words stay forever on my mind because she said them at all.

Listen:

We'll talk about it when we get home.

When we get home. It meant that somehow, she'd found it within her to believe again, to trust, to accept that things were pretty much rotten—no, worse than rotten; they were shitty—but she'd also accepted that she didn't have to just deal with them either. Because it's so easy to get complacent, isn't it? It's so easy to fear improvements, because improvements equal change and change equals believing in a world that you can't quite see yet.

When we get home.

We heard him stirring in the cellar before we left, a rat trapped in a cage. When Mom raised an eyebrow at the sound, I shrugged it off. Our choices were limited now. We had to move quickly and hope we could find our way out of this place before Sykes found his way out of the cellar.

I wished Tina were here to guide us, and I briefly wondered if showing her the cellar had been a mistake. She'd disappeared after without a word. Maybe it was too sudden to be faced with all that. Sometimes you need time.

It didn't matter, though. Tina wasn't here, and I'd have to find it on my own. I started off through the dense trees, trying my best to go in the direction of the quicksand.

We made pretty good time through the swamp. Mom and Anna were silent, and I was thankful for that. So far, both followed me without complaint, despite the sometimes knee-deep water we were slogging through.

After a while, I began to wonder if I was going the right way. Back home, in the woods, we would have been there by now. Things were different here, I reminded myself. Time for sure. Distance probably too. I kept forging on, scrambling up to a relatively dry bank lined with water lilies. It was beautiful, the kind of thing Mom would have wanted to take a picture of in better times. I squeezed between two ancient, kudzu-covered trees when I heard her.

"No."

That was what Anna did when she didn't want to go somewhere. She'd say no and just sit down. I turned—disappointed, but not surprised—to see her sitting right in the swamp water, her dress billowing out like a lily pad, soaked brown all the way up to her shoulders.

I splashed back into the water and went over to her. "Anna," I said, "I'm going to pick you up and carry you. I know you don't like it, but I have to do it. I'm sorry." I reached for her, and she immediately began to wail, beating her fists against my back. I put my mouth next to her ear and said, "Brady. Brady *Bun-ch.*"

She didn't even seem to hear. She was tossing her head wildly. I had to hold her off me to keep her head from colliding with mine.

I struggled forward, back toward the bank, her writhing in my arms. I marveled at her strength. It took all I had to hold on to her to drag her up the bank, and still she screamed and beat on me. One of her fists hit my face, but I ignored it. I wasn't letting go.

A few more steps and I saw it. It looked exactly the same as it looked back in the real world, just as it had the day Dad and I stood nearby thinking of happier times. The creek that ran behind it was similar. It was close, but not exact. The quicksand, as far as I could tell, was identical down to the gritty moistness that looked just solid enough for someone to step on who didn't know any better.

"Why have you brought us here?" Mom said.

I took a deep breath and put Anna down. "Remember when I talked about trusting me?"

Mom just stared. "You don't expect me to . . ." She trailed off, shaking her head.

"It's the way out. I know it sounds crazy, but it's the only way out of here. It's how Seth left." As I spoke, I was acutely aware of the time we were wasting. Sykes would eventually work his way out of the cellar, and when he did, he would come here first.

"Who is Seth?" Mom said. "And why do we care what he did? Oh, Jesus, I knew this was a mistake. Sometimes, Danny, sometimes you just can't go back home again."

I grabbed her. "It doesn't matter how far you've fallen, Mom. You can always come back home."

I tried to drag her toward the quicksand, but she stiffened her body and dug in. I couldn't move her.

"No. I'm sorry, Danny. I'm sorry, I can't be the mother you want me to be."

A wave of something hit me then. It was big and loud and it crashed down all over my head, knocking me off balance. Understanding. I couldn't help Mom any more than I already had. The rest was up to her. And once I accepted this, I felt a sadness, but I also felt a peace. Mom had vanished because she wanted to. I didn't know where she'd gone or with whom, but she had done it of her own will, and if she was going to come back home, she'd have to do that of her own will too. I'd found a way to reach her, to shake her hard, but she'd have to do the rest.

I dropped to my knees, sobbing. My mother had left us. Had she left Anna too? She'd certainly tried. But Anna was otherworldly when she wanted her way. She possessed some kind of cosmic power that would not be denied, not even by her own mother.

Sometimes life is all about timing because if I am honest with myself, I'd come to the realization that we can only save ourselves. I was ready to believe that when it happened.

Sykes showed up.

From behind us, at the edge of the deepest trees, there was a clatter that sounded like a water buffalo trying to find its way out of a deadfall. Splashing and sticks breaking and moaning. Yeah, the moaning, it's still with me to this day.

He came out of the trees, shuffling sideways, and I saw that the last fall must have broken his back or neck or something central because he wasn't quite put together right anymore. From the waist up, he was turned crooked. His legs went one way and the rest of him faced to the right, and if I hadn't been so damned angry and scared, it would have been funny, a piece of physical comedy worthy of the Monty Python skits Cliff and I used to laugh at. But instead of laughing, I reacted.

The quicksand seemed to vibrate in front of me. A snake was near the edge, as if deciding whether to slip in. I watched it, hoping it would go and give me that little extra boost I needed, but it was taking its sweet time, and there was no way to be certain if it was going there or not. And even if it was, what did that prove? That I had about as much sense as a snake? No, this wasn't about sense or reason or thinking. This was about belief. Climbing out of the slip had always been about belief.

I went for the quicksand. I'm not sure if I thought about it at all. It was instinct. I went because in the end, when push finally came to shove, I had faith—enough anyway—after all.

Three steps was all it took and about three seconds to regret it.

I expected Anna, at least, to follow me. This was a mistake. The look of abject terror on Anna's face told me that.

Sykes was still coming, and Mom and Anna could do nothing but run from him. The problem was only one of them was running: Mom. Anna was standing, her fingers in her ears, as Sykes ambled within arm's reach of her.

Mom and I both screamed for her, but it was too late. He had her in his grasp, his leering face inches above her own, and I could see the look of fear wash over her like one of the thunderstorms she dreaded so much. She began to convulse in his arms.

All this while I was sinking. The quicksand was up to my knees. I lunged forward, but I was so firmly entrenched, I couldn't even make myself fall forward. Somehow, the effort seemed to accelerate the quicksand, and it pulled me harder. I was up to my waist in an instant.

"Mom," I said. "Please . . . only you can decide. If you do, take my hand. Please, Mom."

The look on Mom's face was utter anguish.

Anna screamed again, and I heard Sykes laughing.

I sank more, now trying to tilt my head back to avoid the muck creeping over my chin. So much for Cliff's science about only going halfway down. Thinking that gave me some hope too, because it was clear that science didn't apply here, at least the science that Cliff knew.

With a great effort, I was able to turn my head toward Anna, where Sykes held her aloft like a rag doll.

I turned just in time. Otherwise, I might have missed it.

It was a thing of beauty. Like shards of light sliced in long, thick sheets, the girls came.

At first, I didn't even recognize the lights as emanating from the girls. But when they knocked Sykes back, they materialized—girls from pure, white-hot energy. They were like wild cats that had been caged for too long and had forgotten their power. Imagine two tigers that had run wild for much their lives in the jungle, only to be subdued by cruel men and brought into captivity. Any fool could see the power they possessed, but the poor things, driven to apathy from their time inside a cage, had no idea of their own power. These girls were like that. They were bound by nothing, not even gravity, but they didn't know it. One day, they realize the cage has never even been locked, and with the slightest push, they could be free, and opening that cage door is like opening a valve. All the pressure is released. They are free to explode and become who they are. For the girls, the cage had been their own fear, and the release set loose a blast of righteous anger, pent-up fury that literally swooped, blazing, across the sky.

This was what I saw in the moments before sinking under the quicksand. The girls flew at Sykes with a rage so pure, I swore they left streaks in the evening sky that might never fade. All that animosity, aimed squarely at Sykes. I couldn't help but wonder at the justice in that moment. Their very essences seemed to scream through the dusk that he would not hurt Anna like he'd hurt them. It's one of the images I come back to again and again: the raw power, the burning truth. Witnessing something like that changes you in a way that a therapist can never understand. A moment like that transcends reality, memory, rational thought. It felt primal, like God's own justice falling from the sky.

When they came at him, Sykes dropped Anna and fell back, stunned, untouched, at least physically, but I realized as the quicksand took my mouth that power, *real* power, wasn't physical anyway. Real power was all about confidence and faith. And somehow, the girls had found theirs at last. Tina's visit to the cellar, her remembering . . . I'm sure it helped her, but I am equally sure she and Rachel also acted out of a kind of loyalty to Anna. She'd come here because they called, much as they had come here because of Seth.

I watched as Mom hugged Anna close, and the girls swarmed over Sykes, keeping him on the ground through force of will, apparently. I tried to call out, to tell Mom it was going to be okay, that she just needed to take the next step. I wanted to tell her to follow me back home, but the words died in the thick mud.

My nose was next; I felt the grit tickling my upper lip, and then coating it. It felt odd—cool and sticky and calming somehow. My eyes remained riveted on the scene that was playing out in front of me. Rachel and Tina were laughing now, and it sounded like carnival music, full of peculiar angles and absurd joy. They were also floating higher than I'd ever seen them float, surrounded by shimmering lights, two loose conglomerations of fireflies, twinkling in the dusk. The hems of their dresses caught fire and fell like flaming rain.

And then their bones dropped like brittle sticks into the quicksand.

My ears were filling up with mud and the sound of hundreds of souls talking all at once somewhere far away, heard through a wall. The last image I saw before the gritty wetness closed my eyes was of the girls, shouting at Mom and Anna, telling them something. Then they were gone and all that remained were the trees and all the secrets they hold among their clustered branches.

And then they were gone too.

There is a between place. The trees know it. It happens at dusk at that perfect moment between light and dark, when the air is festooned with shadows and the atmosphere is heavy with possibility. Here things are in balance, the world is a slate, without even the slightest traces of the scarred markings you used to believe dictated the way of things. Here, memory is like a stylus that you can use to roam wherever you please.

This is what I found in the quicksand. A place free of the laws of physics, bound by nothing except the limits of memory, hope, and imagination. Imagination most of all. There is a temptation to stay, to live out an infinite life poised on the brink of infinite possibilities. Who knows how long I might have savored the power if I had not felt a hand grasp mine.

Instantly, I knew I wanted to go back home because that hand belonged to Mom, and even though I couldn't see her, I knew she and Anna had decided to join me. Maybe the girls had talked her into it, but I doubt that. More likely, she had decided for herself, decided to give her life one more chance.

Then I heard the high buzz of cicadas and the crackle of electricity. Men's voices, search parties, and the aftermath of a brutal storm, one that I'd narrowly escaped. I listened to it all, picturing the scene perfectly, even down to Sheriff Martin's squad car, which I saw overturned among trees shredded like mulch.

This was my place, my home.

I woke up.

Chapter Thirty-nine

When I opened my eyes, I'm not sure what I expected. What I got was darkness, pure and silent. It took me several moments to realize where I was, to realize that I was back where I'd started inside the storm shelter. I tried to get up, but my body was weak, my mind cloudy. It felt like I'd just awakened from a weeklong nap.

Gradually, I worked my way up to my feet and steadied myself on the ladder. I started to climb when I remembered Pike. He'd been near death when I left the last time, and then when I came back, he'd been gone. Or at least, I thought he had. Suddenly, I wasn't exactly sure of anything.

I paced the shelter two times over and it was empty.

This was good, right? I tried to convince myself. No body meant he was still alive. Still, something nagged at me. Where were Anna and Mom? I remembered—if only vaguely—them joining me in the quicksand. We'd done it. We would be a family again.

But we weren't. I was alone.

Trying to hold off my tears, I climbed the ladder on unsteady legs. My ribs and head hurt. My nose was bleeding. When I opened the hatch, the daylight burned my eyes so badly, I had to close it again. Wincing, I opened it back up just a crack and stuck my head out. In the distance, I saw a line of men trekking through the woods. They had dogs and one of them had a rifle. They were looking for someone.

They were looking for me.

I closed the hatch, shaking. They could find me after I knew where Mom and Anna were, after I'd determined if Pike was alive. Not until.

I went back down the ladder and lay on the ground. I slept. This time, I know it was sleep because my dreams were dreams, and when I woke up, the world hadn't changed a bit.

Well, maybe that's not quite true. A miracle was waiting for me when I woke up.

———

*M*iracle. I don't think Dwight cared for that word much. He once told me he thought it strange that I'd use it to describe Pike's return. After all, hadn't he abducted me? Left me for dead in the storm shelter?

I told him it hadn't been like that.

He nodded. Smugly. Son of a bitch.

There are things about the slip, about fourteen, that I'm willing to consider, to question. Indeed, treading back through those memories is like navigating a rocky sea of unanswered questions. I can accept this. I have to accept it. To do otherwise would be foolish. The swamp, the girls, all of it was open for debate; even if I leaned one way or the other, there was always something waiting to sway me back. But Pike? His honesty, his genuineness, his true desire to help me? No, I don't question this. He wanted to help me. He believed the story he told.

Sometimes, that's all that matters.

———————

There are bad days. More, lately, than ever before. Days when I remember the swamp like a distant dream, and on these days I hit the bar right after work and drink until I'm sleepy, until I can't think of anything except dragging my ass home and climbing into my warm bed. If I'm lucky I'll go right to sleep and dream nothing that I'll remember. But sometimes, even the alcohol isn't enough to keep my mind away, and I make the case in my head, a slow and painful kind of litigation, a weighing of facts versus memory. I build scales inside my head and heart. Try to strike a balance that I can live with. But eventually, I give up. The balance between what I remember and the physical world governed by universal and tenable laws is either too ethereal for grasping or it does not exist at all.

So where does that leave me? To answer that question honestly, I have to consider my greatest fears—that I have in the course of my life slipped away from any universally accepted definition of sanity. Either that, or all of us have been wrong about everything, every notion, every law, every piece of this great pie we accept as reality.

And that's when I remember the storm. The magic that it carries. If there's magic in a storm, why can't there be magic in a storm shelter? Why can't there be magic in anything, really? We don't know.

None of us really know, and finally, I think this is the only comfort I have.

————

Walter Pike shook me gently. He had a flashlight sitting behind him, and his long shaggy hair glowed in its beam, illuminating his haggard face. Haggard, but kind. One of the kindest faces I'd ever seen.

"Damn it, damn it, damn it. I knew you didn't leave me. You slipped. Tell me you slipped."

"I slipped."

He stood up and danced—yes, *danced*—around the shelter. He did this until a coughing fit took him and he had to get some oxygen from his tank.

I sat up. "I don't understand it all, though."

"It's a mind trip, isn't it?" He leaned forward, his face turning deathly serious. "Were they there?"

I nodded.

He waited, his mouth hanging open expectantly.

"I thought I brought them home. But . . ." I trailed off, not wanting to finish the sentence.

"But they didn't come with you, huh?" He looked sad. He sat back and lit another cigarette. "Shit fire. Goddamn shit fire."

"What happened to you?"

"Woke up and found my oxygen tank. Saved my life. You were gone. Slipped, I figured, so I climbed out of here in the dead of the night. Saw my place. Torn to the ground. They're saying it was the worst storm in the state's history. Your place had some damage too, but all in all, you were lucky." He puffed on his cigarette. "Can you tell me about it?"

I told him I could, but first, I thought I needed something to eat. "How long have I been gone?"

"Best I can figure it is three days."

I tried to get my head around this number. It seemed like only a few hours.

"Your daddy made bail. Least that's what I heard one of them sheriff's deputies saying while they were out hunting for us. I found an overturned tree. Hid back behind the roots, right down in the mud, but I could hear every word they said." He shrugged. "Wasn't about to leave until I saw it through with you. When are we going to go back?"

"Back?" The very idea caught me off guard. "You don't understand. There's no going back. I did everything I could do. The rest is up to her."

"Are you sure?"

"Positive."

"I'm sticking around for a few days just in case." He stood and clutched the ladder with one hand, his flashlight with the other. "Can you make it home?"

"I think so. But aren't they looking for you?"

"They are."

"You'd better split."

"Nah, I'll be fine in these woods, at least for another few days. I know them like I was born in them." He grinned, and so did I. As much as I didn't want him to get caught, I was still glad he was going to stick around.

"Give me five minutes to make sure the coast is clear. I don't want one of them cops to start harassing you before you get a chance to see your daddy. I'll whistle when it's clear, okay?"

A few minutes later, I heard the whistle. I climbed out of the shelter and made it about halfway home before collapsing in the mud.

Chapter Forty

I woke up in the hospital with two IVs in my arms. My dad sat beside me, and when he saw my eyes open, he stood up and put his hand on my shoulder.

"Son?"

I think I tried to smile. It was tough. Before the expression could form, I remembered that I'd tried and failed. Mom and Anna did not come back.

He squeezed my shoulder gently. "Thank God." He dropped his face into my chest and began to sob. I put a hand on his head and patted. It was strange, feeling like I was the one with the strength and not the other way around.

Eventually, he sat up, wiping his face clear of tears. He smiled weakly. "I thought I lost you too."

I shook my head. "No, I'm still here."

"I'm so happy."

"You made bail. That's good."

He flushed, embarrassed, and I wished I hadn't said anything.

"Are you okay?" He said the words slowly, as if I might be traumatized. "You can tell me what happened. You can tell me anything, Danny."

"Are Mom and Anna back?"

He shook his head. "Danny, please don't do this, okay? They're gone. I don't know where, but sometimes you have to accept that and move on. Your mother didn't want us in her life."

"I saw her."

"What?"

"She came with me. She may be here. Did you check at home? When have you been home last?"

"Danny, the doctors say you're dehydrated and you've had a severe concussion. I'm sure things have been confusing for you, to say the least." He leaned forward. "Did he hurt you? It's okay, Danny. Just me and you. You don't need to be afraid."

"Did who hurt me?"

"Walter Pike. Who else? If he hurt you, just say the word. Sheriff Martin is already looking for him. They'll bring him to justice."

"He didn't hurt me. He helped me. Pike would never hurt anybody."

Dad scoffed. "History says otherwise. You know he was wanted for murder when he was fourteen?"

"I know. He told me. It was self-defense."

Dad stood up. I could see he was getting angry. "Danny, he's brainwashed you. I don't know how he did it, but it's clear."

I closed my eyes. There was a small part of me that was ready to concede. I'd taken Pike at his word, done exactly as he recommended, and what did I have to show for it? Sleep deprivation? Dehydration? Three days missing from my life?

No. I went there. I saw her. I beat Sykes. I would believe it. I had to.

The doctor came in and talked to Dad. They stepped outside into the hallway, so I couldn't hear what they were saying, but afterward, Dad didn't mention Pike. He didn't seem angry at me either, so I imagine he was told that I was in a fragile state, some bullshit like that. Whatever it was, he laid off me.

Until we were on the way home.

I asked him about the man he assaulted.

"Who was it?"

"I don't want to get into that, Danny."

I sat in the passenger seat, watching the cotton fields go by in long silver streaks.

"But I do. I need to know."

He sighed and pulled the car over to the shoulder. He killed the engine and turned to face me. "I suppose you're old enough to handle the truth."

I waited. For some reason I felt nervous, even though I was pretty sure I knew what he was going to say.

"When you were a little kid, your mother had an affair with a man. His name is Wallace Turner. He's the bartender out at Ghost Bells on County Road Seven. She had been drinking a lot. Using drugs. When I found out, I don't know, I sort of freaked. It wasn't hard to know something was going on. She was out every night—she said it was with her friends, but I knew that was a lie—and I was home every night with you." He touched my shoulder. "Not that I minded hanging out with you.

"Anyway, she eventually told me she wasn't happy. She told me she wanted to leave me. Us." He let the last word linger, and I felt tears welling up from some place deep within me, tears that I'd tucked away for a while, tears that I'd pretended weren't tears at all.

"I couldn't accept it. I went down there one night and followed her out into the parking lot behind the bar. Wallace was with her, and they took turns shooting up. Do you understand what I'm talking about when I say that she was shooting up, Danny?"

I nodded.

"She was using heroin. I lost it. I went for her right then and there. I dragged her back to the car and took her straight to a rehab clinic. Two months later, she came out a different person. At least she seemed different. Life got better. It really did. We started trying for a second child, and after some pain and heartache, we had Anna.

"Anna changed your mother. At first, I thought it was for the better. She was fiercely protective of her. Whatever Anna needed, your mother made sure she had. She took a second job waiting tables to help pay for the tests Anna needed." He shrugged. "But that didn't last. She came home late from work one night, drunk out of her mind. I told her to quit. She quit, but not before making it clear she didn't like being told what to do.

"Then about a year and a half ago, I noticed some of the signs again. She was drinking again, maybe even doing drugs." He clenched his fists on the steering wheel. "I tried, Danny. I tried to pull her back out again, but I couldn't. The man I beat up was Wallace. I shouldn't have. Since I caught them those years ago, he's cleaned up, stayed away from her, I think. But I was so angry. I think she's with somebody else now. I just wish she could have left Anna behind." He let go of the steering wheel and put a hand on my shoulder. "If I could have just done more for her. I tried, son. I promise that I tried. I think that sometimes when a person goes too deep, only they can decide to come back. It has to be something that she wants to do. You understand?"

I did. I understood all too well. Dad wiped away a single tear and started the car. We drove the rest of the way in silence.

———

The roof was partially gone from the house, and Dad had covered the missing sections with black tarp.

"We were lucky," he said. "You should see Cliff's house."

"Is Cliff okay?"

"He's fine. He and his parents were in the basement. Wanna know the kicker? Because they had such a great insurance policy, they'll be rebuilding the whole thing from the ground up. It'll be bigger and better than ever. That Banks, he called to check on you, and then talked for fifteen minutes about the movie room they're going to have. Son of a—"

He finished the sentence. Eventually. But what happened in between his last word and the expletive to follow totally changed his meaning.

Mom stepped out of the house. She was haggard, worn out, maybe even dirty, but she stood there on the stoop in the very place Pike had stood on that stormy night not too long ago. She stood there and smiled.

"—bitch," Dad finished.

I didn't wait for him to stop the car. I opened the door and jumped out while he was still rolling to a stop. I ran as fast as I could and embraced her.

When I finally let go and looked into her eyes, I saw something—recognition, maybe. *She knew.* I can't explain how I was so sure, but I was. She remembered.

"Dan-dan," a voice said from inside the house. "Say 'in the dark.'"

This is how I explained it to Dwight.

I accept that my mother left me. Left us. She took Anna with her. Based on what I remember about that day, it wasn't planned, at least not completely, but something caused her to take Anna and go. If Dwight helped me at all, it was only to see this.

What I also accept is that I had a hand in bringing her back. I can't explain how I used the slip to contact her. I think it had something to do with Anna and those girls and Pike's steadfast belief that she'd be there. The darkness that had fallen over her life had put her there, or at least a version of her, a husk of herself that could at least see me and respond to me. Maybe to her, it was just a dream, but not on my side. On my side it was real.

At least I think it was.

No, not think. Believe. I believe it was real. I have to. The other choice scares me worse than anything else in the world. Not only does it make me crazy, it makes the world sane. It makes a storm just a storm and the past something that can't reach into the future and matter. It makes the wind that blows against my window at night nothing more than a trick of the atmosphere instead of the breath of heaven. Dwight says I'm choosing to believe lies.

Maybe he's right.

Then again, maybe he's wrong.

There is a possibility, however slim. And that's enough for me. Always has been.

Chapter Forty-one

I have said that I believed storms are a kind of magic. There are other kinds too. There's the magic of being young, of believing in things that only a young person can fathom. There's the magic of the unexpected, of returning to a full house, a family reunited despite all the evidence that suggested it would never happen. And finally, there's the magic of memory.

Dwight suggested to me once that what had happened to me was really no more than a series of coincidences from which ("rather nobly," he added) I'd tried to assemble meaning. He would have me see it like this: My mother leaves with Anna. A delusional Walter Pike returns to town and learns that they are missing. This feeds his delusion and his guilt. He contacts me and tells me his story. The timing was perfect, Dwight would say. I was fourteen, an emotional wreck, susceptible to anything. I needed to believe. Add to this the storm, me hitting my head on the ladder, the three missing days in the shelter. My mother and Anna coming back.

"You piece it all together and make something bigger. It's human nature, Dan. It's how religion began at the dawn of time. It's the root of superstitions, fears, any number of things. We take the random and give it meaning. Hear what I'm saying. *We* give it meaning. It doesn't inherently have meaning."

Dwight's a smart man, but he doesn't have any imagination. He forgets about storms. The way they change things, the way they wipe out what came before and make room for what will come later. And what is a storm if not a series of unlikely coincidences? The temperature, humidity, dew point, any number of other factors must be just right in order to produce a big one. Yet they happen all the time. Should we dismiss them, pretend they don't matter?

Maybe we should, but I can't. I'm not one of these people who believes that every storm is a message from God, a deluge of Judeo-Christian reckoning spilled out over a world of sinners. No, storms are nothing like that. Instead, they're puzzles, cryptic labyrinths through which we can glimpse power and transformation, and yes, even meaning. Maybe they mirror the human experience after a fashion, the way lives are shaken free in the wind, the way years pass in torrents, leaving us lightning flashes of memory, fleeting images, seared to the brain for further consideration, electric treasures that wait for us, buzzing dimly. The way (much like the trees) some people fall and others remain standing, at least for a little while longer.

I saw Walter Pike only one more time after that day in the shelter, but he told me something that I'll try to hold on to for the rest of my life.

This was after all the long sessions with police, after the frustration of Mom not wanting to talk about where she'd been, after all the hugs and kisses, and after the moments of stillness when I wanted to pinch myself because a miracle had happened. Not a coincidence. A miracle.

Pike was easy to find. I just walked to the storm shelter. I stood there, looking at the landscape, trying to remember what the swamp had been like, trying to imagine how it had been right here in this very spot, ushered in perhaps by that terrible storm.

Magic. It's there. We just don't look closely enough.

"I hear you had a surprise waiting for you when you got home?"

I turned and saw Pike standing behind me. He still wore the same dirty T-shirt he'd been wearing the day I pulled him through the mud. His oxygen tank lay at his feet, the tubing twisted into a knot, and he was smoking a cigarette. I ran to him. When I got close enough, he dropped the cigarette and stepped on it. He reached out for me. We embraced for a long time, his hand patting my back as I cried.

When we separated at last, I saw that his face was wet too. His one good eye looked at me closely, lovingly, and I knew this would be the very last time I ever saw him.

"Listen to me, Danny. Listen real good."

I nodded.

"You brought your mother and sister back. Never for a second think otherwise. Do you hear me?"

"Yes, sir."

"Do you believe me?"

I hesitated. I wasn't sure what I believed.

He shook his head and squeezed my shoulder hard. "You gotta believe."

"Okay," I said.

"Say it."

"I believe."

"Good. It's going to be hard. I can tell it already is. I was like you. Hell, I am still like you, but seeing this . . . this is confirmation. I just hope I die before I begin to doubt again."

"Don't say that—"

He shook his head violently. "It's the way I feel. Believing in something . . . something more . . . it changes everything. You understand that, right?"

I told him I did.

"What happened to you inside that storm shelter . . . you're going to have grief over that. You think it's hard now? It'll get harder, the older you get, and you'll want to take it and bury it somewhere, like I did those photos. Except it'll be more of a symbolic kind of burial. Do you know the kind I mean? Where something just hurts too much to think about and you push it aside and pretend it never happened?"

I almost laughed. "Yeah. I know what you mean."

"Good. Don't do it with this. That doesn't work." He leaned in, his face almost touching mine now, his good eye locked on mine. I'll always remember him like this. "Here's the key. Remember. Don't forget. No matter what, don't forget."

He let go of me then and stepped back. For a second longer he held my gaze, and then he looked away. He reached for his oxygen tank and tucked it under his arm. He was crying, but he refused to look at me again. He turned and walked back into the trees, and for a moment I entertained the notion that he'd been a ghost all along, just as I had originally thought, but the moment was over. I knelt down and picked up his discarded cigarette butt. It was real. I held it for a long time, and when I stood up, I slipped it into my pocket. I might need it one day.

No matter what, he'd said, *don't forget.*

A nd that is why I'm writing this down. I took some liberties with Pike's story, but I think I got the important stuff right. His voice—that was what had to be there. The details matter least in the end. But I'll never forget his voice in that dark cabin. It swept me along to 1960, until I felt like I knew Seth as intimately as a best friend. Sometimes, I still dream about them both. Though these dreams are simply fleeting images at best, there is always a strong sense of joy in them. I awake from one with a feeling of euphoria that can sometimes last me throughout the day.

There is a flip side to these dreams. A dark one that comes less frequently, but with a startling urgency. In it I am trying to explain to everyone I know about the other world, the world of the shadows that lay just on the other side of . . . what? Words always fail me in the dream, and they fail me now. Upon waking, I realize how ludicrous it all is, and sometimes I find myself bellied up to a bar before four in the afternoon, drinking whiskey with beer chasers and trying to reinvent my past.

There are only a few more things to tell. The first is something I did the day after talking to Pike for the last time. I took a walk deep into the woods, to where the ruins were. I found the remains of Pike's cabin and poked around for a while. For some reason, Tina and Rachel were on my mind. I felt like they were free now, moved on to wherever we move on to, but something nagged me. It was like a sentence without a period. Complete, but not quite. I shrugged it off and continued walking out to Big Creek, where the quicksand was. I took a solid stick I found on the ground and poked at the quicksand. I tried to move the stick around some, but it was too thick. The sand had lost some of its moistness and felt almost like dried mud. Finally, I let go of the stick. It didn't sink. I found a heavy stone from the creek and tossed it into the sand. It too didn't sink.

I'm not sure how, but suddenly I knew what that period was. I knew how I could put it on the end of the sentence.

I was back an hour later with a shovel. It was easy digging because of the softness, but I had to dig for a very long time before I found what I was looking for—the gleaming white of a bone.

I paused long enough to let the adrenaline rush subside before I began to dig again.

Sheriff Martin and Deputy Sims were the first to come out. They parked the squad car out near the cabin and hoofed it over to the creek and the hole I'd dug in what used to be quicksand.

I was waiting for them with Dad. We'd made the call a couple of hours earlier, and the first few people Dad spoke with seemed as if they didn't want to believe that his fourteen-year-old son had managed to dig up two skeletons. Honestly, I suspected they were a little weary of our family, which is something that makes me smile a little when I think about it now. If nothing else, we sure did make Martin earn his salary for a few months. Eventually, Dad talked to the right person and was told somebody would be out when they had a chance. We'd never expected Sheriff Martin himself. His arm was still in a sling from being tossed around by the tornado. It seemed clear he was in no mood to be here.

"Frank," Martin said, and I thought I heard disdain in his voice.

"Sorry to bother you, Sheriff."

Martin grunted.

Sims stood back, not saying a word, just glaring at me and Dad like we were pieces of shit he couldn't wait to scrape off his boot heels. I stood still, right beside the little pit I'd carved out of the ground, wondering how they'd react once they looked inside.

"What you got?" Martin said.

I pointed to the pit, and Martin stepped forward so he could see inside. For a long time, he just stood there.

"Well?" Dad said.

Martin whistled, low, almost to himself. Sims stepped forward. "Well, I'll be damned."

Chapter Forty-two

It took a year or so of forensic work that I don't understand to determine that the bones belonged to Tina and Rachel, though most of the town was like Sheriff Martin—they knew instantly. A year or so later, a man from Nashville, Tennessee, wrote a book piecing it all together, and most of it was pretty damn close to being right. The only stuff he didn't nail were all the parts that happened with the slip. He surmised that the girls had been abducted by Sykes and tortured in the cellar below the cabin, and when he'd killed them, he tossed their remains in the quicksand. He even interviewed me and asked me a lot of questions about Walter Pike. I answered them as honestly as I could without going into the stuff about the slip. He tried to get me to talk about that, but I'd learned from my mother how not to talk about something. Silence. A cold, slightly confused stare. Worked every time.

There's something about turning thirty that makes a person re-evaluate. Eleven months ago, I sat down to decide the things I knew beyond a shadow of a doubt. The list was short, but I did come up with a few things.

I believe there is an afterlife. I believe this world is only as real as you make it. I believe that in certain places, it can always be twilight and that you can make the world whatever you want it to be as long as you are foolish and hopeful. I believe if you love someone enough, you can pull them through a lot of mud, but ultimately, only that person can choose to walk away from it and not come back. I believe in all of this, yet each day I feel these beliefs slipping away from me. Each day I feel my time in the swamp becoming more shadowy, more like a dream than a reality. Then I remind myself that dreams are just a different form of reality, and I feel better.

Mom remembers what happened. I know she does. It's in her eyes, the pregnant pauses she can't fill when I mention something about the time she and Anna went away. The way she always turns the channel when one of the documentaries about the missing girls comes on cable. It must have been a kind of mystery to her, but try-ing to solve it was something she was not willing to do.

I wish I could tell you that we lived happily ever after, that she finally made the effort to stay out of the muck, to stop slipping, but I can't. We had some good times, and my memories of the days after her return are mostly positive, but I won't suppress the negatives. Not anymore. Pike said not to forget.

I'm trying.

Still, as each year passes, I blame her less.

Dad? He never spoke of Walter Pike again. He even asked Sheriff Martin to stop pursuing him. "Maybe he's harmless. Danny seems fine. There's no evidence that he did anything to him." I overheard this one afternoon when Dad believed me to be asleep on the couch.

Anna kept being Anna. Of all of us, she was the least affected. Her world never changed. Her world never will, at least not in this lifetime. There is a comfort in that too, something I envy, because even as I type these words, I am plagued with doubts, pressed down by a feeling that I am wasting my time writing this, or worse, recording the rantings of a lunatic. Thanks to Dwight, I know all the psychological terms, but in the end I don't think they're very helpful.

Last week I canceled my session with him. This week, I'll do the same. I can hear him anytime I need to. I know what he believes and what he'll say. Besides, I'll be on the road for at least the next week. I'm going to Oregon. A little town called Sodaville. It sounds like a happy place.

It's a spur-of-the-moment kind of trip, one that I decided to take after doing some Internet searches a few nights ago. Despite Dwight's admonitions that I leave well enough alone, I Googled "Seth Sykes" and was surprised that only a few relevant hits came back. There was a man in California, a teenager in Ohio, and a poet in Oregon. I did a little more research and found that the poet had written a poem called "Slip." I searched frantically for a copy to read online, but couldn't find one. Coincidence? Maybe. Still, it's enough for me. I leave tomorrow.

Maybe I'll find nothing at all, or maybe it'll be him. That's almost more frightening because then there is a chance he'll tell me how Walter got it all wrong, how none of it really happened like he claimed, and all the things I believe might finally fall down. A house of cards all along.

But when I think like this, I try hard to remember fourteen, to remember faith and a man named Walter Pike and the strange places we're capable of visiting when we're foolish enough to believe.